Cornelius

CORNELIUS LYNCH

ALONG THE RIGHT PATH

Martin, Best Wishes, God Bless, Michael.

ISBN:9781699425763

DEDICATION

To my good and kindly parents, whose selfless sacrifices, endurance and unshakable Christian faith prepared us well for the multi-varied challenges we encountered as we journeyed on the pathways of our lives.

ACKNOWLEDGMENTS

A word of thanks to Sheila Scully for her input and encouragement. Thanks to Peter for preparing the book for publication and thanks to Maria, Fiona, Bláthnaid, Con, Peggy Curtis, and Jim Cooney for their help and advice.

INTRODUCTION

Writing this book was for me a sacred duty. Had I not written it, I would have had to charge myself with cowardice for my uncaring silence, find myself guilty as charged and never again know the fullness of peace in my mind.

The sole aim of this book is to do some good for some really great people that I know and hopefully for thousands of others as well.

This book will be used to raise funds for charitable organisations, with particular reference to groups involved with, Motor Neuron, Parkinson's, Multiple Scelerosis, Alzheimers and Dementia diseases. No profits will accrue to the author.

One

My brother Thomas Martin Kendley, was born on a dark night in January 1946, in a downstairs room of a typical, two storey, country farmhouse of that period - three bedrooms upstairs, kitchen and parlour downstairs, no indoor plumbing, bathroom or toilet, no back door and the front door opening out onto the yard. The downstairs room was actually the parlour but the bed had been moved down there years previously and this facilitated the business of the midwife - or the nurse as she was called at that time. It was a dark night without a trace of a moon or stars and there was little light in the farmhouse - a Tilley lamp and candles being the only sources of illumination. The three older children Nora - myself and Rose were asleep upstairs and while we knew there was some activity downstairs, we were unaware of what was in progress or of what had transpired.

The next morning there was a cover of snow on the ground and the yard outside the house revealed the tracks of the car which had brought the nurse the night before. There was a tall creamery churn in the centre of the yard and clearly the driver - who was my uncle, had used this as a roundabout when turning his car to face it for road again.

Indoors, the house was heated by a great big open fire, that was typical of farmhouses of that time and type. Sitting beside that fire and looking up, one could see the stars in a cloudless sky on a frosty night. The fire was set on the floor and the smoke trailed its way upwards along the back wall, which it had coated with black, tar-like, soot over many a year. There was a hooked iron crane which hung like a gate, right over the fire to swing forward the black kettle or the bastible for baking or the black pot for boiling potatoes or meat.

That evening my father brought in a log about seven or eight feet long and being unable to cut it at the time, he just pushed one end into the fire, with the other end halfway down the concrete kitchen floor and when the bit in the fire was burned, he just kept on pushing it up until it was all gone, leaving but a memory behind. I think it must have lasted a day or two and it certainly was appreciated because the snow remained for quite a while.

We didn't see the baby until the next day and he was wrinkly and red in his face and crinkly in his skin. His hair was black and tight against his scalp, very thin and greasy looking. That was the first glimpse that I had of my brother Thomas.

The snow lasted for a while that January, although I do not know how many days it remained, but I do recall that it changed the appearance of everything around. The hills were white and the trees with slender branches were peppered with a refined dusting of salt-like snow. Everything seemed to be asleep. The larger ash and sycamores had the snow resting on their thick branches - maybe to a depth of about two inches and a five inch deep blanket covered the ground generally. Occasionally more snow fell, lazily drifting featherlike from the sky, falling slowly and gently in the still, unmoving calm. Yes!

everything did seem to be asleep and clumpy coverings of snow lay atop the drooping hedges and furze bushes. All seemed to be comatose in a deep, deep slumber and the trees - rain-washed and winter-bleached, were especially striking by their unmoving stillness, sleeping a protective sleep, deep within themselves.

The cows were kept tied in the stall and I remember clearly the collective munching sound that they made as they chewed and re-chewed the cud. There was warmth there from the shared heat of their bodies and the combined warmth of their breaths. It was a lazy time for them, not only because of the inclement weather but because they were in calf and were no longer regularly milked. My father took the chestnut mare to the river at the lower end of the yard and there she drank noisily as if she was sucking the water between her teeth.

Very few birds were airborne during those days although they did come to eat the crumbs that we threw to them - first the crows to snatch and carry off the bigger pieces and then the smaller robin, wagtail and sparrow. Here and there, occasionally, groups of starlings flew in their own inimitable style, flitting and changing direction and shape in swarmed unison. Overhead, the sky was a dark porous grey - porous in the sense that it was not thick with cloud but seeming as if more snow was up there ready to fall again anytime soon.

Everything did look different, every place white - the fields, the ditches, the road, the yard, the haggard and the hills. Only the larger puddles of water did not have a covering of snow - at least not until they froze, but even then they did not remain covered for very long. The snow on the roofs was most noticeable on the outhouses and the dwelling house and the snow gathered on the windowsills. Footprints of course were also very evident, especially the footprints in the farmyard, as there was constant traffic of humans as well as the tracks of the birds and occasionally the tracks of a rabbit or fox. The smoke from the chimney did not really climb to the sky during those days, seeming only to barely make it to the chimney top and then slowly fall downwards - a sure sign of bad weather the older people said.

Then one morning a great russet red patch in the east of the sky heralded a change in the weather. The day softened and changed and bits of snow began to fall from the hedges and the trees making a soggy, plopping sound as they hit the ground. A light shower of soft rain sprinkled the countryside. The powdery snow on the slender branches was the first to be washed away and then the thicker snow crests on the stouter limbs surrendered, as the thaw gained momentum, and life and landscape reverted back to normal once again.

Within the house, the kitchen was warm with plenty of logs on the big fire and the *gabhail* (armful) of turf that my Dad brought in. There was a wheel bellows there, which we turned to blow air underneath the fire - helping it to light better and making the flames flare up beneath the black kettle or pot.

Joe, our grandaunt, was there. She was a regular who always came to help out when our mother had a new baby. She was a wonderful lady, who wore lipstick and powder on her slightly wrinkled face each day. She smoked fags, sang songs, laughed and was always happy when giving things to others. She fussed around the house and her great passion was for scrubbing and cleaning and always wanting everything to be, as she put it, "as clean as a new pin." While she also liked to have us children looking that clean, actually achieving that was problematic for us, because the ablutions were carried out by scrubbing us, while we stood in a galvanised bath of warm water placed on the kitchen floor.

After a few days my mother was able to leave the bed and come to the kitchen with the new baby and eventually he was put in the cradle. Everybody took turns to rock him and some came to admire him and to say of course who he resembled. These are just some of the thoughts and memories that I have of the birth and very early days of my brother Thomas.

It was a somewhat primitive world into which Thomas was born on that January. There were very few cars, no washing machines, no electricity, no gas cookers or no electric cookers. The bicycle, the horse and trap and the horse and rubber wheeled cart were the most common modes of transport. Cows were milked by hand into buckets, which were emptied into a tall, broad-bottomed creamery churn, with a cloth-clad strainer on top to remove impurities from the milk. The churn was taken to the road to be collected by a neighbour in his Ford 10 jeep and taken to the creamery, where a separation process removed and retained the cream. The churn was refilled with the separated milk which was brought home to the farm for nourishing calves or pigs. That was the life and the world into which my brother first made his entrance. It was, basic, quiet, peaceful, plodding and essentially unhurried.

Fifty one years later, in a modern and vastly transformed world, I was on holiday in the sunny Canary island of Tenerife, when I got a text message on my mobile phone to tell me that, that same brother, Thomas Martin Kendley had just been appointed bishop of the Diocese of Killeenreagh in the Republic of Ireland. His appointment, I was told, was a surprise to many - not only because it was the first time ever that a curate was appointed to that position, but because his approach to his priestly ministry in the parish of Lonerton where he was based, was a source of concern to some, a source of admiration to others and was challenging to a great many more.

Two

My brother Thomas grew strong and with Nora, Rose and myself his siblings, explored our immediate environment - the little river at the bottom of the yard from which we drew water in buckets for the household, the stone ditch gap into the field at the top of the yard where fairy thimbles and a brittle elder grew and the narrow, stony porsheen (little roadway) that led westwards between two high ditches. Imposing large beech and sycamores towered immovable on the ditch around the haggard where the turf-shed was and where the hay was reeked - ever since the bad snowstorm had felled the hayshed some years previously.

From there Thomas the child walked with us further on that wet and stony way, past the gap of the field where the blue cow died and on again to the wider world of the inch field, to the river and the ferny patch, where sheltered yellow cowslips brightly beamed their mellow beauty, from deep among the briars, imprinting their image forever in Thomas' child mind. We saw bushes, trees, briars, furze and occasional tall thistles in the fields, we saw rabbits often, the fox sometimes, trout or eels in the river on occasions and a wily stoat - but only once.

The calm and patient cows were part of our lives and Thomas and the rest of us were skilled at driving them in from the fields to be milked - watching the way they

swayed as they ambled along with full udders swinging from side to side and littering the muddy patches with cloven prints.
Another narrower, more watery stony porsheen swung off to the left along between even higher ditched fields and continued up the hillside to where we cut and saved the turf for winter fires. It was along this stony highway - which our father made with pick axe and shovel and sledge and crowbar, that Thomas walked to school with us, up to where it ended and then followed the soggy path - over the hill, through wet bog-land and down the other side for a long mile of rough terrain, until we reached the rear wall of the school yard beside the main county road.

Thomas learned to climb the stone steps of the barn over the cow byre to the rear and to the right of the dwelling house, where the oats was stored along with other miscellaneous items. It was in that same barn when he was older that he often went to play his violin and hone his musical skills. He was well coordinated and very skilled with hands and feet and he excelled at running and at sport.
As he grew stronger he became adept at climbing the tall sycamore trees on the ditch that bordered the yard in front of the house - the yard in which our father and the workman halter-trained the colt that Thomas loved - some weeks before he was sold, leaving us to grieve in tandem with our chestnut mare. She neighed and galloped in agitation along the meadow ditch as her son the colt, led by a length of rope, trotted after the bicycle of the farmer who had bought him, trotting out of her life and out of our lives too, forever, leaving loss behind.

The road at the lower eastern end of the yard led down to the meadow gap and veered leftwards there to follow the direction of the river to the bridge and uphill to the larger graveled, public road that took our lovely colt away. It would eventually take us away too - all of us, out of our sheltered rustic environment with its secret paths and hides and nests, to traverse the byways and highways of the wider world in the great adventure that is life itself. Thomas took that road too, when he left to study at preparatory school and later when he left for Dublin to train as a primary school teacher and later still he traversed it at many an hour and many a time, as he went to play his violin at gigs and dances at venues throughout the length and breadth of Ireland.

It was while coming on a train from one such gig, at yet another music festival, on a night in May that Thomas, now in his early twenties met Mary for the first time. They were sitting opposite one another for the last leg of the journey from Mallow to Killarney. That part of the track is a monorail and somewhere along the way the brakes were applied and the train lurched to a stop, giving a jolt to the passengers, but not stopping quickly enough to avoid colliding with the cattle that had strayed onto the tracks. Three cattle were killed. It was a long time before information was passed down to the passengers but it was clear that they would be delayed for some time. To make matters worse, the engine was switched off and after awhile everybody began to feel the cold of the clear and chilly night.

Thomas noticed that the young lady seated across from

him seemed to be shivering and so he took his sleeping bag, which was part of his usual travelling equipment, and offered it to her to put around herself. She accepted gratefully. As time went on, Thomas himself began to feel cold and occasionally glanced across at her and wondered ruefully to himself if there was any chance that she might share the blanket with him. Perhaps she was able to read his thoughts or perhaps she had noticed how cold Thomas was, but for whatever reason she lifted up a corner of the blanket and said:
“Look, why don’t you come in here as well? I think there is room enough for two.”

They were warm enough together and after awhile it was getting late and dark, even though it was the month of May. She rested her head on his shoulders as if it was the most natural thing in the world to do and dozed off to sleep and soon afterwards Thomas also fell asleep.
Eventually the tracks were cleared and travel was resumed, but the two young people stayed together under the blanket until the train reached their destination.
"Thanks for the blanket," she said. "It probably saved me from getting pneumonia or pleurisy or something like that."
"You're welcome," said Thomas.
"Do you always bring it with you when you travel to the various venues and music sessions?"
"I never travel without it and I have slept on many a floor from Cork to Donegal."
Their conversation was interrupted by the hoot of a car that was parked nearby.
"Now I have to go," she said, "this car is here to pick me

up. Maybe we will meet again sometime. Thanks again."

Thinking about her later, it occurred to him that something a little special had passed between them there on that train, on that night in May and he experienced a sense of warmth and joy as he thought about her and the manner in which she had rested her head on his shoulder, as if it belonged there naturally. He wondered too if she had felt the same about him and he suspected that she had. He smiled wryly to himself as he thought about the sleeping bag:
"I was very lucky that I bought a new sleeping bag last week," he mused to himself. "I doubt if she would have stayed very long under its tattered, sweaty, ageing predecessor."

A few months later he was playing at a fleadh ceoil dance in Cush with a group of other traditional musicians who had come together for the event. An excellent musician, he was the *de facto* leader of the group. He was renowned for his ability to tailor the tempo of the music to that of the dancers and he had his own methodology for this. He would identify the couple who were the best dancers on the floor and he played to their rhythm and their movement and that always ensured that he had perfect timing for everyone, for every dance.

Every musician knows that there are times when a combination of circumstance, surroundings and their own inner feelings enable them to play music of exceptional and transcendental standard. The musician will be aware of this and the listeners and dancers will be similarly aware. It was like that on this night in Cush. They were a great dancing crowd - dancers who loved to dance, and this further assisted the musicians and lifted their performance.

Since it was a fleadh ceoil, the group departed from the customary waltzes and the two hand reels and played a polka set - a dance for groups of four couples facing each other in a square-shaped formation. The polka set danced on that night was the Sliabh Luachra, a set consisting of six distinct parts, danced to distinctly different tunes with distinctly different rhythms.

Looking down on them from the stage, they presented a fabulous sight. The entire hall was full of dancers who were uniformly disciplined in their movements. All the floor of the hall was filled with sets of four couples - all lively, all disciplined as each couple precisely performed the various moves, while simultaneously tapping their feet in rhythm on the floor. It was energetic, unbridled, skilled, disciplined, wild, respectful and deeply expressive of Gaelic culture, competence and confident self-belief.

Early on, his eyes were drawn to a girl in a group in front of the stage whose dancing was exceptionally smooth. Her movements were effortless, were perfectly synchronised with the music and there was a perfect fluidity about the manner in which her legs moved at the hips and in the steps and flawless rhythm of her dancing of polkas, slides and hornpipes. Watching her body move and swerve, was watching a thing of beauty.

Just as the polka set ended, she turned briefly towards the stage but Thomas was called aside by one of his fellow musicians and when he turned and looked again she was nowhere in sight. He had a niggling feeling that he had seen that face somewhere before and he named her "Dancing Girl" because of her skill and dexterity on the dance floor.

When the night's dancing had ended, people quickly exited the hall, but as always happens, some people gathered around the stage - some to get autographs and others to chat with the musicians. Thomas was bent over, putting his violin into its case when he sensed someone beside him and raising up his head he saw Dancing Girl smiling warmly up at him from the dance floor.
"Do you remember me?" she asked.
"Yes I do", he replied "but I can't remember where it was we met."
"Would it help your memory if I asked you about your blue sleeping bag?"
"It would indeed and I remember you of course - you're the girl from the train."

Later they drove to a quiet place and went through the customary rituals of such circumstances at that time - kissing, embracing, chatting, all with respect and in respect, a little love and nothing more serious than that.
That is how they started together, my brother Thomas and Mary his dancing girl - his greatest love of all.

Within a few months of Thomas' meeting with Mary, I began to notice that a change had come over him. He no longer travelled as frequently to various parts of the country to play at *fleadhanna ceoil* or at *seisiúin* or at various venues and it seemed that he wanted to spend a lot of his time with her and that she also wanted to spend a lot of her time with him. It seemed to me that Mary had put an end to his wild and youthful days of rambling and roving freely around the country, playing music at weekends and during holiday time and that the young man who once was free as the lark in the clear air of summer, had fallen head over heels in love. If proof of that was needed, it was provided one evening sometime later when in the course of our conversation he said to me:

"I'm thinking of building a house."

"Have you a site in mind for it?" I asked.

"I'm in the process of buying a site and I would be pleased if you looked at it and give me your opinion on it."

Three

Bernstadt Hall, the childhood home of Fr. Paul Bernhart Bouvier, was situated at the outer edge of town in a south-facing, two acre site with a gentle gradient. It was an imposing, extra large, squat, two-storey mansion with wide overhanging eaves and magnificent bay windows that drew in the warmth of the sunshine, from east and south and west. There were huge ornately capped chimney stacks mid-height on each side of its large hipped roof. The five ornamental flues that protruded from each stack - testament to an older form of solid fuel heating, reached well above the ridge tile, so as to ensure a good draught in each of the fireplaces in the ten rooms below. Once the home of the land owning gentry, it had been renovated, refurbished and renamed and everything about it and its surrounds reflected impeccability, privilege and wealth.

During the early morning of April 27th 1958, the twenty three year old owner of the house, German born, Mrs. Gretel Bernhart Bouvier felt the first pangs of a long and difficult labour and a long twenty four hours later, at 5.30am a baby boy was born in the luxuriously furnished main bedroom. He would be her only child.

Her father, millionaire industrialist Wilhelm Bernhart, owner of Bernhart Industrial Steel Components Ltd., spared no expense to ensure a safe birth and the room was equipped to the standards of the most up to date labour ward of that era. He also provided a privately paid obstetrician and midwife and this proved fortuitous because complications arose during the birth which might, in their absence, have led to the loss of child or mother or both.

Gretel's husband - tall, suave, debonair Canadian born Pierre Bouvier, who managed the London office of Bernhart Industrial Steel Components Ltd., was unable to be at his wife's bedside due to flight delay. It was late afternoon on the day of his son's birth when he finally arrived at Bernstadt Hall.

He was taken aback at the pallor and apparent weakness of his wife, who could only smile wanly and weakly squeeze his hand as he bent and kissed her.
"You have a son," - her words were faint and barely audible. "Congratulations."
"Congratulations to you," he replied as he attempted to hug her more tightly.
"Gentle. It was a difficult birth. I'm still tender - weak and tender."
"Of course you are," he concurred. "Now you must rest and you will soon be well and strong again."

The midwife placed the baby in Pierre's arms.
"How should I hold him?" Pierre inquired of the sturdy, buxom midwife and she, being equipped with much experience of such situations quipped:
"In your arms of course. Don't worry, he won't break - they never do" and she laughed merrily as she exited the room.

One mid-morning about two weeks later, Pierre was

standing inside the great bay window of their bedroom, happily holding his son in his arms - more comfortably now and admiring the wide and beautiful landscape spread before him. He examined the large neatly trimmed lawn stretching for more than thirty metres southwards, where it yielded to a rougher uncultivated area, designed by nature itself and colonised by wild grasses and fern and thistle and red and white clovers and populated by butterflies and insects and moths. The early summer sunshine was warming the earth that day, nurturing new growth and the daffodils waved their beauty along the periphery of the lawn and driveway. Further down, nearer to the river, foxgloves and clustered primroses on drier earthy banks, proclaimed their loveliness - unrestrained and unabashed.

Pierre stood there for a long time, lost in a reverie of beauty and joy, gratefully holding the baby in his arms, swaying to give comfort to its sleep and so engrossed that he didn't realise that Gretel was standing beside him, until she linked her arm with his in the loving, cuddly sort of way of a caring, loving wife.
"What name will we give to the child?" she asked.
"I think you should choose the name," answered Pierre.
"I would like to call him Paul," she said, "the name of the great missionary of the early Christian Church. Paul Pierre Bouvier - would you like that?"
"Yes it is a worthy name, but I think it would be appropriate to bestow your family name on him. After all, it was your father that brought us together. Paul Bernhart Bouvier - how does that sound to you?"
"That sounds just right," said Gretel. "It has a nice balance

to it. And now, because I'm still a little sore and tender, I must ask you to stoop down from your great height and let me kiss your handsome face."

Four

It took about three months before all the legalities were completed and the necessary loans sanctioned, and so it came about, one warm day late in spring when he returned from school, Thomas was thrilled to see a big, yellow bulldozer engaged in clearing and levelling the site. How wonderful the red earth looked piled up to one side and he could clearly see where the broad, strong blade of the bulldozer had levelled the area in which the house was to be built. It was a great thrill to behold.

He took off his jacket and shirt and went to work tidying up the loose earth. It was good to feel the flexing of muscles and sinews and the blood pumping freely in the veins of his strong arms and hands, as he rhythmically worked the shovel. The sun shone warmly on his back and Thomas felt that it was a good omen of things to come. He felt good - tired but good.
"It is a nice site for a house," remarked the bulldozer operator, after he had put his machine on the low loader. "It is good to see a young man building a new home in his own parish."
"The site is nice," agreed Thomas "and you've done a good job clearing and levelling it."
"Practice makes perfect," the man replied. "I wish you good luck with the building."
"Thanks," said Thomas, "a little good luck can help a lot."

Two or three evenings each week Thomas and Mary would visit the site to see the work in progress and it was a great excitement for them to see the first rows of blocks put in place and the outline of the various rooms being visible for the first time. Later the outlines of the window openings were taking shape and they were so excited each day to see something new as they travelled the road towards the house.
"Look," exclaimed Thomas excitedly one day, "the lentils are in place and the walls are built up over the doors and windows."
"It looks like a great big concrete box," suggested Mary.
A few weeks later the gables towered above everything and they were able to see the house long before they reached it.
Mary was thrilled one evening to see that the roof tiles were in place and the final outline of the house was clear for the first time. When the windows and external doors were fitted, Thomas remarked:
"The house is sheltered and protected from wind and rain now and the internal work can go on, regardless of the weather conditions."

Work continued steadily and each time they came, much to their delight, they would see new progress.
"Oh look the fire must be lighting, look, there's smoke coming from the chimney," Mary exclaimed one evening as they approached the house.
"That is not a real fire as such," explained Thomas, "the builder probably lit some papers and wood shavings to test the draught in the chimneys."
It was a pleasant surprise for Thomas and Mary to see the smoke coming from their own chimney for the very first

time and it was a special day for them.

After they had become engaged they chose and bought the paint and we all helped out with the painting and decoration. They bought the furniture in accordance with their means, a tiled fireplace and eventually it was finished, beds put in place and everything almost ready for the day of the wedding.
"Happy?" asked Thomas.
"The happiest girl in the world," said Mary and she threw her arms around him and kissed him in front of everyone causing him to blush a little - but of course he had no reason to complain.
This period of their lives together was exciting and happy each and every single day.

The wedding of Thomas and Mary took place two years after their first meeting. It was the happiest day of their lives and they sang together in the back seat of the car as they were being driven to the hotel:

"Along the wooded pathways where the wildflowers grow,
A strolling hand in hand my love and I we used to roam,
"A walking on life's pathway and never to let go,
Like lovers in the woodlands where the wildflowers grow."

It was a wedding typical of weddings of the time. Mary's sister was the bridesmaid and I was the best man. The marriage was in the late forenoon followed by dinner and reception in the early afternoon.

There was music and dance after the meal with a local

band playing a mixture of country and western and Irish céilí music and the floor was full of dancers throughout the evening. Some of the guests who were notable singers, did their party piece and some traditional musicians took to the stage to play for the polka set. As well as being an excellent musician, Thomas was also a very fine dancer and despite being slightly encumbered by the long wedding dress, both Mary and himself acquitted themselves admirably on the dance floor.

In accordance with the custom at that time, some friends of the bride and groom tied several tin cans, small buckets and other noise making accoutrements to the honeymoon car with strings and some of the girls wrote 'just married' on the doors, sides and windows with lipstick.

By 6.30pm that evening Thomas and Mary had left for their honeymoon amid shouts and cheers and entertained by the raucous noises of the tin cans dancing off the road behind them. They stopped after a few miles to untie the pots and cans and headed to their hotel to sleep together, for the very first time, since they had been under the sleeping blanket on the train on the occasion of their first meeting, two years previously. Mary snuggled over near to Thomas as he drove and in their unbounded joy, they broke into song once more:

"Along the wooded pathways where the wildflowers grow,
A strolling hand in hand my love and I we used to roam..."

My brother Thomas was twenty three years old and his beloved Mary - his 'Dancing Girl' was twenty one when they became man and wife.

Many of the wedding guests were country people and they had their chores to do including milking the cows and by 7.30pm everyone had left to go home. It was a fabulous day.

Five

Gretel Bernhart was involved with Bernhart Industrial Steel Components Ltd. from a young age and frequently accompanied her father Wilhelm to trade fairs, shows and conferences all over Europe. Although they rarely travelled to North America, it was on one of these rare trips that she met Pierre Bouvier, the man who would become her husband and father of her only child.

It was at the Montreal Trade Exhibition and they were there primarily, to seek out opportunities to supply steel components to the oil industry with a particular focus on companies involved in exploration. In the course of his search Wilhelm Bernhart came across the exhibit stand of PCOG - Petroleum Canada Oil and Gas - a small company which according to its own promotional literature, had exciting plans for exploration and drilling in western Canada and which was at that time focused on raising the necessary capital, which would enable drilling to commence.

The man fronting the professionally presented exhibits attracted much attention. He was tall, well built with broad strong shoulders, wore his clothes well, was trim, tanned, had a smooth and handsome face with a prominent nose, was thirty five years old, was shiningly bald at the front and top of his head, was professional, polished, attractive and exuded confidence, competence and assurance.

"Yes, PCOG is planning extensive exploration in Western Canada - principally in Alberta and we are currently well advanced in our preparations to commence drilling two wells," Pierre explained.
"What are your prospects?" asked Wilhelm.
"The prospects are very good. Initial soil sampling and geological studies point to success."
"Have you done test drills?" Wilhelm inquired.
"Some, yes!"
"And the results?" asked Wilhelm, whose knowledge of such matters was in the realm of the elementary.
"The results indicate the likely presence of oil and gas in commercial quantities."
Pierre's responses were smooth, slick and reassuring and Gretel, who was standing some distance away, observed the ease and confidence with which he answered all questions. Her father was a somewhat dour, solidly built, imposing man and others were often apprehensive or fearful in his presence - but not so this man. Gretel was impressed.

The highlight of the trade fair was the mid-week dinner provided by the Canadian Ministry for Trade and Commerce. The PCOG representative who was seated beside Gretel, introduced himself in his customary warm and friendly manner:
"Pierre Bouvier of PCOG - Petroleum Canada Oil and Gas," he said extending his hand and holding hers in a comfortably firm grip. "I saw you at our exhibit stand today."
"Gretel Bernhart, of Bernhart Industrial Steel Components Ltd.," she replied. "and I am pleased to make your

acquaintance but I was not at your stand today."
"Yes, you are right of course and I stand corrected - you were not at our stand but you were in the vicinity."
"Yes! I was waiting for my father Wilhelm Bernhart. I remained aloof at some distance and didn't realise that you had seen me."
"I did see you - as the song says - from the corner of my eye. I also noticed how beautiful you are and I'm very pleased to have this opportunity to talk with you."

Pierre had been keenly aware of her presence as he chatted with Wilhelm Bernhart at the PCOG stand that day. He knew instinctively that this was not a woman that would be easily impressed by a new acquaintance and as they conversed through dinner and beyond he recognised that Gretel commanded respect - she expected it and got it. She was deep and serious beyond the norm but she also had a sense of fun, was a good conversationalist and Pierre resolved to see more of the daughter of the president of Bernhart Industrial Steel Components Ltd.

Six

After they returned from the honeymoon Thomas and Mary went to live in their lovely new dormer house at the upper end of their u-shaped valley.
"Welcome to your new home Mrs. Kendley," said Thomas as he easily scooped Mary up into his arms and carried her across the threshold, while she clung on with both arms around his neck.
"You're a strong man Thomas Martin Kendley," she said "and I am happy to be your wife."

It was a great thrill for them to move into their new house. He was proud of the home that he had built for her and they were happy there. It was special to them and in the spring and summer, the sun shone on the house practically all day long. Thomas and Mary had come from humble circumstances and their new house with its stylish furnishings and modern facilities was a big improvement on what they had been used to in their respective family homes.

They had both come from families in which prayer was important and in which the family rosary was recited each night and so, they just naturally followed the custom in their own lives. Each night Thomas and Mary knelt on the kitchen floor, resting their elbows on chairs or in the sitting room in front of the fire and recited the rosary and family prayers. Mary taught Thomas a prayer that would be a help and comfort to him throughout his life and they always recited it each night thereafter for as long as they were together:

"Like as the shepherd to his sheep,
So is the Lord my God to me.
Attending to my ev'ry need,
A resting me in pastures green
Near waters still he leadeth me,
My weary spirit to make clean....... "

"These are the happiest of times," declared Thomas to his Dancing Girl, as he reflected on their first breakfast together in their own home, on himself leaving for work, on their first dinner together and then sitting on the new sitting room suite, in front of the open fire ablaze in the brand new tile and marble fireplace.

"It is a time of great happiness," she replied "and a time of great love between us. Let us build a house of love together."

Their first baby miscarried after seventeen weeks and another two years had passed before they learned with great excitement that they were to be blessed with - not just one child but with two.

"Thanks be to God," they said, "God is opening another door to us - twins to make up for the baby we lost. It is exciting news"

The twins were born to Thomas and Mary in the spring - first the girl who lived for about thirty minutes, and a boy who was stillborn. The trauma and the sadness surrounding that event was deep and long lasting and

silent.
In those days people didn't talk much about things like that - so if a child was stillborn, or died during birth or just before the birth, it was taken as being part of life and it was very much handled within the immediate family, so there were no ceremonies or Masses for such events at that time. The death of a newborn baby was not perceived as a major tragedy - a disappointment surely, everyone understood that - but the expectation was that you would get on with life and pull yourself together.
"You're young and have lots of life ahead of you," you would be told. "There will be other children."
You were expected to trust in God that everything would be alright and move on with life and avoid dwelling too long on mourning. Mary and Thomas did not grieve or cry in the presence of each other. A private ring corralled such grief in that era. It was wrapped, put aside and buried deep and not acknowledged - but from time to time in later years, it would recur with poignant pain - triggered by a memory recalled or a casual remark or a story long gone cold.

I accompanied Thomas to the hospital to collect the bodies of both babies and we brought them home in their little white coffins in the back seat of his car. We spoke only sporadically because Thomas was deep in thought and besides, there's only so much one can say in situations like that. At one stage Thomas remarked:
"Our Catholic faith is the greatest of gifts but I think that some of the Church's teachings are at variance with the spirit of God Himself."
"Do you want to explain what you mean?" I asked.

"I learned in school," he said "that children who die before they are born are excluded from heaven and have to spend their eternity away from God in Limbo - all because they had died before they could be baptised."
"I learned that too," I answered, "but I think it has changed since the Second Vatican Council. I'm not entirely sure that it was ever an actual agreed dogma of the faith"
"I couldn't accept it anyway," he said. "That teaching would mean that our little baby boy would be in Limbo forever, while his twin sister, who was baptised before she died, would be in heaven forever in the full presence of God."
"No human parent would impose so harsh an eternity on their child," I said, "so how could God our all-loving Father do it to them. I'm sure positive certain, that they are both among the angels of God in heaven."
"That's my view too," he said, "but I asked the nurses to baptise both of them just the same."

At the graveyard, the priest was there waiting - good man that he was and the gravedigger had dug a space big enough for the two little coffins to be laid side by side.
"It's not very deep," Thomas remarked.
"That's the normal depth for children," the gravedigger assured him.
Afterwards, we returned to our homes and Thomas went back to the hospital to comfort and console his beloved Mary.
"I asked the nurse to baptise them as soon as possible after being born and she told me that she did that and she named them Veronica and John - just as we had requested," explained Thomas.

"We have two angels in heaven," she answered.
"We have. It will make dying easier when our time comes, because we will meet them again."

Thomas was asked to return to the hospital before Mary was discharged and the doctor had disappointing news for him.
"It would be unwise to try to have any more children because it might be risky," she explained.
The doctor who was clearly a very good and genuine Christian explained that there were natural methods of contraception which could be used and these were explained more clearly by their General Practitioner. And so that is how they went about their lives with quiet sadness of course at the loss of the miscarried baby, at the loss of the twins and accepting of the prospect that they would not have any more children - but life goes on and they were prepared to accept their lot in life.

Seven

Gretel and Pierre continued to meet throughout the year after the Montreal Trade Exhibition. Their meetings alternated between the Bernhart family home in Ireland and Montreal, where Pierre lived and where the humble offices of PCOG were situated.
Wilhelm had some misgivings about his daughter's suitor.
"What is your overall opinion of Pierre Bouvier?" he asked his wife Ericka one night after they had retired to bed.
"He's really a very handsome man and a gentleman too I think. Why do you ask?"
"I have some niggling doubts about him."
"What sort of doubts?"
"He's very polished and suave - very skilled with words."
"And what is wrong with that?"
"It's just that he's elusive, hard to pin down on many issues and his skill with words enables him to escape without revealing very much about anything - particularly about the progress of his company PCOG."
"I think he is very romantic and very caring for Gretel. He is always a perfect gentleman."
"Yes! - but that's exactly why I am worried. He is too good to be true," replied Wilhelm.

Eventually, Pierre's attentiveness to Gretel, his obvious thoughtfulness and unfailing courtesy convinced Wilhelm that she had met a man who truly loved her. They became engaged on the first anniversary of their meeting at the

Montreal Trade Exhibition. Marriage was impractical while they lived so far apart - one in Ireland and one in Canada and Wilhelm discussed this dilemma with Pierre one evening over drinks in the lounge of the Bernhart family home.

"I am concerned that there is not a good basis for marriage while you and Gretel live so far apart. Gretel is a director of Bernhart Industrial Steel Components Ltd. and cannot go to live in Montreal - except for an occasional few weeks."

"Of course not," replied Pierre, and after some quick, opportunistic thinking continued: "and unfortunately, I have a contract with PCOG that ties me to Montreal for another three years."

"Can you opt out of the contract?"

"There is no opt out clause and directly breaching the contract would involve financial penalties."

"If you cannot opt out of your contract and cannot be appointed to Europe by your company, I as a caring father to Gretel cannot consent to your marriage in such circumstances. It would not work."

"There is another option," said Pierre.

"Please elaborate."

"A prospective employer could buy out my contract from PCOG. With this arrangement, I would get letters of commendation and a guarantee of verbal confirmation for any prospective employer, regarding my ability and competence."

"And this would also cost money, yes!" declared Wilhelm.

"Yes, ten thousand Canadian dollars for each of the remaining years - for a prospective employer, but I believe that I could negotiate a better deal if I was to buy myself

out."
"And if a prospective employer bought the contract, its terms would be binding on you - if you did become his employee."
"Yes!"
"Well then," said Wilhelm, "perhaps there is another solution to this problem and I will think on it."

Two months later, a meeting of the board of directors of Petroleum Canada Oil and Gas (of which Pierre was the sole owner), approved the plan to release Pierre from his contract (which he himself had just recently drafted), for an agreed sum of twenty thousand Canadian dollars. Wilhelm promptly paid up, Pierre became an employee of Bernhart Industrial Steel Components Ltd. and the money eventually made its way by devious, circuitous routes into Pierre's personal bank account.

Two major difficulties had been overcome for Pierre – he was now in full time employment with Bernhart Industrial Steel Components Ltd. and he had at last become a man of means, with some real money in his pockets.

PCOG ceased trading after Pierre’s departure – in fact, it never had begun to trade publicly. He transferred ownership of the land bank in the badlands of Alberta from the company to himself.

Eight

Thomas and Mary took very seriously the warning of their gynaecologist, that any more pregnancies could have serious health implications for Mary. They observed the guidelines of their family doctor but despite all their precautions, Mary became pregnant again.

As it transpired, all went very well with the pregnancy and in due course, a baby boy was born - to everybody's great delight and joy and the warning of the gynaecologist was deemed to be wrong or so it seemed and it faded from their minds. They christened him Enda but immediately began to call him Indie and that became the name by which he was to be known thereafter by everyone.

In the first week or so after the baby came home, they were very concerned and nervous. They were alert to every move he made at night and both jumped out to tend to him at the slightest move, but they soon settled down as they became more accustomed to meeting his needs. Presents began to pile up as grandparents, aunts, uncles friends and neighbours came to see the new baby and congratulate the grateful parents. It was a glorious time for them but tragedy would soon strike again.

Mary Kendley died one day while Thomas was at school. It was the determination of the doctors that death was due to

a condition that develops following childbirth in a very small number of cases.
This determination came as a hammer blow to Thomas, as the warning given to him by the gynaecologist after the birth of the twins flashed across his mind.
"You must avoid any more pregnancies," the gynaecologist had said. "It could be risky."

I won't go into the deeply emotional details of the grief and desolation felt and expressed by parents, siblings, friends and by Nora, Rose and myself - I simply can't because it is too painful. Besides there is a privacy in the grieving of the person and I want to honour and respect that. It is enough to state generally that the grieving was communal, contagious and that it pierced the hearts of everyone. The rest is easy to imagine. The great sadness of the wake, of the funeral, of the family members – her brothers, sisters, father and mother and the heartbreak that they clearly felt and exhibited. The baby was a source of grateful distraction and consolation especially to Mary's parents and siblings, in the great loss, emptiness and sadness that followed - but time moves on. There isn't a choice. The great wheel of life turns without ceasing - it turns for those whose time it is to come and for those whose time it is to go and for some it turns long before their time has come - or so we think.

On the day of the funeral, after the burial the crowds were reluctant to leave - feeling perhaps that the enormous loss of someone so young and so beautiful required them to stay awhile longer. They hoped that their presence would be a source of comfort to the bereaved or that they could

give consolation by words that were repeated over and over a hundred, thousand times:
"I'm so sorry Thomas... I'm sorry for your sad loss... It is a severe blow.... She is up there in heaven with the angels... She will look after you all from heaven... She will not be far away.. The dead are very near us.... She is up there now with the twins and she is happy... It was so tragic the way it happened.. Your baby boy will be a comfort to you..."
Yes! the baby would be a comfort to him. He would mind him and look after him. He must focus on that.

Nine

The year preceding the marriage of Gretel and Pierre was one of great happiness and frenetic activity. Wilhelm bought Bernstadt Hall and Gretel took charge of refurbishments, decoration and furnishing. Pierre was fully occupied in London setting up the new office for Bernhart Industrial Steel Components plc., designing and printing new promotional literature and installing up to date communications infrastructure. Despite all this he managed to regularly come and stay with the Bernharts and spend time with Gretel, while she occasionally spent weekends with him in London.

Gretel's father Wilhelm was still perturbed by instinctive niggling doubts about his future son in law.
“He is so very smooth,” Wilhelm said to Ericka one evening as they sat in their drawing room.
"What do you mean by that?" asked Ericka.
"He is altogether too agreeable and has the ability to be eloquently persuasive about diametrically opposing propositions. I always suspect such people," Wilhelm replied.
“But dear, aren't these the very attributes that made him an excellent promotion officer for our company?”
“He is doing good work for us," agreed Wilhelm, "but I fear that he himself will always be his own first priority."
“Is that not true of everyone?" asked Ericka. "How else would you expect him to be? Everyone must look out for

themselves, as the proverb says: every man for himself and God for everyman."
"That is not the proverb," joked Wilhelm.
"Well if it isn't it ought to be," quipped Ericka.
There was no arguing with that.

In contrast to the wedding of Thomas and Mary, Gretel and Pierre's wedding celebrations were formal in all aspects. Music was provided by an orchestra, the dancing was formal and impressive - the ladies in elegant gowns swishing almost at floor level and the men in black swallow tail coats and striped grey trousers added to the opulence and style of the occasion. It was impressive but very different indeed from the wild freedom of the Siege of Ennis and Polka Sets at the wedding of my brother Thomas and Mary - his beloved Dancing Girl.

If the year before the wedding was happy, the first year of married life was even happier. Pierre dutifully flew home to Bernstadt Hall each alternate weekend and Gretel went as often as possible to London to stay with Pierre - faithfully until her pregnancy was at an advanced stage. When their son Paul Bernhart Bouvier was born, both husband and wife felt great joy and thanked God for this blessing.

In October of that year, the baby was six months old and Pierre was at the big bay window, hands deep in his pockets, looking across at the gently sloping hillside with its many coloured groves and fields of faded green and at the meandering cattle that invariably grazed there. Today he saw but didn't notice them. Neither did he notice the orange beaked blackbird and his dark brown female mate scratch for worms from the soil beneath the weeping willow or the large, feathery rook stamping on the lawn for worms directly in front of the window.

His mind was drifting across to England - specifically to issues surrounding the tender he had submitted to the Secretary for Defence for the manufacture and supply of steel components for the military. As if that was not enough distraction, he was also disturbed in his mind by an increasingly frustrating personal issue in his marital relationship with Gretel. Due to complications and difficulties she had suffered as a result of the difficult birth of Baby Paul, there was a temporary cessation in their physical love life.
This was beginning to be the cause of tension between them and it was this tension and frustration that most dominated his mind on that July morning - as he gazed unseeingly out the bay window, so intent on his thoughts that he didn't hear her approach until she reached up and kissed him.
"You are admiring the beauty of the world," she remarked.
"Not only the beauty of the world" he answered in his smooth tone of voice, "but the beauty of my wife and wishing we had better news from the doctor."
"I know it is not easy for you" said Gretel. "I will speak to her this week. Perhaps she will have good news."
"Yes, I hope so," Pierre replied. "It would not be so difficult if you were not so beautiful."
She put her arms around him then and rested her head on his chest and they stood there for some time and then the nursemaid entered and handed the baby to Pierre.

"Go to Daddy," she said and the world regained its splendour. All of nature responded and sang its harmonies in the crisp sunny morning - made brighter by the happiness of a father holding his little son tenderly in his arms.

Baby Paul whom his father called Peaboy, continued to develop and to always be the focus of someone's attention in Bernstadt Hall or in the home of his grandparents Ericka and Wilhelm. He was slow to learn to walk but once he did, he was constantly on the go, legs spread wide, hands held at shoulder height with the palms turned outwards to help his balance. He explored everywhere within the house and paid attention to the finer detail of objects and pictures by close visual scrutiny and often rubbing his fingers along their surfaces, in an act of tactile learning, which perhaps reflected a keen and inquiring intellect.

Ten

Thomas of course, was a teacher - this was his vocation in life and teaching had to be done regardless of personal circumstances. School is a great place to get serious issues from the mind because you are so busy and life is so frenetic when you are dealing with a classroom full of lively children, that you don't have time to think about your own troubles. Cill Gobnait N.S. was a rural school and everyone in the school community and beyond was enormously kind and caring to him. The children knew the awful thing that had happened to him and they were kind to him and with very few exceptions, were very obedient and helpful.

Indie commenced school at the age of four years and travelled in the car with Thomas. His journey to school every day was through elevated landscapes with many beautiful views of climbing hillside fields and lower greener ones, along the banks of a winding stony river. There were occasional broader panoramas from the top of a rise in the road, interspersed here and there with white or yellow coloured houses and clusters of trees, sheltering sheds and other farm buildings.
Along the road he encountered a variety of people - roadmen with their shovels cleaning out the water tables or cutting protruding briars and brambles with a scythe or long handled bill hook.
Thomas always allowed plenty of time for the journey to

school. He was almost certain to encounter delays in the form of slow moving vehicles - a tractor and trailer laden with milk churns on its way to the creamery or people standing on the road while the cattle went across or driving out the cows after the early morning milking. It was useless to fret and fume when a herd of cows was ambling towards you, filling the entire road. Cows with swinging udders walk at their own pace and are entirely unconcerned about the stresses of the morning motorist hurrying for work. Thomas knew that the best way of dealing with this situation was to switch off the engine and wait until the cows had gone past. This allowed him to relax, roll down the window and have a few brief words with the farmer-drover as he passed by:

"Good morning, Den. A lovely morning."

"Good morning Master; 'tis a lovely morning, 'tis indeed a lovely morning, you may say that Master - a lovely morning indeed."

"How's the farming going Den?"

"Disastrous! Disastrous! No good at all master. No money making - no money at all."

"No money at all Den - that's very bad indeed."

"Indeed, it is you that has the fine job, Master, three months holidays every summer."

"I know Den - every July and August."

"And a big cheque coming every week to you Master while the poor farmer must wait for fair day."

"Wait awhile Den and I'll get a few pounds from my pocket to give you," Thomas would say jokingly.

"That would be very good Master, very good indeed and 'tis you could well afford it, but I have no time to wait for it today, I must run after them cows before they pass the

gate of the field and head for Cork or Killarney."
"Some other day so, Den."
"That will be grand Master - grand altogether," laughed Den as he ran in his wellington boots to catch up with the cows.
Thomas often laughed at this conversation because he knew and Den knew, that the farming was going quite well at that time and that Den was one of the wealthiest men in the parish.
"The poor mouth," laughed Thomas, "an inheritance from the era of the landlordism in Ireland. It served us well."

Thomas was very friendly with the musical McMahon family, who had five children in the school and they frequently invited him to their home for sessions of music and song with other local musicians. One of their five children - a boy named Packie, had Down Syndrome. He was much loved by his siblings, parents and neighbours and he loved everyone in return, loved listening to the music and always became excited whenever Thomas visited the family home. Sometimes Thomas left his violin there and when he called again, Packie would approach him with the violin and say:
"Master, play a tune. Play a tune master. Play a tune for Packie."

Occasionally a local dance would be organised in the Community Hall beside the school. Thomas and the McMahons often played there and local people and parents and their children came and danced and sang songs. It was usually very pleasant and fabulously friendly and homely. Meanwhile, Indie was growing stronger and

Thomas became more content and more at peace with himself.

Eleven

In the years that followed Thomas acted on his resolve to compensate Indie for the loss of his mother and he did all that he could to be both a father and a mother to him. Thereafter they were together whenever and wherever possible - if he was travelling or at a football match or simply walking in the countryside, Indie was there with him and they grew together like two good buddies.

The river Shourna runs through the outskirts of Sheffin where we live and it is a very good fishing river. Thomas spent a lot of time fishing there in the years after Mary's death, even fishing at night sometimes when Indie was staying with us and getting to know his cousins.
"The bank of the river is a great place to experience peace," he often said. "There is just you and the water and the very sound of silence itself - expressed in the combined swish and ripple and gurgle of streams far and near."

When Indie was eight years old he began to accompany his dad when he went fishing. Some would say that this was a dangerous thing to do and Mary's parents often expressed concern:
"For God's sake, will you mind that child on the river," Mary's grey-haired mother frequently admonished.
Thomas assured them that he would mind him and that he would teach him to be safe and careful.

"I know you will teach him well," said Mary's father, "but he is still only a child and you can't always trust a child to remember what you have taught him."

Thomas did teach Indie the craft of being safe and also some of the craft of being a good fisherman. He showed him how to cast, how to pull the fly along the stilly pools and how to let the light current carry it along temptingly for a hungry trout. He showed him how to make the cast go a greater distance by holding his hand and elbow rigidly and he occasionally allowed him to wind in an exhausted trout to the river bank after it had been played and made tired and weary by skilled rod work.

Often when they returned home after such outings, Thomas would take down the violin or concert flute and play from his vast repertoire of tunes. He would close his eyes as he played and visualise again the couples on the crowded dance floor, moving in perfect time to the music - waltzes, two hand reels, the Siege of Ennis, four hand reels, the wonderful haymaker's jig and the various reel and polka sets that were wild and free and disciplined and respectable. There was something joyous and intimate about it all that was indelibly written on his memory - always ready and waiting to be re-visualised by the power and nostalgia of the music.

They were very happy times for Thomas and Indie and they became really good buddies. His focus was on Indie and the future looked happy and bright, but it was not to turn out that way.

Twelve

Gretel was very happy. She cut down on her workload with the company and delighted in caring for baby Paul. Thus she was fairly compensated for the deficiency in her physical relationship with Pierre. Besides, she was stoical and accepting by nature - apart from a habitual tendency to blurt out at times without appropriate restraint.
Unlike Gretel, Pierre had no such compensations. Even when he did come home to Bernstadt Hall, he found her absorbed with caring for the baby and unable to share much time with him and he frequently returned to London in a state of frustration - something that did not go unnoticed by Shirley, his office secretary.

Shirley Greene was blonde, attractive and unlike Gretel, was naturally ebullient, affirming and soothing and she was secretly obsessed with Pierre.
She questioned him many times after his return from his weekends at Bernstadt Hall:
"You look tired this morning Pierre. Did you have a good weekend? How is the baby and how is your wife?"
She soon deduced from his responses that all was not well in the relationship between this fabulously handsome man and his wife and she was secretly pleased about this.

Pierre continued to immerse himself in his work. He was still as attractive as ever, a focus of feminine attention at trade shows and conferences but he protected himself from romantic involvement by not socialising at night and going early to his room. There were a number of regulars - men and women who did the rounds of conferences and shows on behalf of their companies and while some women flirted teasingly with him, he didn't falter. He looked forward to resuming full marital relationships with Gretel and waited for the prescribed time to pass.

"I know you have been anticipating the resumption of our full loving relationship," said Gretel after they had finished supper in Bernstadt Hall one weekend.

"Is there still a problem?" Pierre asked.

"I am afraid so. The doctor advised against any further pregnancy for two more years. I know this is disappointing for you and it is also disappointing for me"

"I want a second opinion."

"I thought of that and I got a second opinion.

"And?" prompted Pierre.

"She confirmed the prognosis."

Pierre didn't answer and she was worried by his silence.

"It would be easier to plan our relationship if your work was here. Maybe my father can find a position for you here at home."

"I am doing the work I was contracted to do in the UK." answered Pierre. "I never break a contract. There is always a price to be paid by those who do."

Pierre felt aggrieved and sore in his feelings. Two more years was a long time to wait and he felt that Gretel was being unreasonable."

"There is some obstacle in everyone's life" she replied "some cross to carry. On the scale of life's sorrows, it is not too heavy a burden to bear."

Pierre did not respond. He felt she was rejecting him, casting him aside. He grew more frustrated and angry within himself:
"I will go to the guest room," he said. "It is best that way."

The thought that he was being wronged by his wife burrowed deeper into Pierre's mind and developed into a conviction that she had broken the very terms of their marriage contract. He repeated again to himself the words he had spoken earlier:
“There is always a price to be paid by those who break a contract."

Pierre had worked very hard at his job in England. He had a stand at all the prestigious shows where engineering and mechanical equipment of all sorts were exhibited. His aim was to establish Bernhart Industrial Steel Components Ltd. as a significant player in the larger industrial manufacturing sphere and his work was making a positive impact. The submission of a tender to the British Ministry of Defence was a major progression and if successful, would lead on to more lucrative opportunities for the company in the future. New orders were already coming on stream and back in Ireland, Wilhelm Bernhart was well pleased.
“Pierre is doing quite well,” he remarked one evening to Ericka as they relaxed in the drawing room of their palatial home. "He is working quite hard for us."
“That is good” she answered, “but I am concerned that his work is keeping him away from Gretel. They no longer spend weekends together as frequently as they used to.”
“Well she cannot travel to London on weekends like she used to - she has a baby to care for now," argued Wilhelm.

“Yes, but now Pierre only comes home one weekend in three or sometimes just once a month. I am concerned about that. There are many temptations out there."

"It does not have to be that way," stated Wilhelm. "He must cut down on his work for the company each weekend. I will tell him that."

“It isn’t the work that is causing him to stay away from his wife," said Ericka.

“What do you mean?"

“Gretel’s doctor has told her that she must avoid becoming pregnant for at least another two years.”

“I see,” said Wilhelm.

“Gretel favours natural family planning," said Ericka.

"So what," observed Wilhelm. "We had to do the same in our lives."

“The situation is not the same," explained Ericka. "You were living here with me but Pierre is in London five days each week. This is causing tension in the marriage."

“Has Gretel spoken to you about this matter!" asked Wilhelm.

"Yes! She wants to adhere to the teaching of the Church. Pierre does not."

“I see the problem," said Wilhelm. "The situation is difficult, especially when you are young but a good man will always do what must be done, just like I did – if he truly loves his wife.”

“But, my darling, you were solid and dependable and deeply caring.”

“And you think Pierre is not dependable and deeply caring.”

“He is not," answered Ericka. "He is caring and dependable but only in the right circumstances and besides, he is very handsome and some women are drawn to him."

"And in the present circumstances, you think he will be too weak to resist them?"

"Yes," said Ericka. "I think your original assessment of him is correct - Pierre will always put Pierre first and foremost because Pierre is, and always will be, his own very first priority."

Thirteen

Thomas' son Indie was drowned during the summer of his ninth year when he fell into the flooded river, after the bank on which he was standing collapsed beneath him. They were fishing together here in the river Shourna. Indie was using the new fishing rod that his father had bought him for his birthday - a nice colourful plastic spinner that could be used with a lure, a worm or with a bubble for fly fishing. Indie was beside himself with delight. He had also got a pair of small waders and they made a happy sight as they headed off for the river - the small little fisherman accompanying his tall Dad, both wearing waders and dressed for the task - both carrying their fishing rods.

The weather was very warm that summer and as sometimes happens in heavy weather, there was a sudden and sustained thunderstorm and a cloudburst in the hills that caused a spectacularly high flood some days earlier. The water levels in the Shourna reached a record height and high up on the trees that grew in the bank, one could see the driftwood and the bits of flotsam that proved the water had reached that level. If you didn't see the flotsam on the trees, it would have been hard to believe that the water had risen so high, but it did and the flotsam proved it.

On that fateful July day, a warm sun shone strongly on Thomas and his son Indie, penetrating their outer garments and spreading its warmth along their backs and shoulders. Indie was full of excitement - his first day out with his very own fishing rod. He had often been with his father prior to this and he often used his father's fishing rod, but now, he had his own and he felt big and grown up and proud. The flood had not fully abated and was perhaps a foot or so higher than normal and the water was greyish brown and swiftly flowing.

They commenced fishing above the bridge where the river is wide and not very deep. Perhaps it is at that point, twenty metres wide and they were there a little while and Thomas did a huge long cast right across the river, under the tree branches on the far bank. Immediately he felt the tug on the line and he reeled in a fine trout. It was a wonderful sight, seeing the silver bellied trout dancing in the water with its tail splashing hither and thither all the way across the pool, fighting to break free of the hook and line. After that, they caught no more trout there and they moved to the other side, just below the bridge. It was a stone bridge, with beautifully crafted stone arches and robust limestone capping, chest-high on top of its battlements.

They went across the road and settled in below the bridge at one of their favourite spots. It was a very good spot to get trout, because sometimes in the rise or fall of the flood there was a little whirlpool there and the whirlpool brought worms with it and deposited them there and the fish came to feed on them. When you dropped in a hook baited with a worm there was a great chance that a fish would take the bait and you had a trout in no time at all.

Thomas told Indie to get out the container of worms, which he had kept in oatmeal for some weeks to toughen them and he affixed one to the hook of Indie's rod and Indie cast it in.
"Be sure to keep back from the edge of the bank," Thomas warned him, before he himself went about thirty metres downstream to cast in his own bait and return to Indie - having placed his rod in a leaning position against a barbed wire fence. That way, he hoped to get a trout in his own rod while he returned to supervise Indie.
It was during that brief absence that the awful accident occurred. The big flood had eroded away the earth beneath the bank where Indie was standing and when, for some reason he stepped too near the edge, the bank fell into the swift flowing current, bringing Indie with it.

There was a large crowd at the Indie's funeral mass. At times like this, many people support the bereaved by their strength, their silence and their consoling words but others add to the grief by being sad and overcome with emotion themselves. As is usual at times like this, the tragedy became a topic of conversation and discussion and there was a mixture of opinions.
"He should never have brought that child fishing - that child was too young for that."
"Ah he was trying to be a father and a mother to the child and he did his best for him."
"The question is, could he have saved him if he plunged into the water?"
"I'm sure that he would have done that if he could."
"If he plunged in, he would have been swept away and drowned - so we would have a double tragedy instead of

one."
"Maybe he would have been better off to have been drowned. He is left with a heavy cross to bear."
"God will help him. They say that the Lord fits the beast for the burden."

Mary's father was sharply critical of Thomas.
"You were warned that that child was too young for going fishing. We warned you a hundred times to be extra careful because you can't trust a child to remember what you have told them - I told you that time after time. I'll be honest with you and tell you straight out that I will find it very hard to forgive you - ever."
"Don't blame yourself too much," her mother had said. "Try to think that Indie is with his mother in heaven and with the twins and with your first baby. They are all there and they are very happy. Think of it like that. It will bring you consolation. We will try to think of it like that too, but our hearts are broken, broken beyond repair. We will never get over all this tragedy - never."

Fourteen

Back in England, Pierre Bouvier relaxed the disciplined regime he had practiced at social events generally and reverted again to the ways of his bachelor days. He no longer avoided the social events at trade fairs and soon he began to experience old excitements in the company of the women who were regularly drawn to him.

It was in Liverpool that Pierre first broke his marriage vows. He justified his actions by blaming Gretel. Even so, he was remorseful and vowed it would not happen again - but of course it did. It was easier the next time round. He ceased attending mass and while he did occasionally pray on his knees to ask God to help him overcome his weakness, the potency and excitement that engulfed him made him weak and unable to resist temptation.
His visits home became more infrequent. Gretel developed a testiness, was sometimes harshly irritable and began to resort frequently to the drinks cabinet at home and in the office.

Ericka could read the signs and realised that drastic action was required and she outlined her solution to her husband Wilhelm, as they sat in their fireside chairs one evening:
"Pierre must be brought here to work," she declared to Wilhelm, "if he is not brought back, our daughter's marriage will not last I think."
"But we do not have a role for him here," argued Wilhelm.

"Well then, you must create a role for him. Make him a director - the company needs to consolidate its progress and expansion at this time. He is the man to do that."
"Who will take over the London office?" he asked.
"Let Shirley Greene do that. Most of his promotional work is done now. She is well capable of consolidating the progress that has been made and of keeping everything on an even keel."
"If we win the Ministry of Defence contract, we will need him here to oversee production," said Wilhelm.
"He must be brought back here whether we do, or do not win the contract. It is here he should be with his wife and his child."
"We must handle this carefully," mused Wilhelm. "Confidentiality is essential. We will reveal our plans on a need to know basis only - for the time being at least. Pierre does not need to know right away."

Two weeks later the Secretary of Defence notified Bernhart Industrial Steel Components Ltd. that its seven million pounds tender to supply hardened steel components for military hardware had been accepted. It was the breakthrough into big league business that Pierre had dreamed of and worked for but he felt it had come too late for him. His marriage was seriously impaired - possibly to the point of no return.

Ericka and Wilhelm were delighted to have won the contract and informed Pierre that they were hosting a dinner to celebrate his great achievement with some close friends and family. They did not tell him that they planned to make him a director of the company and that he would be coming home for good to Bernstadt Hall to his wife and to his beloved Peaboy. They wanted it to be a surprise for him. Shirley Greene in the London Office was the only one outside of the immediate family who was informed of the planned changes.

Gretel was elated and delighted and it was at her suggestion that everyone was sworn to secrecy about the new appointment. It would be a fabulous surprise for Pierre. They would then be able to plan their relationship and resume the fullness of their love life. Everything was looking bright again.

On the morning of the day of the celebration, Gretel received an anonymous typewritten letter outlining allegations of frequent indiscretions and infidelities by her husband Pierre Bouvier, in various cities in England, including an ongoing affair with his secretary Shirley Greene, a married woman and a mother of two children.
Gretel was shell shocked.
"Be careful how you handle this," warned her mother. "It is an anonymous letter and it may be untrue and may well be malicious."
"I have suspected that he was being unfaithful for some time," said Gretel. "I sensed it."
"Even so," replied her mother, "you must not mention it to him tonight. Let some time elapse. Keep it to yourself for awhile. Pretend that you know nothing. Soon your husband will be home with you and no longer in the way of temptation."
"It will not be easy for me to hold it all in," Gretel declared. "It will not be easy."

"It is the best way to deal with it," said Ericka. "Many good things have come together for us at this time. Sales in the U.K. have increased hugely, the Ministry of Defence contract has come through and most important of all we are able to employ Pierre here at home where he can be with you and little Peaboy as one happy family. Pierre himself has done much to achieve this."
"I know and I acknowledge his achievement but I can't stomach his being unfaithful with so many different women. If it were only one woman, it would not be so filthy."
"Look on the positive side. He will soon be home with you permanently, once he takes up his directorship. Concentrate on that," advised Ericka. "Give it time."
"You know that I can't hold my tongue at times and I tend to blurt things out regardless of the consequences," said Gretel.
"I know, but you must keep your tongue under control this time. Blurting out could destroy everything."
"I will try my best," she promised.
"Oh! and one more thing," said her mother, "avoid drinking too much alcohol. It diminishes our ability to control our emotions and is very good at loosening tongues."

Gretel was taken aback at this reference to alcohol. During the past twelve months she had developed a liking for wine and spirits. She had secretly overindulged at times but she didn't realise that her mother was aware of this.
"It seems that mother knows more about me than I thought," she mused silently to herself and then said aloud: "Your advice is good and I will do as you suggest."

Throughout all of that day Gretel's feelings were turbulent and alternated between happiness that Pierre was coming home and anger at his infidelity. She was disturbed and shaken and she fortified herself with frequent visits to the drinks cabinet for moderate amounts of vodka and orange.

Gretel tried hard to be pleasant at the celebratory family dinner and had more vodka and orange to keep her spirits up. She tried as hard as she could to remain calm, but she was so obviously testy and a little drunk during the meal, that Pierre took her home before the meal had ended and before the surprise announcement of his appointment as director could be made. She was sullen and in a bad mood on the short journey to Bernstadt Hall and refused to talk to him.

Later, when Pierre joined her in the bedroom and put his arms around her in a comforting way, she lost her reserve and became reckless and unable to stop the harsh words tumbling in torrents from her mouth:
"Take your filthy hands off of me," she ordered in a slurred voice.
"Filthy hands!" exclaimed Pierre in surprise.
"Your hands are filthy from the women you've been with in cities all over England."
"I have not been with women all over England," Pierre protested.
"Oh yes you have," she screamed, "and I have a letter here to prove it."
Pierre was taken aback, but remained cool and calm.
"O.K. I admit that I have been unfaithful a few times, but

not with women all over England."
"And I suppose you haven't had an affair with your secretary Shirley Greene either."
"I have not."
"Liar."
Pierre refrained from further argument.
Gretel was visibly shaking with anger and emotion and having lost all restraint, recklessly ordered Pierre out of the bedroom.
"You are not sleeping in my bed tonight. You can sleep in the guest room and while you are there you can think about your mistress Shirley Greene and all the other women you've had in Liverpool, Manchester and all over England. Now leave this room because you are not worthy to be in it. You are an adulterer and you are not a fit person to be a parent to your son."
"I did not have an affair with Shirley Greene," protested Pierre again.
"Liar," she screamed. "You lying adulterer."
Pierre turned and walked out of the room without another word, closing the door quietly as he left.

Fifteen

After Indie's funeral Thomas had just five weeks to come to terms with his new reality and prepare himself mentally to return to the task of teaching the children in September. In the circumstances he did remarkably well. He went on a pilgrimage to Knock, as he was advised to do, by an old man who came to comfort him:
"Go to where the help is," the old man had said. "Go to Knock. The help is there."
Well, he did go and he got great consolation there and inner spiritual strength.

He appeared outwardly calm but there was a traumatic turbulence underneath and some of his actions reflected the depth of revulsion and self-blaming that was going on in his mind. One evening when I called to his house he was out in the back garden. He had a little fire going and I couldn't fail to notice the pieces of his fishing rod amid the flickering flames. I didn't comment on that and he didn't either. Then he said:
"The concertina and the flute are inside. I want you to take them to your house because I won't be needing them again."
"I would prefer if you kept them here," I answered. "Maybe, sometime in the future the humour will come upon you to play them again."
"No, I am finished with them," he stated trenchantly.
"I will leave them here with you anyway."

"If you leave them here," he said, "I will just put them in the fire with the fishing rod. Please take them. Maybe your children will play them sometime."

Well I brought them down because I thought it was the right thing to do. I wondered why he didn't ask me to take the violin but I learned later that he had given it to McMahons and told them to keep it, in the hope that one of their family would use it.
"I am finished with it," he said, "my soul is dead to music. I will never play again."
These were some of the punishments that he imposed upon himself, punishments for his negligence, as he saw it, punishments for his failure to protect his child and punishment for the cowardice he had shown.

One gloriously warm evening towards the end of the summer holidays, he was at the back of the house digging out stones and breaking small rocks with a sledgehammer and crowbar. There was much beauty all around him and the blackbird and thrush were singing and a skylark in the high heavens profusely pouring out its warbled notes, but Thomas was unable to focus properly on his work and he neither saw the beauty nor heard the heavenly refrain. The weight of what had happened was pressing in on him incessantly and as he worked he was talking aloud to God and he complained angrily about the burden of grief that had been imposed on him:
"You are God, who is supposed to be good and just and loving and caring to us. Well you haven't been very good and caring to me, have you? You've taken our first baby, the twins, my wife and my child - is that good and loving

and caring? Why did you do all of that to me? Why? Answer me that. I've always done my very best and always worked hard and have always been good to everyone. Well you have not been very good to me. You've stripped me of all that was important and dear to me in my life. Is that the reward I get for being good and honest? That's a nice reward alright."

The more he spoke like that the angrier and more helpless he became. A wrong spirit took hold of him and he was gripped by great bitterness and frustration and he began to scold God and hate everything else - his new house, the garden, the beautiful gate. At some time in this madness he walked to the front wall of which he had been so proud and began to pound it with the sledgehammer, leaving dents in the plaster and he kept on pounding it and pounding it and cursing life and his misfortune.
Holes appeared in the wall as the sledge broke through the outer part of the concrete cavity blocks and still he kept on pounding with all his force, again and again and again until the energy subsided and the moment of madness had passed and then he threw himself on the ground and cried out loud and his body shook and shuddered until the tension had eased. When he stood up again, he felt sorry for what he had done - the wall had done nothing to merit this. The moment had passed.

Later he put the sledge and crowbar into the shed and went for a very long walk in the hills. He was hungry and he realised that he had been punishing himself for weeks by eating little more than a starvation diet. The isolation of the hills soothed his mind and the large barren open bog-

lands aroused in him a feeling of calm and he began to feel sorry that he had scolded God and blamed Him for everything:
"Dear God, I'm sorry for being so angry with you and for blaming you and for scolding you, but I know that you will understand. I know that the misfortunes that I have encountered were not caused by you. They were accidents of life or of experience or of human failure - nothing more. I know that you are the source of all that is good and decent and holy and that by virtue of the selfless good that is in me, I am inextricably and eternally linked with you. I know that for sure and for certain."

As he walked he came upon the narrow upper reaches of a river, flowing beside a stone, boundary ditch in an area that was relatively flat and so the water was not deep and it was spread wide among a multiplicity of cobbled stones and smallish rounded boulders. Gazing on the stream and walking beside it, it occurred to him that this stream had been there for a hundred thousand years or more and water was flowing there all of that time and it had a permanence.
"It was there generations before me," he said aloud, "and it will still be flowing away merrily, freely, carelessly, unworriedly on its way, generations after I have passed and gone."

And so in this place with nothing but stillness all around, no one in sight, no house, no animal or bird, a sense of the great permanence that there is on earth and in such places came over him and with that a sense of the very brief span of the human life and the great impermanence that there is

in the lives of all humans. Just as that wide mountain stream would have great torrents of brown foaming water tearing down in times of storm and rain and thunder, it would in a short time revert to its more tranquil ways.
"It is thus with the tragedies of human life," he mused - "The raging floods of tragic events, the raging storms that tear and wound the heart, the foaming waters of turbulent emotions and of a deeply troubled mind and the eventual return -with the help of God and the passage of time, to calm tranquility and a clean-washed soul."

He talked aloud as he walked along, careful about where he put his feet, for the ground was soft and boggy.
"I know that suffering is a part of life, perhaps even a necessary and inescapable part of life, but why Lord, why? A consequence of evil perhaps or its fruits or maybe it counters those who do evil, maybe it balances out the harm that they do."

For awhile after that day, Thomas was calmer in himself and more accepting of what had happened to him but he continued to blame himself for Indie's death and to see himself as a coward because he failed to risk his own life to save him. He persisted with this conviction and continued to inflict upon himself the punishment that inevitably accompanies such a destructive and negative belief.
He repaired the damage that he had done to the wall, but the signs remained to be seen and served occasionally as a reminder to him of his journey through his own personal valley of darkness.

Sixteen

Pierre did not go to the guest bedroom, after Gretel in her drunken state had ordered him out but went instead to the nursery. He stood there for a long time looking at his two and a half year old son asleep in his cot, watching his little chest rising ever so slightly with each peaceful sleeping breath. He wanted to take him in his arms but decided against it. It would make what he was about to do more painful, so instead he lowered the side of the cot and bending down planted a tender kiss on the forehead of his sleeping son.
"*Au revoir* little Peaboy," he said aloud. "May God bless you. I hope we will meet again sometime, someday, somewhere in the not too distant future."

After Pierre had left the room, Gretel threw herself across the bed and fell into a drunken stupor. She became sick sometime later and her head was reeling, so she knelt at the toilet bowl, vomiting until her throat was sore and her tongue felt dry and swollen and water streamed from her eyes and streaked her makeup and mascara and her mouth was filled with a sour and bitter taste. Her eyes burned and her head ached and she fell into a fitful sleep.

When she finally awoke around 9.30am a strong sense of foreboding gripped her, a sense that she had crossed her own personal Rubicon to a much changed landscape, now equipped with hard-learned lessons and the harsh realities

of outcomes of stupidity, of awful intemperance and of failure to exercise restraint.
"Pierre, Pierre!" - she must go and talk to him and tell him about their plans to make him a director of the company and how they will be able to live like husband and wife again and rear baby Paul, giving him two fulltime parents instead of one at home and one away as at present. But what had she said to him last night? Did she really say that he was not a fit person to be a father to little Peaboy? Oh dear! She must go to him and explain.
She walked with wobbling steps past the nursery where baby Paul was cooing happily to the nursemaid:
"Thank God for that" - but she must go to the guest room to Pierre and explain everything to him.
When she finally opened the door, she saw that the bed had not been slept in. Pierre wasn't there.

After he had fondly kissed his child on the forehead, Pierre had quietly left Bernstadt Hall, travelled by taxi to the airport and was lucky enough to get a standby seat on a flight to London.

Around the time that Gretel was on her wobbly walk to the guestroom on the morning after the ill-fated celebratory dinner party, her husband Pierre was closing the door of the safe in the London Office of Bernhart Industrial Steel Components Ltd. having just deposited two envelopes therein.
The larger of these contained two documents - his letter of resignation from Bernhart Industrial Steel Components Ltd. and a photocopy of a bank draft in favour of Pierre Bouvier in the amount of £140,000.

The second envelope contained a letter to Mrs. Gretel Bouvier, Bernstadt Hall. It was a loving and tender letter in many ways and Pierre freely admitted to his innate inborn flawed weakness for involvement with women. There was no criticism of Gretel, much praise and kind words for her parents, deeply painful acceptance of her criticisms that he was not a fit person to be a father to his son and the last paragraph which read:

"A time comes in the life of everyone when they must pause and examine what they are doing, consider where they wish to go and what they wish to achieve and whether they are on the right course to reach their potential and goal. That time is now for you and for me and we must address it singly and separate from each other. We are wiser now than we once were, for life has taught us lessons that are only found in life and one of these lessons is that a price is always paid when we breach a sacred trust.
It would be nice to think that we could go back to earlier dreams and hopes now deferred, but we cannot. Circumstances and the consequences of folly have prohibited that. It is inappropriate that a child of such a truly Christian family would be parented by someone who had so wronged his mother and so I take you at your word and leave now before he is old enough to have concrete memories of me. I ask that you would not blame yourself or worry about me. I have other dreams and I will cast myself upon the sea of life and let its flowing tides take me where they will.
Finally, I commit by contract in the form of these written words, to render financial support to you and to my son."

Signed with love and sadness,
Pierre.

Days and weeks of trauma followed in the homes of Gretel and of her parents. She begged her father to try to find Pierre and explain how they were planning to make him a director of the company and to bring him back to Bernstadt Hall, to herself and to little 'Peaboy.'

Wilhelm did try, utilising all his contacts in Germany, France, Canada and the U.S.A. He tried and tried until he was weary and began to realise that he was getting old and feeling the effects of his years.

It was his wife Ericka with her customary incisive intuition, who grasped the stark reality that Pierre would not be coming back:

"He will not be found," she declared. "He is a good strategist remember and I expect that he would have an effective exit strategy planned. I do not believe that he devised his exit plans in the brief few hours after the dinner party. His contingency plans were thought out well in advance I think. The preparation of the £140,000 bank draft is proof of that. No! He is gone - I'm certain of that."

Pierre's letter to Wilhelm Bernhart was deft, respectful and courteous but coldly calculating as the following excerpt shows:

"I expect that you were cautious enough to study the detail of the contract which you bought from PCOG. If you did carefully read it as I had advised, then you will be familiar with the terms of Appendix 3(a) regarding my entitlement to a 4.5% bonus of the additional profits generated for the

company arising from my work and a sum of £140,000 sterling has accrued in that regard. In the circumstances I'm sure that you will understand why I arranged this remuneration through the London Office."
"Let me assure you that I dearly loved your daughter Gretel. I freely admit that I posses some natural attribute that makes me attractive to women. I know that many men would regard that as a blessing, but let me assure them, that it is not a blessing but a curse - because it is an attraction based on good looks, a fleeting transient attribute, which when it fades, these same admirers fade with it. It is only a love that is based on the inner spirit of the human being that endures and that is most worthy. That is the love that was shared by Gretel and me and I regret that circumstances, differing beliefs and my innate weaknesses destroyed it."

"Finally, as a decent human being, I know that you may have some concern for me although you may also have a great deal of anger. Do not worry. I am a good strategist. I will find a way to make a living. Maybe my childhood dream of an oil discovery that delivers a handsome number of barrels of crude will come true one day."

Unknown to her parents, Gretel employed a firm of private investigators in a desperate effort to locate her husband. She was so desperate that she was prepared to beg him on her knees to return. But it was not to be. They did find airline records that showed him travelling from London to Amsterdam, to Montreal, to New York and latterly to Rio De Janeiro where ownership of land in the badlands of Alberta were transferred for a nominal sum to

Senhor Pedro Rodriguez a citizen of Brazil - and there the trail of Pierre Bouvier disappeared without trace. It was the last straw and Gretel accepted the inevitable.

Wilhelm Bernhart withdrew his tender with the Ministry of Defence. The company ceased its quest for new business in the United Kingdom and Europe and concentrated on fulfilling its existing overseas commitments. He devoted much attention and time to his grandson Paul Bernhart Bouvier. Maybe, just maybe, he would one day become the C.E.O. of Bernhart Industrial Steel Components Ltd. in succession to his grandfather.
"It is only a dream," mused Wilhelm, "but it is a dream that keeps me going all the same."

Seventeen

Many friends and neighbours, old and new, helped Thomas in the first year after Indie's death. I was always very close to him in a brotherly sort of way and along with my wife Hannah, I did my best to help. Our sisters Nora and Rose helped too, in so far as they could but since Nora lived in Washington and Rose in Edinburg and each had families of their own, that help was not as great as they would have liked it to be. The local priests helped and they were good to him but it was in his school community in Cill Gobnait that he received the most effective and powerful help of all. They were comforting and consoling for the most part. Parents who came in the evening to collect their children, frequently called in to have a word with Thomas, to console him with encouraging words or just engage in normal conversation..

Rossa Lee was one of the people who called to him most frequently. Rossa had one daughter who was two years older than Indie and they had come to live in the area five or six years previously. She told everybody that her husband was away at sea but nobody had ever met him because he never came home.

One day Mrs. Dynan, one of the older teachers had some surprising news for Thomas.
"That Mrs. Lee is a very nice woman," she began.
"She certainly seems very nice," agreed Thomas.
"I hope you won't mind me saying this to you Thomas,"

she continued, "but there is talk around the place that there is an affair going on between yourself and Mrs. Lee."
"That's news to me," declared Thomas.
"I know that it is," said Mrs. Dynan.
"Is this rumour widespread?"
"Well, as you probably know by now, people around here don't talk very much about matters like that, but I was asked to let you know that this is what is being said - by some people at least."
"Mrs. Lee calls in for a chat after school fairly often, especially since Indie died but a whole lot of other people do the same," explained Thomas.
"I know, and all I am doing this evening is making you aware that this rumour is there."
"I appreciate that. Should I mention that to Mrs. Lee?"
"That is something which you must decide for yourself, but if I were you, I wouldn't say anything - just be careful to maintain a professional relationship - sit on the other side of the table sort of thing - if you what I mean."
"It is good advice. I will be careful and do as you suggest."
"Look, I hope you won't worry about that."
"No! I won't. Everything will be alright."
"It will of course," affirmed Mrs. Dynan, "everything will always be alright anyway in the end."

Gradually Thomas began to drink more steadily and he physically began to show the signs of it. He assiduously avoided drinking in the pub local to the school in Cill Gobnait but on one evening, when he was feeling particularly low, he was overcome by a sense of recklessness and he called in and one thing led to another.
"To hell with it," he said. "What the hell difference is it

going to make anyway where I drink my whiskey?"
The company in the pub was good and he temporarily forgot his troubles and lost his sense of time and responsibility, but worse still, he forgot his sense of his own place in the community. People wanted to buy him drink. Some wanted to 'stand to him' as a token of gratitude for some favour that he had done for them:
"You must have a drink from me Master. We are very grateful to you for all that you did for our children."
Others wanted to 'stand to him' but didn't because they were concerned about his status as the schoolmaster and they didn't want to see him becoming intoxicated and compromised. They were also concerned that he would not have had a lunch or dinner and would advise him saying:
"Master, it is bad to drink on an empty stomach."
"Master, you need to be careful because you must drive home."
A few others who were motivated by a different design, were quite pleased to see the master brought down a peg or two and winked conspiratorially at colleagues as they said:
"Have another one Master, one for the road. We might all be dead by tomorrow."
"Have another one Master. A bird never flew on one wing. You might as well be hung for a sheep as for a lamb."

Alcohol cultivates a carefree 'devil may care' atmosphere in a pub. It deadens the senses and impairs judgement and while Thomas didn't want to drink it all, he didn't want to refuse either and eventually it was obvious to everyone - except to Thomas himself - that he was drunk, that he was not in a fit condition to remain in the public bar and that he was totally incapable of driving home. The small minority who disliked him, smirked behind his back and nudged each other with their elbows, while those who cared for him began to plot a strategy for getting him out of there, before he was seriously compromised.

The lady who owned the pub was a very kind lady and she coaxed him in to the kitchen and he fell asleep on the chair while resting his head on the table. She discussed the matter briefly with her husband and didn't really know what to do but after awhile, having recalled the rumours of a romantic affair that had been circulating he said:
"We will ring Rossa Lee and ask her if she will come down to him. She will know what to do."

Eighteen

Paul Bernhart Bouvier grew up short and sturdy with the Germanic facial outline of his maternal grandfather Wilhelm Bernhart and he bore no resemblance to his father the tall handsomely built Pierre Bouvier. He had the serious nature of his mother and a tendency to have a fixation on rules - an attribute which would cause significant problems for himself and for others in the future. Later on in his life some of the gifts and aptitudes of his father Pierre - a learned flexibility and an ability to adapt, to change and to compromise - would come to the fore and help propel him into positions of great responsibility.

Although Pierre Bouvier had disappeared without trace, support money in the form of bank drafts arrived each year from a trust fund established for the purpose of assisting Gretel and Paul. Neither Gretel nor Wilhelm nor Shirley Green nor any of his English women friends would ever see him again, but Paul - his beloved 'Peaboy' was destined to meet him in circumstances stranger than fiction could ever have conceived.

From his earliest days in primary school Paul Bernhart Bouvier was calm, self-assured, content in himself and sure of his own ability.

He consistently achieved first place in all subjects in all

school tests, in all grades. He was less talented at sport and games but he played them reasonably well. Although he was below average height, he was sturdy and was not easily shouldered off the ball. On one occasion when a bigger boy, who was regarded as a bully, began pushing him about roughly, he retaliated forcefully and the bully became more understanding towards others thereafter.

When at last he was finishing primary school, Gretel received from the wise old sixth class teacher, a report that was remarkably similar to the one received eight years earlier, when Paul was in infants: "calm, content, confident, competent" were top of the list of positives while scrupulousness about adherence to the rules by himself and others was something that could at times be problematic."

"It is remarkably similar to the very first report I received from Sr. Emmanuel when he was in infants eight years ago," Gretel remarked. "It seems that his ways haven't changed very much."

"My life's experience as a teacher suggests to me, that the basic attributes of children don't change very much, from the day they enroll to the day they leave," the wise old teacher remarked. "Their deepest, inbuilt characteristics remain durable and strongly influence their behaviour, throughout school life and beyond."

"Maybe this is true at all ages," suggested Gretel, thinking ruefully of her own lifelong inability to restrain her tongue in times of emotional turbulence and the awful trouble it had caused to her marriage.

"The school of life teaches us many lessons as we journey through, and these lessons do ameliorate our faults and

strengthen us in our weaknesses," said the wise old teacher, "but they surface again at times and take us by surprise. So, yes, I think you are right and I agree with you because I know it from the experience of my own life."
"And so do I from the experience of my life," said Gretel, "so do I."

During his teenage years Paul spent most of his free time helping his grandfather in his factory. He was happy working alongside Granddad Wilhelm - walking through the factory floor, supervising, making sure that all procedures were adhered to.
"Adherence to procedures is an absolute requirement. Many of our components are a product of the skills of different operatives who work on them at the various stages, until they reach finishing and completion. Any deviation from the specifications at any of the stages, will result in a flawed product and this means we don't get paid, we lose money and our reputation is damaged."
"I fully understand that," affirmed Paul.

He came to admire his mother's extensive knowledge of the business and her practical no nonsense approach to whatever needed to be done. Listening to her at times as she spoke to customers on the telephone, he realised, the extent of personal knowledge she had of them and the assurances she confidently provided:
"Work on your order is on target - all is as you specified. Production of the high load-carrying capacity ball bearings is nearing completion and that consignment will be dispatched on Friday. Production of the heavy load category roller bearings has already been completed and

that consignment is being dispatched today."
Sometimes after such a conversation she would replace the handset, turn to Paul with a satisfied look on her face and smilingly say:
"Competence like that inspires confidence."

Nineteen

Rossa Lee brought her car around to the rear of the pub and entering the kitchen she instantly took in the scene - Thomas leaning on the table, the half empty cup of tea in front of him, the dampening sawdust scattered around his chair on the floor, all told their tale. He had sobered up a little and was awake at this point in time. The landlady was standing beside him with the teapot in her hand while her husband remained in the background. Thomas was helped into the car and Rossa drove him to her home, while another of his friends followed with his car.

She tried to help him into her home, but he staggered backwards, swung around in a semi-circle and fell into the flower bed beside the footpath just outside and muddied his suit. When he finally got himself standing upright, he kept on repeating the same few sentences over and over again as if they were the only ones he knew:
"I am ashamed of myself Rossa. Thanks for helping me."
He did vary the order of the words:
"Rossa, thanks for helping me. I'm so ashamed - so ashamed. Thanks Rossa. Thanks. I'm so ashamed - so ashamed."

She left him in a chair beside the kitchen stove until he slept off the worst of the drunkenness and then she made him some tea and he became reasonably sober and lucid. At this stage it was getting late and she took him to the

room downstairs which she used for herself since her husband had left her. She took off his shoes. It was only then he realised the mess he had made of his suit.
"My clothes are dirty," he said, "I must clean them. I can't go to school like that in the morning. I will drive home after a few hours sleep and get a change of clothes."
"Oh no you won't!" she declared, "you are in no fit state to drive a car. Do you want to kill someone on the road? Stay right there where you are."
"But I can't walk into a classroom with muddy clothes."
"And you won't either. Take off the clothes - shirt and all and I will come back in a few minutes to collect them and put them in the wash."
"I'm so ashamed," he said.
"No need to be ashamed," she said and then in her soft, empathetic voice she added:
"Be under the blankets when I get back."
When she returned, she placed all of the items that were in his pockets on the bedside locker and left to put the clothes in the machine.

He could not sleep because of the shame and embarrassment that he felt. He thought of Mary his beloved wife and of Indie and of how he had failed them and the excessive volume of alcohol that he had consumed depressed his spirit and so when he thought of them and of his parents - who once had such high hopes for him, he was filled with remorse and self blame and a feeling that he had let everyone down, that he had failed everyone and his self-loathing increased and in that state of mind sleep was impossible.
He was still awake when she returned, having put his

clothes in the wash and he was underneath the bedclothes as she had instructed him. She dimmed the lights and sat on the bedside chair, looking towards the end of the bed so that he was not able to look directly at her face.

"Your clothes are in the wash," she said "and I will put them in the dryer in an hour. They will be ready in no time at all."

"I'm so deeply ashamed," he said. "It was not enough that I should fail my wife and my son and my parents, but now I have let down the children in the school and their parents and everyone in this community and in the parish."

"It is only yourself that is saying that," Rossa said, in that soft and caring voice that reflected her deep and kindly nature.

"It is myself that knows," he answered "and no one knows better."

And then, at that time and in that place, with that kind, empathetic woman sitting on the bedside chair, his alcohol filled brain finally yielded up the key to the emotional lock that had for so long suppressed and imprisoned his anguished feelings - and they were released in a torrent of words, unstoppable as the flowing waters of the pebbly mountain stream.

"I caused the death of my wife and the death of my son," he said. "Shame is not enough. I deserve a greater punishment than shame."

"Shush now, you did not cause the death of your wife."

"I caused the death of my wife, through my own selfish action, despite being advised by the doctor not to try again to have a child, after the death of the twins."

"Why did the doctor give that advice?"

"She said that the same would thing happen again, that any

future pregnancy would end just like the twins and therefore we should not try for a baby again."
"And you did as she advised!"
"We did. exactly as we had been instructed and it was all to no avail because Mary became pregnant and Indie was born and then I come home from school one day and I find Mary on the floor dead - as a result of a birth related haemorrhage and a fear clutched my heart that I had caused her death by making her pregnant. As I was leaving the graveyard on the day of the burial, a woman accused me of causing Mary's death."
"What did she say?"
"She said I killed my wife."
"A woman said that?"
"Yes! She was tall and thin and sallow in the face and wearing the black clothes of a widow and there was dry bitterness in her voice."
"She must have been evil - been devoid of all feelings," said Rossa.
" Maybe so but I was found guilty by her in her bitterness. My fears had been affirmed, my guilt had been pronounced. There was no judge to pass sentence on me, so I passed sentence on myself and I have punished myself ever since nourishing the burden of my guilt."

Rossa remained sitting on the chair while he spoke, gently rocking to and fro, not able to see his face clearly in the semi-darkness, listening in silence, feeling a deep empathy and affection for the man beneath the blankets in her bed.

He spoke of how he had seen Indie's hand gripping the fishing rod just above the water, as the current swept him

down on the far side and how he himself was too cowardly to risk his own life to save his son.
"I should have plunged into the flood," he said, "and if I was swept away and drowned, I would have died a brave man. How many thousand times since then, have I plunged into that river in my imagination and been brave and heroic - but the fact is that I had not taken the risk. The Dad to whom Indie cried out for help, was nothing more than a coward."

Rossa did not answer, because a great lump of emotion had arisen in her throat and soft, warm tears trickled slowly down her shadowed face.

"Ever since then," he continued, "I have considered many actions that I might have taken on that day and imagined how things might have turned out differently - that the lorry with the foreign registration plates stopped when I reached the bridge and the driver had accompanied me in my desperate run down the far side of the river bank and we saw Indie caught in the branch of a tree, just above the level of the water and when we pulled him out, the driver, who was trained in First Aid, revived him by mouth to mouth resuscitation and Indie was soon able to stand up again and I took off my coat and put it around him and we went home together - but of course it was not so, it didn't happen thus. Indie was dead and no amount of imagination would ever change that cold hard reality. The lorry had already crossed the bridge when I climbed out on to the road and despite my frantic waving and shouting the driver did not stop. He probably never even saw me in his rear-view mirrors as he focused on the road ahead and journeyed on his way."

Twenty

Gretel, Paul, Ericka and Wilhelm Bernhart attended the sacraments and Sunday mass faithfully and regularly. Their prayer life was interlinked with their private lives and with their business. They were guided in all things by truth and the light of faith and a percentage of their profits was always allocated for charitable causes and for those in need.

Despite her directness and tendency to blurt out on occasion, Gretel possessed a strong spirituality which influenced her throughout her life and this trait was also deeply imbedded in Paul - as they were to learn on one fateful day to their dismay.
"He has a strong innate spirituality," Ericka remarked that Sunday afternoon, as she and Wilhelm and Gretel sat restlessly in the lounge in Bernstadt Hall, having just heard some startling news, "I have always felt that quality in him."

Paul had left the room a few minutes earlier, having informed them of his intention to become a priest - leaving stunned silence in the room behind.
Neither Gretel nor Wilhelm responded so she continued:
"That strong spirituality directs and compels him on the road he has chosen and we must be sensitive to that and respect it."
"He is very young - only seventeen" said Gretel whose feelings were in turmoil, torn between spiritual joy and

hollow disappointment that he would not be the taking over the company to which he was the sole heir. She had worked for this and nourished and prepared him for it and her father had done likewise.

Wilhelm coughed and cleared his throat:

"Maybe we should ask him to test his vocation, by working with the company for a year, before taking action on his decision," he suggested. "He is very young as you say - only seventeen and he has had little experience of life in the wider world."

"My fear," said Gretel, "is that having commenced studies in the seminary, he would discover that he did not have a vocation at all."

"Then he could come back to the company," said Ericka.

"Not without a third level qualification," said Gretel.

"I will speak now on this matter," said Wilhelm, "because I did not speak in the past when I should have. I propose that Paul would attend university and attain his degree and work with us in the company in his spare time. This would give him experience of life and four years to consider his vocation. If he still wishes to study at the seminary, he would have so much experience behind him, but most importantly he would have a qualification to fall back on - if he should ever wish to leave religious life."

"That is the wiser course for him to follow," said Ericka.

"Yes," agreed Gretel, "it is the wiser course but I don't think that he will follow it. I think his mind is made up and it would not be easy to change it."

Gretel discussed Wilhelm's proposal with Paul and while he saw the merit and wisdom of it, he was not prepared to wait four years, before beginning to follow his dream of becoming a priest.

"I intend to commence my studies at the seminary in September" he stated but I will ask the university to keep my place in reserve for me for one year. If over that year I decide to leave the seminary, I will have the option to pursue an engineering course at the university."

Paul got his way.

Wilhelm and Gretel continued to manage the business with enthusiasm for a few years after Paul's departure but their hopes that he would return to the company diminished with every passing year.

"He will not be coming back to us," stated Ericka during dinner with Wilhelm and Gretel one evening.

"I am not yet sure of that," said Gretel.

"I believe that Ericka is right," said Wilhelm, "I think he will not be coming back. He has given his life to God and not to us. We must respect that."

After that evening, something changed in Wilhelm Bernhart and he was never quite the same. His enthusiasm for his work with the company began a slow but steady decline and he lost the 'fire in the belly' that had helped make him a successful industrialist for so many years of his adult life. He was well into his seventies and over the next few years he began to grow slower in his movements. He exercised less and less and became overweight and deteriorated physically. Ericka worried a lot about him and she herself developed chronic arthritis in her knuckles and knees and feet.

It was consideration of their failing health that led to a re-organisation of the company. Gretel became the company's Chief Executive Officer in place of her father Wilhelm. He and Ericka bought a villa in Lanzarote along the coast to the west of the Puerto Del Carmen - to which they commuted regularly and the warmth of the climate brought relief to Ericka from her arthritic pains.

Twenty One

Rossa Lee listened until Thomas had finished speaking and for a while there was such stillness in the room that the ticking of the small bedside clock seemed strong and loud. She felt a deep empathy for Thomas, but she knew that showing him pity would not help him and so she wiped her tear stained face with the palm of her hand and spoke to divert his focus from his own sorrows.

"I too have known pain" she said, "I have known sorrow, betrayal and abandonment, and because of that I am able to understand for you."

She spoke kindly to him, slowly - often pausing between sentences - as if she were choosing her words with great care and there was depth and wisdom in what she had to say. The gentle softness of her voice caressed and soothed his mental anguish like a healing balm.

"You are punishing yourself too harshly," she said. "Do you not know that you do not have the right to do that?"

"But I deserve to be punished," he said.

"Perhaps you do," she said, "but punishment is up to God alone. It is not for you to decide."

"I merit the punishment because of my cowardice."

"Let God be the judge of that. You were not as much of a coward as you have made yourself out to be. You made a choice. If you had plunged into the river, you would have been swept away and what good would that do? You simply chose another course of action because it offered the best hope for saving your child. That is all you did - you chose the best option and that does not make you a

coward. You must always judge fairly. Justice must always be applied - even if is yourself that you are judging."
"Neither did you kill your wife," she said. "It took two of you to create the child that you both named Indie. Your wife's death was a consequence of circumstance and nothing else. You have found yourself guilty of a crime that you did not commit. You are punishing yourself without mercy and in doing that, you are injuring your spirit and the spirit of God that is in you. You are injuring your soul and that is a real and very serious sin."
"Sometimes," he said, "I think that there is no God."
"Oh yes there is a God. God is in you. You are a son of God - didn't you know that? Don't be so foolish as to deny the very existence of the goodness of God which is a part of yourself. To deny God is to deny yourself."
She said many more things that helped him in the calm and peaceful darkness of that night and as she spoke a palpable spiritual, loving atmosphere saturated the air between them. Both of them felt it and they did not want it to end because it aroused pleasant, hope filled, peaceful, loving feelings. She explained that he had descended into his hell and that now he had reached the end and it would all be upwards from there on. She explained that he needed to pray and needed to understand and fully realise the truth and that the truth would set him free. She said so many things but one of them would recur to him again and again in the weeks and months that followed:
"You might need to look again at the road that you are travelling. It may be that you are being directed to another road in life. You may need to think about that and seek out that other way."

He had remained so still in the bed that she thought he might have fallen asleep and so she decided to leave quietly to get his clothes from the dryer but as soon as she arose from the bedside, he spoke:
"I thank you for that. In my heart I know that you are right and it is also true that I have injured my spirit and to injure the spirit is a serious sin, or so the bible says."

She lapsed into silence again and the atmosphere became a spiritual, caring magnetic field transmitting loving, healing, goodness in continuous electrified currents streaming between them. They were both aware of this; both of them felt it but neither of them spoke of it.
Old familiar feelings began to filter through him and slowly, ever softly, the demon of self hatred began to lose its grip, as it was weakened and overcome by the love of that good and caring woman.
"You have blamed yourself for far too long," she said. "You must let go - you simply have to let it go."
And so he did begin.

Later she knelt beside the bed:
"I want you to pray with me," she said.
"I have not prayed in a long time," he answered.
"Well it is time you did," she asserted. "The time has come to pray again but it must be a prayer of great depth - in which you finally let go of your own willfulness and place your trust and faith in God who will always guide you like a shepherd guides his sheep - even in the most difficult times, as you walk the darkest valleys of your life."
"I know the prayer," he said.
"Now let me hold your hands in mine as we say together

from the depths of our hearts:

Like as the shepherd to his sheep,
So is the Lord my God to me.
Attending to my ev'ry need,
A resting me in pastures green
Near waters still he leadeth me,
My weary spirit to make clean.

He leads me on the path of right,
He's true and faithful to his name.
And should I walk the valley's night,
Its evils will not frighten me,
For with his crook and staff nearby,
He keeps me safe and comforts me."

The rising sun was brightening the eastern sky and the birds were singing the first fulsome notes of the dawn chorus and Thomas was breathing lightly in his sleep when she finally left the room. She went silently to her daughter's room, slipped quietly under the blankets and fell soundly into sleep.

His freshly washed clothes were on the dressing table when he awoke. His shirt and tie were spotlessly clean and his shoes were polished. When he was dressed she gave him the breakfast.
"Thanks for washing the clothes," he said.
"You need to shave," she said. "Here are some razors that my husband used to have. I think it is okay to give one of them to you."

As he was leaving the house he noticed a picture, which he thought resembled Holy Mary. It was a picture of a woman with spattered bloodstains on her clothes, hands and face and a scratch down the side of one of her cheeks.
"Is that a picture of Holy Mary?" he asked.
"Yes it is," she answered. "For me that picture reflects accurately what the mother of Jesus must have looked like after He had died. She had endured deep sorrow in her life. It shows her as being in her fifties and shows what she must have looked like, after the crucifixion of her son and after she had cradled his lifeless body in her lap and arms."
"It is very different from the usual pictures which show Mary as young mother, always cleanly dressed in blue and spotlessly clean," Thomas remarked.
"For me, this picture accurately depicts Holy Mary after the brutal reality of the crucifixion" said Rossa. "That was the Holy Mary I could identify with - someone who had passed through the troubles and trials of life and was marked and scarred by them - but not defeated."
"It is a good picture to have," said Thomas. "It reminds us, that the tribulations of others may be far more painful than our own."

Later she said goodbye to him at the door and he thanked her very sincerely.
"I am truly grateful for all that you did for me last night and since then. I don't know how I will ever repay you."
"Think nothing of it. I am glad I was able to help. I am mindful of the words of the prayer of St. Francis that 'it is in giving that we receive.' By helping you sort out some of your troubles, I also helped myself to clarify and cope with some of mine."

He put his arms around her and she held him for a long time and then pushing him gently away she said:
"Now before you leave, I want to ask you not to come here again."
"Why do you ask that of me?"
"Because that is what is best for both of us. I think your soul is destined for a different path and I would never want to hinder that. Besides, I have faith that one day my own husband will return to me."
"I think my soul is dead."
"No it isn't. You just need to look deeper inside yourself to find its beauty and its wonder."

Just then Rose Anna - a truly, amazingly well balanced twelve year old came to the front door.
"Are you feeling better now?" she asked. "Mammy told me that you were not well last night."
"Yes, I'm better now and I thank you and your Mammy for keeping me and looking after me."
"You are welcome," said Rose Anna. "I will see you later. Enjoy the rest of your day."
They waved goodbye as he drove off and they remained standing there at the doorstep until the car had gone out of sight. Then they turned and went silently inside.

As for Thomas, the tide of his life turned that night and nothing would ever be the same again. On that night he had been saved from destruction by a guardian angel in the person of Rossa Lee. The self imposed, curse-spell of self-blame and punishment was broken by the selfless love and deep faith of a good and caring Christian woman.

He did as she had suggested and searched deeper within himself to find the beauty of his soul that had been so deeply injured. He trained himself to listen to the nourishing, healing words of the spirit of God, that gradually grew stronger in the goodness of his heart and his wounded soul slowly began to be healed and become wholesome once again.

Twenty Two

Paul Bernhart Bouvier was ordained a priest in 1984, for the Diocese of Killeenreagh, when he was just over twenty five years old. His maternal grandfather Wilhelm Bernhart had died one year earlier and two years after the ordination, his mother Gretel sold Bernhart Industrial Steel Components Ltd. in a deal that made her a multi-millionaire. After she had securely invested her money in gilt-edged bank shares, she went to live with her mother in their villa in sunny Lanzarote.

They lived very happily there, came back frequently to Ireland and met regularly with Fr. Paul. On one of those trips, Ericka sold the home that she and Wilhelm had shared for so many happy years. On another, later occasion she was diagnosed with cancer and although she returned to Lanzarote, she came back to Ireland for hospice care and died a short time later. Gretel keenly felt the loss of both parents who had died within a few years of each other. She remained in Ireland for a time but eventually went back to Lanzarote and lived alone in the villa that she had inherited from her parents.

From the beginning of his priestly life, Rev. Fr. Bouvier was on a personal mission to do all in his power, to reverse many of the changes in the Catholic Church, that had emanated from the Second Vatican Council, which closed on 8th December 1965. He favoured the full restoration of the Traditional Latin Mass and the re-imposition of the rigid guidelines for the reception of Holy Communion. He was committed to preservation of the traditional Christian family, supported by the sacramental Christian marriage of a man and a woman. His zeal for reversing the changes of Vatican II arose in part from his inbuilt understanding of the value and necessity for rules, but perhaps more so from the conservatism that prevailed in the seminary during the period of his spiritual formation and training.

He was warmly welcomed as a young curate at first in all parishes to which he was appointed. He was a brilliant speaker, was very humble, lived simply and was indeed very friendly and very holy in a prayerful way. He celebrated mass with deep reverence, attended to the sick in hospitals and homes with joyous commitment and fervour. He was generally popular with the youth, and many young girls in particular, practically adored him.

Despite all that, his tenure in parishes was generally of brief duration - mainly because of complaints about his apparent fixation on returning the Church to pre-Vatican II times. Some of the complaints related to his use of Latin for large segments of the mass, but most focused on his rigid attitude about the preparedness of the people to receive Holy Communion - a rigidity that caused some to feel excluded from the sacrament and by extension, excluded from the Mass and from the Church.

By the time he reached the age of thirty three, eight years after his ordination, he had served in five different parishes, having been transferred on four different occasions. This was certainly quite unusual. He was asked

to attend at the bishop's residence to discuss his appointment to his sixth parish and Bishop Tranton, having commended him on his good work with the young people, the sick and elderly, advised him in a fatherly sort of way:
"Fr. Paul, I fear that your zeal for the law and the rules, exceeds that of your namesake, the illustrious Saint Paul, prior to his conversion on the road to Damascus. As you know, he felt that it was his absolute duty to see that the law was obeyed in its detail and applied without mercy."
"Saul was applying the Jewish law, but I am applying the law of Jesus Christ as laid down in the gospels. There is a difference," stated Fr. Paul.
The bishop looked briefly out the large, ceiling-high window with its drab unvarnished shutters and yellowed sashes before refocusing his keen intelligent eyes on the holy and zealous young priest, who was sitting stiffly on the unkempt outsized chair.
"Agreed." said the bishop. "Yes there is a difference, but there is also one big similarity."
"What is the similarity?" asked Fr. Paul.
"Lack of mercy," answered the bishop. "Before his conversion on the road to Damascus, Saul applied the law without mercy. I fear it is the same with you and I am praying for a great conversion for you too - good and holy man that you are."
"I think it is the Church and not I that needs the conversion, but if it is me, then I'm sure the Lord will arrange it," answered Fr. Paul
"We will pray for it" said the bishop, "and now I ask you to take up your appointment in Lonerton Parish at the weekend three weeks hence. The parish priest, Fr Towman

is moving on in years but he is very wise and I ask that you would listen with care to his advice."

Twenty Three

The night that Thomas spent in the home of Rossa Lee was a turning point in his life. He had descended as low as he could go, literally to the mud, but the experience of that night had changed his life forever.
He took the Pioneer Total Abstinence Association pledge not to drink alcohol again and he remained faithful to that promise for the rest of his life. He resumed active involvement with the Church and the sacraments and renewed and strengthened his faith in God. He began to look deeper within himself, to be more solitary and began to go frequently to the hills and to isolated places for very long walks - often spending more than a day reflecting in the peace and solitude that such places offered.

On one occasion he was walking a forestry road in the absolute wilderness and apart from the trees there was nothing in sight, nothing to be heard, not even the bleating of a sheep or the call of a bird. He came to a fork in the wooded road and because it was secluded, hemmed in and without any visible landmarks, he was unsure of which road he should take and this dilemma triggered the recollection of words spoken by Rossa Lee:
"I think your soul is destined for a different path. You just need to look deeper inside yourself to find its beauty and its wonder."

Here, now in this wood-enclosed junction, he had to make a choice of another sort:

"Should I continue on straight ahead or should I veer off to the left?" he asked himself aloud, "which path is the right one to take?"

Eventually he chose the path to the left and after three quarters of a mile, he came out of the forestry and knew that he had chosen well:

"Ah, the two lakes," he said, "I recognise you like old friends."

There was a lake on each side, where the graveled road leveled at the summit of the hill and a broad expanse of heath and heather-covered blanket bog stretched far away into the west. He could see the outline of the rows of long turf banks, where he had worked when he was young and he stood there now, absorbed in reverie of ways and times long lost and gone forever:

"Many the long day I spent on those turf banks," he said aloud, "happy enough and carefree, without a penny in my pocket - cleaning with the hay knife, hands blistered from cutting with the *sleán*, spreading with the two pronged pike, spitting on my hands to get a better grip on the handle and later on turning and footing the drying sods. There used to be crowds there then - family groups in every bank, boys and girls, young men and young women, gregarious, talking loudly as they worked, their voices carrying from one bank to the next. I see them still and hear their voices echo in the caverns of my mind and I will bear them always deep within my being - because in truth they are a part of me forever."

He stayed there for a long time, resting his hands on his walking stick. He looked admiringly into the distance, at

multiple hilltops, in varying shades of smoky blue, in the south and the south west. He was enchanted by that panorama, stretching away as far as the eye could see - all beneath the bright blue sky with small white clouds that cast faint shadows on the hillside and multiple peaks that raised their heads above each other - like great, gigantic eggs in a great, gigantic basket.
"The wonder of it all," he exclaimed. "The awesome wonder of it all."

His stance was that of a countryman, for that is what he was - straining his eyes to see further but after awhile, his attention strayed and he looked instead with his mind's eye on the past and present of his life - and there, solitary and alone, standing in that gravely road, on that gently sloping heath and heather covered hill, he became convinced that the time had come to take a different pathway, on the journey of his life.
"I've given enough of my life to education and to schools," he proclaimed. "The time has come for me to take another road. Goodbye to all of that. It's over. I'll go anew upon a different route and I will see where it and God will lead me."

In July of that year, three years after Indie had died, school principal Thomas Martin Kendley handed in his resignation to the board of management of Cill Gobnait National School. He made preparations to enroll in the seminary and he commenced his studies that September when he was forty one years old.

In the interim he had painted the house and cleaned it up

very well. He cleaned the room that Indie used - cleaned the cot and cleaned the bed and dressed it with newly laundered bedclothes. Everything was in order and spotlessly clean and fresh - 'clean as a new pin' - as our old grandaunt Joe used to say when we were children all together in our farmhouse family home. He painted the exterior of the house and while he was painting the garden wall, he saw the marks that he had made on it with the sledge years earlier, when he was overcome with frustration and near madness by all that he had endured.

"The poor wall," he said. "Look what I did to it and the wall never caused me the slightest offence."

He smiled as he looked at the sledge marks and was grateful that all of that had passed and that he was fully alive once more.

"Thank God," he said. "I thank you that I was able to accept the weakness of my own humanity. I thank you for all of your blessings to me. I have learned much humility but I paid very dearly for it."

Twenty Four

One year after the ordination of twenty five year old Paul Bernhart Bouvier, my brother Thomas and six other students started in the seminary. Aged forty one, Thomas was the oldest of them, but he found the studies very manageable. He had always been an intelligent and competent student and study came very easy to him. He settled in easily to the routine of early morning prayers, matins and lauds, morning mass, vespers in the evening time and compline - the night time prayer. Meditation on the sacred scriptures was an important feature of each day and I think this was easy for him too, because he had developed a habit of deep reflection during the last year, before deciding to go to the seminary.

We visited him in the late spring of the following year. It was our first visit and he looked very different, dressed in the long, black cassock with a cincture around his waist. He seemed at peace within himself and we also shared in that peace.

The years passed quickly enough. By the time he was ready for ordination, six years later, only two of the six that had started with him remained and they were all ordained together in the seminary chapel.

Thomas did not come to his home parish to celebrate his first mass, as was the established practice at the time but stayed in the seminary and celebrated his first mass there. He continued to work there and five weeks had passed before he returned to his home.

A night of celebration was organised in his home parish and my sisters Nora and Rose came from their homes in Washington and Edinburgh bringing their husbands and children with them.
"It is a great pity," said Nora, "that Dad and Mam didn't live to see this day."
"They are with us in spirit," replied Rose and we all agreed with that sentiment.

I know he enjoyed the night's celebration, but I am certain that the celebration organised in the little billiard hall beside Cill Gobnait school, where he had taught for so many years, meant more to him that anything else. There was a large attendance. There were many old friends that he recognised easily and many of his past pupils whom he also recognised, but there were others who had changed beyond recognition - some because they had grown from the little children into adulthood and other, older ones who had married and attended with their wives and children.
It was a night of many speeches, but it was also a night of music, song and dance, of great freedom, celebration, a great display of talent, and a great use of talent by so many people, young and old.

Thomas did not play music nor did anyone ask him to play because everyone was aware that he had abandoned all music following the tragic drowning of his son Indie. They also knew that he had done this as a punishment for himself, arising out of that tragedy. At that time he had asked me to take his concertina and concert flute and he left the violin with the McMahon family, who lived in the school community in which he taught.

The McMahons were great musicians and in the days before Indie's tragic death, Thomas had spent many happy hours in their family home, playing music with them and with their neighbours. He frequently visited them and he recalled how Packie - their beloved son who had Down syndrome, would approach him with a violin and say:
"Play a tune Master. Play a tune for Packie."

All these years later, many people felt that it was a great loss to humanity that Thomas had given up playing music. He was a gifted musician with a national reputation. Occasionally well intentioned people tried to persuade him to break his self-imposed ban but his answer was always resolute:
"My soul is dead to music," he would say. "I will never play again. I'm done with all of that."

During the tea break the chairs were arranged in semi-circular fashion around the dance floor and the hall was filled with the lively buzz of conversation. Suddenly the talking petered out into silence, as the people observed Packie McMahon walking across the floor, with the violin and bow in his hands. He stopped in front of Thomas, held the instrument out to him and said in his habitual way:
"Play a tune, Master. Play a tune for Packie."
There was silence because everyone was aware that Thomas had not played a single note of music since Indie had died. He was taken by surprise at first and he was reluctant but Packie was insistent:

"Play a tune Master, play a tune for Packie. One tune for Packie Master."

Thomas knew that he could not refuse to play for Packie, who loved everyone and was beloved of everyone. Even though he was completely unprepared for this turn of events, he accepted the violin from Packie, placed it snugly beneath his chin and closing his eyes he played the very beautiful *Cualan*' - a mournful and hauntingly beautiful slow air.

Music can touch and heal the soul in a way that only musicians know and it was thus with Thomas as he touched the strings and moved the bow with finely honed dexterity. Those who sat beside him were moved also in their souls and watching him as he played, clearly saw the tears that forced their way from underneath his tightly-squeezed eyelids and roll slowly down his cheeks. There were tears in many eyes and strong men swallowed hard and women wept soft tears of joy and normally boisterous boys and girls stood in awe as a man was freed by his own sweet music, from a demon that had constrained him for so long.

There was rapturous applause and so he wiped away the tears and commenced a lively polka. Other musicians came up to play beside him and the people clapped their hands and tapped their feet in rhythm. Dancers took to the floor and danced joyfully in perfect timing to the magic of reels and polkas and hornpipes, played with skill and talent rare.

When it was over there was a spontaneous eruption of loud and sustained applause because everybody knew, that through the magic of his music, Thomas had achieved a great victory and broken the shackles of the ghost of failures past. The last remaining element of his self imposed punishment was excised that night, broken by the caring innocence of an adult with the mind of a child and by the incomprehensible wonder of traditional Irish music played on the strings of the heart.

There were presentations to Thomas at various stages during the night's entertainment - including a simply wrapped gift presented by a beautiful young lady, whom he recognised immediately as Rose Anna Lee because of her unmistakable resemblance to her mother Rossa. She had grown into a beautiful young woman.

"Mam asked me to present this gift to you and she knows it will have a deep and special meaning for you in your life as a priest."

"Thank you very much, and thank your mother for me," said Thomas.

"I think she would want us to open it," said Rose Anna. "Shall I open it for you?"

"Please do," said Thomas.

"It is a copy of a picture that you admired once upon a time and we know that it will always mean a lot to you."

Thomas held the frame in both hands and gazed on the picture of a middle aged Holy Mary with blood spattered hands and face and the long scratch on her cheek and the signs of sorrow and struggle in her time worn face.

"It will always be special to me," he said. "It will remind me that Mary the mother of Jesus suffered much and experienced pain and sorrow and hardship and heartbreak. Thank you. Thank you so much."

Later on, Rossa did approach him accompanied by Rose Anna and a bespectacled frail looking man.

"This is Samuel, my husband who has returned to me to stay. I would like you to meet him. He is not well at this time."

"I am pleased to meet you," said Samuel in a trembling voice. "I have heard many good things about you," and he extended his left hand to weakly shake Thomas' outstretched right hand.

"My health is not as robust as it used to be," he said and Thomas noticed how he kept his trembling right hand tightly against his body.

"Fr. Thomas, I am very happy for you," said Rossa. "You know all those years ago, I tried to explain to you that the tragedies of your life, awful though they were, had provided you with a kind of freedom. It was a freedom from prideful constraints of any kind, freedom from the demands of self, total freedom that only true humility can bring. It is that total humility, devoid of any trace of selfishness, that enabled you to be ordained and that same, stripped-bare humility, will make you into a great and wonderful priest."

"Freedom also brings responsibility," replied Fr. Thomas.

"Yes, the responsibility was on you to use that freedom wisely and that is what you have done."

Rose Anna gave him a hug.

God bless you Rose Anna," he said.

"And God bless you too Fr. Thomas," she replied. "May God bless you always."

Twenty Five

Newly ordained Fr. Thomas Kendley, was appointed junior curate in Lonerton - a position left vacant by the promotion to senior curate of Fr. Paul Bernhart Bouvier, who at that time had been in the parish for two years. Fr. Thomas was forty six years old and Fr. Bouvier was thirty four.

Lonerton was a predominantly suburban parish, with a population of five and a half thousand. It had a medium sized church with a magnificent stone steeple of cut sandstone and it had been built in the previous century, when Lonerton was a one street village, some three miles from the city. For many years that church would be full to capacity for each of the four Sunday morning Masses, full to such an extent that ushers were needed to find seating for the unpunctual.

"Now, at this present time," the people told Fr. Thomas, "there are but two Masses and the church is half empty."

That statistic was all the more surprising, because the population of the town had increased exponentially, due to urban expansion and the transformation of the little village into a satellite town. Various theories were offered to explain this reduction in mass attendance:

“It is the young people Father. They don’t believe in anything anymore. They don’t believe in God or anything else."

"The young people nowadays have no need for prayer. They have everything they want and have no need for God."

"I don't know what change has come over young people, Father, but they don't go to Mass anymore."

Fr Thomas heard the same narratives at the first meeting of the priests in the parish, which was held in the Spartan-like church sacristy, presided over by the parish priest Canon Towman - an ageing, big, heavy-set man with a broad, strong face and a large head with a bounteous covering of unkempt wavy, white-grey hair..
The canon outlined the current state of affairs in the parish:
"Times have changed, Fr. Thomas," he said. "The same need for God isn't in peoples' lives anymore. They don't believe in the simplicity of the message anymore. They don't accept mysteries. They are educated. They ask questions. We are not giving them answers."
"They are too much given to having their children play games on Sunday mornings and many of the games and training sessions are now taking the place of the Sunday Mass," stated Fr. Bouvier. "The Church should take a stronger line with such parents."
"I cannot see Fr. Thomas," said the canon, "how the faith can be kept alive in this parish into the future, but I have to trust in God. Sure enough many people have stopped coming to Mass and to the sacraments. Some of these feel disconnected and some others feel excluded."
"That is their choice and their loss," said Fr. Bouvier. "They are depriving themselves of the opportunity to participate in the sacred liturgy and that is their own doing. If they choose to remain disconnected from the Church, that is their choice."
"I would not place all of the blame on the people," said

Canon Towman mildly.
"We can encourage them and of course we should, but there is not much we can do if they stay away and won't come to church?" said Fr. Bouvier.
"We must go to them," said Canon Towman. "That is what I would do if I were younger and more agile, I would go to them. That's what Jesus did. He didn't stay in one position or in one place and wait for the people to come to him. He went to the people. He told the apostles to go and teach all nations and so they went to the people. Fr. Thomas, I believe that this is what we must do now, we must go to the people but I know that Fr. Bouvier doesn't share my view. Perhaps Fr Thomas, you would consider taking on the role of being a link person with those people - those disconnected and excluded people."
"You mean a sort of ambassador," inquired Thomas.
"Exactly," said the canon, "an ambassador to the disconnected and excluded."
"I will be happy to give it a try," replied Fr. Thomas. "I will go where I am sent, but not with the title of ambassador but as a servant."
"I wish you luck with that," commented Fr Bouvier with a resigned air of pessimism. "It will take a miracle to convince some of the hard cases in the Calcutta and Harlem estates to turn away from sin and return to Christ."
"Calcutta and Harlem?" repeated Fr. Thomas quizzically.
"Nicknames for two housing estates in Cooley Park," explained Fr. Bouvier, "insulting nicknames that I do not approve of, coined by local wags because of the anti social behaviour and drug dealing that has given these estates a bad reputation."

"During the last thirty years," Canon Towman explained, "two large publicly funded housing estates have been built in the eastern end of the town, large numbers of houses built very close together with very little space and very little play area. A lot of wonderful people live in these estates - industrious, hard working, decent, good hearted and generous. Some have been unemployed for a long time, faced with soul destroying boredom and a sense of not being useful. But for all that, they are fundamentally decent human beings and many bring up their families with discipline and respectability."

"I'd certainly admire them for that," answered Fr. Thomas. "It sounds like a good place with good people."

"There's also a downside," interjected Fr. Bouvier.

"Yes there is a downside," said the Canon.

"Anti-social behaviour, theft, drug-related crime and intimidation," said Fr. Bouvier.

"Some of the younger generation see themselves as victims," explained Canon Towman, "victims of the state, victims of the system, victims of government, and of those whom they perceive as being super rich and wealthy and some see the Church as part of the system."

"This belief may encourage unsociable behaviour," suggested Fr. Thomas.

"Or it may be a phase of life that they go through and leave after awhile to settle down respectably and bring up children of their own," replied Canon Towman.

"Is poverty a factor in all of this," asked Fr. Thomas, "poverty or a sense of poverty?"

"Poverty was never an excuse for criminality and bad behaviour," said Fr. Bouvier. "I know some very fine

people who were reared in dire poverty."
"True," said the canon, "but times change and a different ethic can be dominant during different periods of time."
"There are many different personalities in every estate, in every family perhaps," said Fr. Thomas. "You find the good and the bad wherever you go."
"Whatever, the cause is," said the canon, "the Church must be there trying to bring healing and peace."
After repeatedly checking his watch, Fr. Bouvier asked to be excused:
"I'm afraid I must leave you" said Fr. Bouvier, "I must attend a meeting."

After Fr Bouvier had left the canon continued:
"At the other end of town, to the west there is a private housing estate. The people in these estates own their houses, in theory, at least. They borrowed money and they bought the house and it is theirs as long as they keep paying a large mortgage for all of their working lives. They have all the appearances of wealth and success. They have a good car. They go to work each day, usually the father and the mother. Many of them work hard but at weekends they play golf and games. About fifty percent of those families attend Mass, but the other fifty percent reject some of the teachings of the Church and they will only attend for family events such as baptisms, First Holy Communion and Confirmation. The same lack of play space for children is there and the same lack of shopping and recreational facilities and the green area around each house is little bigger than a good sized bedroom. In both areas, there are people who feel excluded from the Church because of divorces or other circumstances of their lives.

We must try to connect with them also."
"It seems to me that the greater challenge is in the estates in the eastern side of town and I will gladly go there and give it my very best," said Fr. Thomas. "Would Fr. Bouvier be willing to take on the role of link person with the estate in the western end of town?"
"Fr. Bouvier is a great man in many ways," said the canon. "He is an authentic 'turn away from sin and be faithful to the gospel' type of priest."
"And there is nothing wrong with that," said Thomas.
"You are right of course, but the problem lies in the way he goes about it. He is committed to ensuring that everybody is cleansed from sin, as he sees it. He goes by the book but does not temper it with mercy in the broadest sense of the word."
"Are you implying that this is the reason why some people won't go to mass?" asked Thomas.
"No! not totally, but it may be a factor all the same," said Canon Towman. "Fr Bouvier is a good and holy man but he is young and inexperienced and displays a lack of understanding on some sensitive issues."
"Sensitive issues, such as the relationship of husband and wife, intimate and otherwise?" inquired Fr. Thomas?
"Exactly that," replied Canon Towman.
"I understand those difficulties very well," stated Thomas. "As you know I was once a married man and my personal experience helps me to understand."
"Then there is the real issue of couples cohabiting, particularly those whose marriages have broken down," said Canon Towman.
"These are sensitive matters and often complicated," answered Thomas.

"I know," responded the canon. "I know that some won't go to mass, because they feel excluded or condemned for something that they see as not being their fault."

The canon sat hunched forward in his chair and as he spoke of these matters, his big strong head was bowed and he kept his eyes focused on his strong hands that were joined on the table - as if he were uncomfortable and uneasy with the subject under discussion. He paused awhile and then continued:

"And so, Fr. Thomas, here I am, a man, pushing on for seventy three years, with arthritis in the knuckles of my hands and in my knees and the parish for which I am responsible is on a downward curve socially and in Christian life and practice. I have given all of my life to the Church and to God. Fr. Bouvier is good man, who has been sent to me by the bishop to be my senior curate and he, in his own goodness and in his own idealism, wants people to be pure and free from sin and that is an admirable aim. He sets that ideal as a precondition for receiving Holy Communion and our church is not very full any more, but he is convinced that he knows best. Do you understand what I am trying to say to you Thomas?"

"You are telling me that there is a lack of understanding and perhaps a lack of empathy, that there is too much emphasis on some Church regulations and that God's mercy should be applied more liberally."

"Exactly," said the canon. "You understand it well. That is why I am giving to you the responsibility to create an environment of personal and communal wellbeing among the disconnected and excluded people of this parish. Think about it Fr. Thomas. Make plans and we will talk about it again."

They walked out the chapel yard together and stopped to survey their surroundings.
"We live in a beautiful land," said the canon pointing to the beautiful and varied panorama of fields on the hillside to the north - pasture green, tillage brown and some golden with uncut barley or oats."
"Yes indeed," said Thomas, "and it is important that we take the time to admire and enjoy it. May I compliment you on how well your church yard shrubbery and flowers are maintained," said Fr. Thomas.
"That is the work of one good man who dedicates his spare time to that work out of respect for the Lord and out of the sheer goodness of his heart. You will no doubt meet him soon enough because he comes to early mass each morning."
"I look forward to it - what's his name?"
"Whiston, Eddie Whiston but everyone calls him Whispy and he doesn't mind that. He is the kind of man that if you meet him once, you will always recognise him again and it will be unlikely that you will forget him. So I bid you good bye for now," said Canon Towman. "I hope you get on well with Fr. Bouvier."
"Good bye," said Fr. Thomas. "I'm sure I will get on fine with him."

Twenty Six

Five foot seven inch Eddie Whiston was a working man, of average build with steely strength in his sinews and muscles toned from a lifetime of manual work. He was easily recognisable by the tradesman's navy overalls and French style beret, which he wore each working day. Known locally as Whispy, regarded as being a little innocent at times he was seventy one years old when his deep abiding love for his one and only daughter drove him to embark on a course of drastic action that, for a brief period of time, made him a household name throughout Ireland and beyond.

He was neither slightly built nor stout but was firm with a physical strength that belied his stature - always in a hurry to go somewhere or do something, always walking quickly and he talked quickly, definitively, strongly. His straight, oily pepper-grey hair was always tidily trimmed and combed, his eyes were strongly blue and his smooth skinned face and hands were tough, tanned and darkened brown.
His voice was clear and his speech distinctive but characterised by pronunciation in which 'd-sounds' were dominant and 'th-sounds' absent. He never learned to read, could write his name competently, could accurately use a rule and measuring tape in his carpentry and building work and he displayed a quick and lively intelligence.

As regards living a Christian life, Eddie diligently adhered to the commandments. He firmly believed in God, faithfully knelt and said his morning and evening prayers, recited the angelus, went to confession once a month, always went to Mass, received Holy Communion and was strictly honest in all his dealings. He was careful to avoid calling God's name in vain or in anger, drawing instead from a repertoire of same-sounding substitutes - jaycus for Jesus, cripes for Christ and he always referred to the devil as 'the diggle.'

He was everyone's handyman. He drank stout sparingly, wouldn't touch spirits, was good company and interesting to have a drink with in a pub. He had a strong sense of justice, a clear view of what was right and wrong and was likely to react angrily to any form of unfair treatment of anyone and so it wouldn't be unusual, for someone passing by a street-side pub door, to hear Eddie's raised voice:
"No! Dat's not right at all. Dat's not fair. No wan could stand over dat. I don't agree with dat at all. Dat's right wrong altogether."

He never learned a trade but he was a veritable 'Jack of all trades' and he worked over a wide area in the parish and beyond. He was - as he said himself, 'never idle' - for he was well handed, with a natural belief in his own ability. He never learned to drive, so if jobs were local, he walked to his work, if they were within a four or five mile radius he cycled, but if the distance was greater or if heavy tools were needed, the employer usually collected him by car. He shared the meals with the employing family, always showed respect and was respected in return.

His wife Nora was a lovely dark haired woman who was as neat and tidy and good and honest as himself. She was as good, caring and faithful a wife to Eddie as he was a husband to her and they were always good humoured and happy. They had one daughter Teresita or Tessie as they called her, whom they both loved dearly and whom they reared well and certainly didn't spoil.

Tessie, their only child developed into a very beautiful girl, with an easy and attractive personality and even though there were many solid young men who would woo her, she married Max Delown, a lanky smooth talking, soft, putty-faced young man, who was always clean and well dressed, impeccably groomed, smelled of aftershave and scented body sprays, was very plausible and didn't have a penny to his name. They lived in her home with Whispy and her mother and two of their three children, a boy and a girl were born there.

Max kept a distance from too much involvement with the children and tended to come and go as he pleased, something that was possible due to the assistance that Tessie's mother and father provided with minding the children. No one would blame him for keeping a low profile while living with his in-laws, but there were some who suspected that he was not a paragon of marital fidelity and that he was having affairs with other women.

Eventually, assisted financially by Tessie's father, the young couple got a house of their own on a rent to purchase scheme. Their third child, a boy was born about a year later and very soon after that Max told Tessie that he didn't love her any more, that he was leaving her and going to live with someone else. He returned some nights later, collected his belongings and left without even saying goodnight to his children.

After her husband had walked out on her, Tessie continued to pray daily as she always did and to attend Mass and receive Holy Communion each Sunday, as she had done throughout her life. She prayed for many things, for her children and when she came to accept that her runaway husband would not be coming back, she prayed that she would meet a good and decent man who would treat her with respect and who would be a role model and father for her three children. Her prayers must have been answered because almost two years after her husband left, she went out for the first time with big Dan Hayley, a sound and solid country man.

Dan was a big, strong, tough man - tough in the sense that he was not easily disturbed and was not given to unnecessary and useless worry. He was a caring man and in due course he moved into Tessie's house, but not before the divorce proceedings which her husband Max had initiated had been concluded. Her parents were disappointed about the divorce but accepted that it was probably the prudent thing to do, considering the fact that Max Delown wanted a share of the ownership of the house - a disgraceful claim they thought because he had not contributed a single penny to its purchase or upkeep.
"There was no real alternative to a divorce," Tessie declared. "Max was in England with his new woman and was making demands for money in lieu of what he considered his share of the house."

Tessie and Dan lived very happily together and had two sons of their own and all of this time Tessie continued to attend Church and the sacraments, as she always did. Subsequent to the decree of divorce, they decided to get married, but since divorced Catholics are not allowed to remarry in the Church, they were married in a civil ceremony. Tessie continued to go to the sacraments as she had done right throughout her life. This put her in conflict with the teaching of the Church namely that anyone who was divorced and remarried outside the Catholic Church was banned from receiving Holy Communion. The parish priest Canon Towman was very lenient in regard to implementing this ban and he was never known for having refused Holy Communion to anyone.

Twenty Seven

A chance encounter in the island of Lanzarote initiated a chain of events that would bring about a major change in the life of Fr. Bouvier's mother Gretel. The death of her father, Wilhelm Bernhart had already led to major changes in Gretel's lifestyle, including the sale of the company that she loved so much and a change of residence from Ireland to Lanzarote, where she moved to live with her mother Ericka. She had been busy with the affairs of the company all of her life and she struggled to adjust to her leisurely life in retirement. This struggle was exacerbated after Ericka's death. She felt the loss of her mother very keenly and she frequently felt isolated, lonely and alone.

As if all of this turbulence wasn't bad enough, a major crisis in the financial and banking sector massively reduced the value of her so-called gilt-edged bank shares and she incurred a massive financial setback. Her income was drastically reduced. She had enough to enable her to live comfortably but she had no more than that.
"I was good at making money," she mused ruefully "but I was very bad at investing it."
If the worst came to the worst, she could begin to utilise the lump sum, that still arrived annually, from the trust fund established by her former husband, Pierre Bouvier. Up to that time, her pride had prevented her from using it and she had instead given it all to various charities.
"How ironic it would be'" she mused "if I had to depend on that money to sustain me in my old age."

This musing unleashed a flood of associated thoughts, from that section of her mind where memories of Pierre Bouvier and their life together were stored.
"I wonder if he is still alive?" she soliloquised. "The fact that his promised financial support comes every year suggests that he is alive and the reduced allowance after Paul reached the age of twenty one affirms that. On the other hand, the money comes from a trust fund and that would be operative even if he was dead. I wish I knew. Despite all our efforts to trace him, his trail went cold in Brazil and no trace of him was found thereafter except the for the divorce papers, which were forwarded to me from a lawyer in Mexico. I know one thing for sure and that is that I dearly loved him with all my heart. My feeling is that he is still alive. If it were otherwise, my deepest instinct would affirm it. I'm sure of that. Wherever he is, I hope he is happy. Maybe he is lying out on some warm sunny beach or sipping martinis at the poolside bar. If he is, then he is far happier than I am - here all alone, while my only son is a priest working for God in a parish in Ireland."

On one occasion Gretel was acting as host to four Girl Guide leaders in her Lanzarote villa and she took them to Montana De Fuego, for a spectacularly exciting bus tour of that awesome and unique volcanic landscape.
Later, she joined them in the queue of tourists waiting to ride the camels on the sandy, red, lower slopes of the hill of Timanfaya. There were twelve camels, each carrying two passengers, riding side-saddle. Her four young friends partnered off together and when she reached the front of the queue she glanced worriedly at the stranger with whom

she would be sharing a camel and opted out at the last minute.
"The senora does not like to ride with you, Senor," said the camel handler as he placed a bag of sand into the other side-saddle to balance the weight. He had just finished tying it when Gretel, dressed in attractive creamy-white casuals, came forward once more:
"I have changed my mind," she said, "I will go after all."

Once aboard, she looked again at her riding companion, a tanned fit looking man whom she judged to be late fifties - about her own age.
"*Lo siento* - I am sorry," she said, "I was a little apprehensive."
"*De nada.* Perfectly understandable," he answered. "May I ask which caused the greater apprehension, the camel or myself? I hope it is the camel, because I think I am a little more handsome than he."
She looked across at him with concern and saw the broad smile on his face and then he laughed a mirthful laugh and she herself laughed too.

At the end of the ride, the camel knelt down to allow them to alight but stood again before Gretel had finished extricating herself from the saddle. Her seat began to slide down her side of the camel but she was saved from further embarrassment by her riding companion, who placed his strong hands beneath her arms and lifted her to the ground.
"Easy does it," he said, "it's tough being a camel you know," and they laughed together again.

They met again later at a roadside cafe where they stopped for refreshments - the tall strong man and the good looking woman of average build and height whose natural seriousness was evident in her strong firm, clear skinned face and pale blue eyes.
"I noticed that you are sitting all alone in the bus although you have some young people with you," he remarked.
"Yes," she replied. "There are four girl guides with me but they are paired off in other seats."
"I too am alone," he said. "Perhaps I could sit with you for the remainder of the homeward journey."

Later that night as she lay in bed in her villa her mind turned to the pleasant stranger who had made her laugh and brightened up her day.
"I was startled at the sound of my own laughter," she thought. "I hadn't heard myself laugh for many years, probably not since Pierre walked out of my life."
She felt giddy and a little elated - perhaps from being with four vivacious young girls, but she knew in her heart that there was more to it than that. The stranger had a calmness and a peace about him.
"I'm glad you climbed aboard that camel," he had said as he helped her alight at her bus stop, "you brought pleasure to my day."
"And you brought pleasure to mine," she replied.
"My name is Jack Donoughue," he said extending his hand.
"And I am Gretel," she said, "Gretel Bernhart Bouvier. *Buenos noches senor.*"
"*Hasta luego* - see you later," he said and he waved as the bus moved away.

After awhile she turned and quenched the bedside lamp, snuggled up cosily under the light bedclothes and said half aloud to herself:
"I think that today I met an extraordinary man."

Twenty Eight

"One bright sunny evening, Eddie Whiston was driven home by a farmer after a long day of plastering a milking parlour and his hands and wrists and legs were stiffly and sore. He was tired and he felt the dryness of dusty cement in his hair and the caked sweat that clung uncomfortably to his face and forehead and around his eyes. There were signs of dried mortar and cement on his overalls and his face was stained where the sweat had washed down the dust from his cheeks.
"I'm looking forward to a good wash and rest after the supper," he announced to the farmer as he closed the car door.

He sensed a tension in the house, even before he saw Tessie, standing red-eyed by the kitchen sink and Nora standing beside her with one foot resting on top of the other and one hand resting on the worktop.
"Is something wrong," he asked.
Nora began to answer but Tessie cut across her after she had finished dabbing her eyes with a hand towel.
"Nothing is wrong Dad," she answered. "Actually I was just about to leave when you came in the door. Dan will be home soon for his dinner."
"No further questions," answered Whispy. "I know when to keep my mouth shut."

As soon as she had left he repeated his question.
"What's the trouble with Tessie?" he asked.

"It's Fr. Bouvier," said Nora. "He called Tessie aside after mass this morning, and told her that she is excluded from receiving Holy Communion, because she got a divorce and remarried outside the Church."
"And did he give her Holy Communion today?"
"He did, but he said he cannot do that anymore. Church rules forbid him he said."
"Did she explain to him that her husband left her and she had to get a divorce to protect herself and her children? Did she tell him that?"
"No! She was so surprised and upset that she didn't even answer him."

Nora and himself called over to Tessie's house after supper. Tessie was very distressed at this turn of events and she was hurting in her soul at being banned from meeting Jesus in Holy Communion. Her husband Dan and her mother Nora accepted the situation stoically but Whispy blew a fuse when he fully realised the seriousness of what had happened.
"Dat's right wrong altogether," he exclaimed vehemently and driven by anger at what he perceived as unjust treatment, he went immediately to talk with Fr. Bouvier.

"I find it very difficult to cope with de treatment being meted out to my daughter Tessie," he began, in a conciliatory tone of voice.
"Your daughter is excluded from Holy Communion, because of the circumstances of her life," explained Fr. Bouvier calmly.
"But de circumstances of her life are not of her own making," said Whispy. "Her husband deserted her, leaving

her to rear dere tree children and forcing her to pay money for his share in de house, something he never paid a penny for."

"I am sympathetic to her situation," said Fr. Bouvier, "but I cannot change Church teaching."

"It was all outside her control," stated Whispy in exasperation.

"That may be," said Fr. Bouvier, "but I have to implement Church teaching. I'm sorry but that's outside my control."

Whispy talked to the parish priest, Canon Towman in the sacristy after mass on the following morning.

"You know well Eddie that I never refused to give Holy Communion to Tessie," said the Canon, "but my hand has been forced in the matter by Fr. Bouvier and I can't be seen to be openly opposing the official teaching of the Church and going against my own senior curate."

"I can understand your position," said Whispy.

"If it were up to me," said the Canon, "I would not refuse Holy Communion to someone presenting at the altar, whom I knew to be trying their best to live a good Christian life."

"Can't you tell Fr. Bouvier to do de same," said Whispy. "You're de parish priest and he is only de curate. You're de boss."

"Unfortunately it is not that simple. The reality is that Fr. Bouvier is simply implementing official Church teaching and I can't go against him in that."

In the days that followed, Eddie Whiston's mind was in a state of turmoil and he was unable to sleep at night. He was never very good at keeping matters to himself and he

talked freely about the issue. He was so distressed at the unfairness of it that he even spoke of it in the pub, in breach of the conventional wisdom that politics and religion should never be discussed in that venue.
"I tink dat dey have no right to exclude anyone from Holy Communion and dey shouldn't do it," he would argue.
"Why do you say that, Whispy," someone would ask.
"Because dey are preventing a good and decent person from going to meet Jesus in Holy Communion."
"What can you do about it?"
"I don't know yet, but I'm not going to take dis lying down. I have a great mind to get a placard and protest outside de church gate."
"Maybe you should," said a slightly tipsy customer "and who knows we might join you."
"I'd say now that very few would join you, Eddie," commented the lady publican. "People do not like to go against their priests."

Towards the end of the week, Eddie became convinced that he should act in the face of the injustice that was being done to his daughter, as he saw it. Using his skill as handyman carpenter he designed an attractive placard and attached it to a five foot length of two by one and because of Eddie's low level of literacy, his wife Nora wrote the message on it.
"Do you want me to come with you?" she asked.
"No Nora," he answered. "One of us is enough to be sticking his neck out."
"You know I would stand with you, if you want," she replied.
"I know dat," he said, "but I tink one of us is enough."

Eddie Whiston made his stand with his placard on the footpath directly opposite the chapel gate at each of the Masses on the following Sunday. He chose to stand across the road from the gate because he did not want to cause any obstruction to anyone attending Mass. The message on the placard could be clearly read by all:

DON'T STOP PEOPLE FROM MEETING JESUS
DON'T STOP JESUS FROM MEETING PEOPLE

The news of his protest spread quickly around the parish and it was a topic of discussion in homes, pubs, shops, marts and fairs. Eddie and his daughter Tessie were widely known and widely respected in the parish and beyond and while there was some ridicule by a minority, there was a great deal of sympathy for her and for him - as a father fighting for fair and just treatment for his daughter.
"What would you do if she was *your* daughter?" was a question repeated again and again.

Within two days the local newspapers had reported on the protest, by midweek a picture of a grim faced Eddie Whispy holding his placard was featured in the national daily newspapers and in the front page of all of the national newspapers on the following Sunday.
Radio stations sent reporters to record interviews with Eddie Whiston and they conducted *vox pop* interviews in the shops and streets and markets. National television stations sent camera crews and within ten days his protest was being reported as an item of interest in television newscasts in various parts of the world.

Twenty Nine

Fr. Thomas used his car for his first visit to Cooley Park. There were some lovely well-kept houses there but neglect was also evident which pointed to a lack of unified community spirit and a lack of respect - evident in the pervasive graffiti, in the neglect of some properties, particularly in the middle and lower east end sections: boarded up windows, some broken windows, broken doors, broken fences, abandoned cars - some with wheels as flat as pancakes and some with engines and bonnets missing - obviously there for a long time and dogs roaming freely along well worn muddy paths.

"It hadn't always been like that," said a local councillor whom he consulted. "Cooley Park was conceived and built with great idealism, believe it or not. It was built by well intentioned planners and local authorities who had the belief that people would be happy if they were provided with modern homes with modern facilities and initially, people were happy and content."
"What changed?" asked Fr. Thomas.
"The First Estate residents had come from houses that were inferior to the new houses that were given to them in Cooley Park and so they were relatively happy. Many of the couples were young and when the children grew up, the first problems began to emerge. The planners had thought of the needs of the people within the homes, but I think it would have been better if more provision was made for play areas and other facilities including shopping

facilities - basic things that would help knit the community together."

"Was that omission corrected in the other two newer estates?" asked Fr. Thomas.

"No! The opposite in fact. The gardens were smaller, the houses less private and there was nearly double the amount of houses per acre. The newer sections of Cooley Park, particularly the Calcutta Estate, were a product of an era when there was pressure to produce the highest possible number of houses at the lowest possible cost and the plans, construction materials and density reflected that."

"Is unemployment a factor?" asked Fr. Thomas.

"It was not a problem for the older residents because there was seasonal work from farmers and there were lots of manual labour type jobs and people were kept busy and felt more useful," answered the councillor.

"So unemployment is a problem for some at this time," suggested Fr. Thomas.

"Yes. There's more automation in factories now."

"Farming methods have changed and men are no longer needed for manual labour like in former times," suggested Fr. Thomas.

"There's also a lot of regulations that prevent young people from getting summer jobs and that sort of thing," said the councillor.

"Expectations are also different, I suppose," said Fr. Thomas.

"Yes! Times change and people change with them."

"And we must move with the times as well."

"Exactly," said the councillor.

Fr Thomas' plan of action for Cooley Park involved knocking on doors and calling to each house and he worked his way methodically from the last house at the lower Calcutta estate upwards through the middle Harlem estate and then to the homes in the First Estate beside the main road.

Generally, the reception was friendly enough. The inhabitants were generally a younger generation but there was an evident disconnect between them and the Church and between their outlook and the Church's teaching on certain issues, particularly relating to banning people from receiving Holy Communion:
"I am banned from going to Holy Communion, because my first marriage broke down and I'm now living with someone else."
"But you are still welcome to attend mass," said Fr. Thomas.
"I know, but it is not the same when I am banned from Holy Communion."

Some doors were not opened of course and he took note of those and came back again and again and in that way he managed to establish contact with most people, introduce himself and let them know that he was there to help.

Some houses were neatly painted in the middle Harlem estate but a lot were generally grotty and some boarded up, pretty much the same as the houses in the low lying Calcutta estate - neglected, reflecting lack of money or carelessness, lack of esteem and lack of pride of place. In contrast to many others, number 39 - the last house in the lower end of Harlem - closest to Calcutta, was particularly well maintained, clean, with a well kept garden, a neatly trimmed miniature lawn, richly coloured flower beds and rambling roses round the door.

Thomas had picked up some vibes about the occupants of this house from a number of householders but got specific information from two women who were chatting over the garden railings one evening:
"Did you call to Number 39?" asked Julia, a tall, pleasant, smiling bespectacled lady.
"Not yet, but I will," replied Fr. Thomas.
"We think you should that know that the ladies in that house are - well - they are a bit different," she said.
"Different! In what way?" asked Fr. Thomas.
"It's the work they do, their profession so to speak," she replied.
"Their profession!" repeated Thomas.
"She's trying to tell you that they work in the city at night, in the street - if you know what I mean," interjected Josephine, a medium sized, slightly built, slender lady with lipstick and a liberally powdered face.
"I think I do know what you mean," said Fr. Thomas.
"Now to be exact, only one of them, Jordana the poor thing actually works in the streets; she's the smaller, stouter one," explained Julia the smiling lady. "The tall good looking one is Alessandra. She's a capable lady and a very nice lady too. She is an escort and she also gives martial arts and self defence lessons in the city."
"She's from some country where the communists were in charge," stated Julia. "Some say that she was in the resistance movement in her homeland and that the man she loved was killed by the secret police."
"I wonder why she chose to come here to Lonerton?"

asked Fr. Thomas.
"Maybe she is trying to get away from her painful past," suggested Josephine. "I think she was tortured, you know."
"Oh dear! That's terrible," replied Thomas.
"We wanted to give you that information before you visited them," said Julia, "so that you would know what to expect when you call there."
"Thanks," said Fr. Thomas. "It is good to be forewarned. We'll talk again."

Many of the children in Cooley Park did well at school, but some of the others who did not do well in life, blamed the 'system' and gravitated towards crime and anti-social behaviour.
"Sometimes government services bring people from the city areas who have anti-social problems and give them houses in Cooley Park, sometimes without consultation with the local schools or community," complained one middle aged lady as she and her husband stood at her front door talking to Fr. Thomas.
"Some turn out very well," said her husband "but others bring their problems with them and make matters worse for the locals with their misdeeds."

Long periods of unemployment and habitual dependence on the welfare of the state for most of their lives, had disempowered some of the residents, depleted their self respect, stifled any progressive initiative that they possessed and some became hostile in their attitude.
"Giving everything to people can be destructive," said one local shopkeeper to Fr. Thomas one day. "It can make people feel different and colour their attitude and

encourage a belief that they have an entitlement to almost everything."
"It can also stifle initiative," interjected a customer. "If they get work, they will lose their benefits, so they are trapped and generally hemmed in by the system."
"They can grow up without having to be responsible for provision for their own needs," continued the shopkeeper. "In essence they are deprived of the need to be responsible and deprived of the satisfaction of achieving for themselves."
"That may be an over simplification," suggested Fr. Thomas.
"I know," said the shopkeeper, "but I think there is some truth in it as well. Think about it."

Overall Thomas encountered very little hostility. The vast majority of the people were friendly and good humoured and seemed happy in themselves. A minority were sullen and some were unresponsive - they listened to what he had to say, took his card and shut the door without a word. A minority blamed everyone except themselves for their own lack of success in life and expressed this in sweeping and generalised, condemnatory statements:
"I blame the government. They're only interested in helping the rich people."
"The politicians are all the same. They only look after themselves. I blame them."
Others blamed the schools and the education system.
"The teachers I had were no good; that's what happened to me."

Some had a firm belief that there were large numbers of

extremely wealthy people out there and if the government would make them pay more taxes the citizens of Harlem and Calcutta would get their fair share of the wealth of the nation.

Anthony Joseph Moran, low-sized, in his early sixties who modelled himself on Trotsky the Russian revolutionary, was the most extreme of these Harlem residents. Just like his Russian idol, he sported an imposing moustache and a goatee beard, and round rimmed spectacles similar to those worn by Trotsky - the ardent proponent of world communism who was exiled by Stalin and assassinated in Mexico in 1940. Anthony Joseph Moran was so vociferous and strident in his praise and propagation of the views of his idol, that the locals nicknamed him Trotsky Moran or just Trotsky for short.

"I will not be inviting you in," he declared to Fr. Thomas on the doorstep. "God - what God? There is no God. All that stuff that the Church teaches about God is a load of old rubbish, a silly old fairy tale to frighten children and gullible people into doing what the pope and the bishops want them to do."

"I only called to introduce myself," said Fr. Thomas.

"Well, you have some neck, you who are a member of the bourgeoisie controlling Church, coming down here to the working class who are exploited by you and everyone of your class and creed."

"Very well," said Thomas. "I will leave my card with you. Please feel free to contact me if ever I can be of assistance."

"Keep your card. I will not be contacting you or asking you for assistance," Trotsky declared, "and now I bid you good day," he concluded, as he turned abruptly away and closed the door in Thomas' face.

Occasionally when Fr Thomas was invited in to a home the discussion turned to the problem of drugs and drink in the estate and the disrespect shown by a gang who were intimidating ordinary decent people. The name Bowzer Diggins came up most frequently in that context and it was clear that he was regarded as a bad influence in the estate, that he had generated a great deal of fear and that no one was prepared to confront him:
"This place has gone to the dogs since the Diggins family were brought out here. Now most members of the family are alright in fairness to them but Bowzer, the big fellow, he is a bad boyo."
"That Diggins fellow is going around the estate with a gang of lackeys who do his bidding. They are intimidating decent people in the estate, especially the young and the elderly who are not able to defend themselves."
Drug dealing and outdoor drinking parties also featured in the complaints:
"Drugs are being bought and sold every night in Dealers' Alley and indeed it is no strangers that are at it. They say Teveena Scrahill's son Shawny is a supplying and dealing drugs."
"The poor decent woman, she raised him on her own and gave him everything that he wanted, and look at him now - bringing harm to the neighbourhood and shame to his poor mother."
"Almost every night there are young people, some as young as thirteen or fourteen taking part in drinking parties."

"As young as thirteen or fourteen," exclaimed Fr. Thomas. "Where are they buying the drink? Surely it is illegal to sell alcohol to anyone under the age of eighteen."
"They are not buying it themselves. The older ones like Bowzer Diggins' lackeys are buying it and selling it on to them at a profit."

In the better off First Estate, the one nearest the main road, the residents were more affluent, generally more senior, had attitudes more positive and there were general expressions of satisfaction with life. The concerns expressed in the First Estate were similar to those of the others with anti-social behaviour, graffiti, disrespect and intimidation topping the list. Shawny Scrahill was acknowledged to be a drug dealer and Bowzer Diggins was acknowledged to be a sinister influence on the entire Cooley Park.

Thirty

When Fr. Thomas did call to Number 39, Alessandra herself opened the door and she was a surprise in many ways. She was strikingly beautiful and her clothes accentuated a beautiful figure - well fitting jeans, and long sleeved, low necked blouse. Her golden blonde hair was neatly styled but was not tightly cropped or anything like that.
"Do come in," she said in a business like tone of voice, and in an accent which Fr. Thomas thought to be East European.
"Thank you," said Fr. Thomas.
"Did you vant to see me or Jordana?" she asked.
"It would be nice to talk to both of you," replied Fr. Thomas. "I am Fr. Thomas Kendley and I am the new curate in this parish. I am just calling round to introduce myself."
"Oh!" said Alessandra. "I did not know you ver a pryist, because you ver not vearing ze clothes of a pryist. I am sorry I thought you ver - someone else."
It was not difficult for Fr. Thomas to sense that there was something different here.
"Vould you like some tea or coffee?" she asked,
Fr. Thomas, realised that there could be gossip if he spent too long in this house but he ignored the concern.
"Yes! I would like a coffee, thank you," he said and thus began a relationship and friendship that would endure throughout their lives.

Alessandra was quite natural and open with Fr. Thomas

about herself, once she realised that he was a priest or 'pryist' as she pronounced it and there was no resentment there. She was very respectful and also very open about her work:
"I am an escort," she explained.
"I see," said Fr. Thomas, who was a little fearful that he had landed himself in an awkward situation.
"I accompany individual men to functions or celebrations - usually business functions. These are usually men who are unmarried or who are vidowed or divorced. I dress elegantly, I talk vit them and their friends or colleagues, I dance vit them and entertain them."
Fr. Thomas wondered if he should say: "that's interesting" or "it sounds exciting" but in the end he just said:
"I see" and then his stalled mind came up with practical question:
"Are you ever subjected to intimidation or danger?"
"Yes but only on a few occasions. I am skilled in martial arts and I am vell able to defend myself."
"May I speak with your friend?" asked Fr. Thomas.
"Jordana is not really my friend. I give her permission to use my house because she don't have a place to stay but I vill go to her bedroom and ask her if she vould like to speak vit you."

Looking around the room while she was gone, Fr. Thomas noticed the overall neatness of the room, the comfortable black leatherette seats, the ghetto blaster compact discs player, television, neat stacks of compact discs, flower vases, candle holders, a small statue of the Infant of Prague and a leather covered bible which had the appearance of having been used a lot.
"Jordana is not vell and she do not like to talk vit you

today," Alessandra stated on her return to the room. "Maybe another time. She vorked late last night and she is - how do you say - cold turkey, depressed."

Later she walked to the door with him:
"Thank you for calling," she said, "you vill be velcome to call again. Next time do not come until three o'clock afternoon, ven Jordana vill be up and about and she vill talk vit you, I think."
Fr. Thomas was glad that he had accepted the offer of coffee. It afforded him an opportunity to chat with someone, whom he recognised immediately as being unusual, and it gave him an opportunity to get new insights into her life and the life of Jordana.

He continued his work of trying to establish links with the residents of Cooley Park and to link them more closely with the Church in Lonerton. There were a lot of houses and it was very slow work. He went back again and again and it was very tedious trying to start a relationship with some. He did get a good overall picture of the place and he did get a good understanding of the people and in particular he got a good understanding of their attitude to the Church.
"There is no God there," argued one individual. If there was he would not allow the awful things that are happening in the world - so there is no point in going to Mass."

Others held the view that the Church was only for the better off people, that the priests kept all the money that was collected every Sunday - something which was

definitely not true. Occasionally someone would ask:
"Why don't the priests come down to us?" - to which Thomas would quietly respond:
"I am a priest and I am here with you."
"Ah yes," he was told, "but you are only coming down here for a few hours. We need a small chapel of our own down here."
That comment stung him deeply but it also provoked him to make a promise.
"I will try to spend more time here. Maybe we could establish an office here where you can come and visit and meet and discuss and pray also of course."
"Well, that would be very good indeed, but I know it will never happen."
"I'll try my best," said Thomas.
"I know you mean well, but you would never get the parish priest or the bishop to agree to that."
"Wait and see," said Thomas.
"Well, I will wait and see, but I'll only believe it when I see it."

Thirty One

When Fr Thomas called again to Number 39, Jordana was unwilling to come from her bedroom to talk with him, even though he had called in late afternoon - as recommended by Alessandra.
"I think she is not vell today," explained Alessandra to Fr. Thomas. "I think her spirit is in a veak place."
"I'm sorry to hear that," replied Fr. Thomas. "Tell her that I understand and I will pray that she gets well very soon."
"She vill have to go to vork tonight, even if she is feeling low," stated Alessandra.
"Can she not stay home and rest?"
"No she cannot stay home and rest."
"Why not?" asked Fr. Thomas, "surely she is her own boss."
"She has two bosses," explained Alessandra," but she herself is not one of them. One is her pimp who takes much of vat she earns and ze other is her addiction vich takes everything else."
"Addiction to drugs."
"Yes. That is her other boss."

When Fr. Thomas finally did meet Jordana, he was surprised at how wrecked and wretched she looked. He was sitting in one of the leatherette chairs in Alessandra's house and she sat smoking and resting her elbow on the corner of the table opposite him. Her dressing gown was partially unbuttoned leaving her knees and legs uncovered and Thomas could see that they contained many scratches

and puncture marks.
"I will make a cup of coffee for you as soon as I've finished this," she said holding up the rolled cigarette with her brown-stained fingers and the sleeve of the dressing gown slid down to her elbows, revealing more marks and scars.
They talked for a long while and many times she smiled a hurting, 'covering up smile' - trying to be pleasing even in her awful physical and painful, emotional state.
"I was in a steady relationship once," she told him. "We even had a house for a while. He didn't want children but the contraceptive didn't work and I became pregnant. He began to beat me after that as if I was to blame for getting pregnant and one night we both were high on drugs and spirits and he beat me badly, belting me hard around the stomach and the next day I began to lose the baby. I think that was what he wanted."
"Did you stay with him after that?" asked Thomas.
"No! He left for a while but he came back after a few months and said he was sorry and that he would never beat me again and so I took him back."
"After all he had done," said Thomas."Why did you take him back?"
"I suppose I loved him. I suppose I needed him, needed someone to love me."

It was Alessandra who filled in the gaps in Jordana's story on another occasion when Jordana wasn't there.
"That no good boyfriend vas not good," she explained, "but Jordana could not see that. He vas desperate, he needed money for drugs and that vas how she began to vork as a prostitute."

"Are you saying that she became a prostitute to get money to feed his drug habit?" asked Thomas.
"That is vat I am saying but in ze process she also became addicted."
"They are not together now," ventured Thomas.
"No, He became too violent so she left him and I took her in - but he is still her pimp."
"Can assistance be got for her?" asked Thomas, "in some rehabilitation or detoxification centre?"
"Maybe you could help vit that," said Alessandra "but I fear it is too late."
"I will do my best," promised Fr. Thomas.

In between visits to Number 39, Fr. Thomas gave a progress report on his mission to Cooley Park, to Canon Towman and senior curate Fr. P. B. Bouvier.
"Thanks Fr. Thomas," said the canon. "Your report has confirmed for me my belief, that the people of Cooley Park are good, decent, salt of the earth people - as good and as kind and generous in their hearts as any people anywhere."
"There are some notable exceptions," prompted Fr. Bouvier.
"That's true," answered Canon Towman "and it is the evil power of those exceptions that we must overcome, with the help of almighty God, without whom we could do nothing."
"Those women in Number 39 are a bad influence," declared Fr. Bouvier - one is an escort and the other one is a harlot and a.."
Before he could finish his sentence Canon Towman brought his big opened palm down forcefully on the table

and with a trembling voice and a face flushed red with distress he reprimanded his senior curate:
"Do not use that word to describe that good and decent girl," he stormed vehemently, "she may be down on her luck, but she is a child of God just like you or me."
"Bu- but she is a prostitute," protested Fr. Bouvier.
"Yes, but remember this: her poor mother cradled her in her arms in the moments after her birth, just as lovingly as your beloved mother cradled you."
"She is a prostitute now, and that is an undeniable fact and she is a bad influence in the estate," argued Fr. Bouvier.
"So what do we do with her?" asked the canon. "I need only ask myself one question to find that answer - what would Jesus do? The gospels tell us that he did not condemn, he forgave and treated with respect. He did not judge mercilessly, which is what you Reverend Father Bouvier are often inclined to do, judge without having due regard for mercy."
"I follow the teaching of the *magisterium* of the Catholic Church," answered Fr. Bouvier "and I make no apology for that."
"Ah! Yes, but you forget the merciful teaching of Jesus Christ who died an awful, gruesome, horrible death for all of us," answered Canon Towman. "It is the example of Jesus that we must follow. He showed love and respect for the prostitute and we must do the same for that poor fragile woman. There can be no love without mercy and as a priest, you ought to know that."
"You sound as if you know her," commented Fr. Thomas.
"Yes I do know her," answered Canon Towman. "I baptised her when I served as a curate in the parish where her father and mother lived with her other siblings - two

boys and another sister. Her parents were a bit disunited. She was christened Jordana. I remembered the name well because it was an unusual name at that time. She was about thirteen when I left that parish. She was of a tender nature and disposition, easily hurt but too timid to retaliate or defend herself and she would hide her hurt behind a forced, joyless, mirthless smile. The poor child. It hurts me to think of it. She was subservient, always anxious to please - over-anxious I thought, as if she thirsted for approval and affection. It was as if she had judged herself to be of little value, to be inferior to others, and as a result considered herself unworthy of being loved - even by herself and so she craved for love and appreciation from outside."

"Do you know how she came to her present state in life?" asked Fr. Thomas.

"She became rebellious at home in her early teenage years and by the time she was seventeen, she was associating with types of people who were not fit company for her. She dressed like them, copied their lifestyle, did alcohol and drugs and soon disassociated herself from the norms of the society into which she was born. She derided her Christian faith and was convinced that it was old fashioned and that her new way of life was modern and free. She was wrong of course. Her new found way of life was not freedom but a trap, a prison, an enslavement from which she has not yet escaped. The poor child, the poor, poor child became no better than a slave."

"Have you met her since she came to live in Cooley Park?" asked Fr. Thomas.

"Yes! She came to the house to see me and to ask me for money - a substantial amount? She said she owed the

money to a drug dealer and she would be beaten up if she didn't pay or have her face scarred or maybe be killed."
"Did you give her the money?" asked Fr. Thomas.
"I did - I arranged to have it delivered to her debtors, but not before I had got advice from the gardai."
"It is a tragic story," said Fr. Bouvier. "Now I understand why you do not want her called a harlot."
"I don't want to hear that title applied to anyone," responded the canon humbly. "I will say no more about Jordana for now," he continued, "but I regret that I was unchristian earlier in the way I spoke to you Fr. Paul. I ask for your forgiveness and for your blessing."
Having spoken thus, Canon Towman rested his hand on the table for support as he knelt on the floor and bowed his head.
"Please do not kneel," said Fr. Bouvier and he swallowed hard. "You don't need to do that."
"It is my role as a priest to bring healing and never to hurt and so I must kneel, not only for forgiveness and a blessing but for a deepening of my humility and for protection from the twin evils of arrogance and pride. So I beg for your sacramental forgiveness and your priestly blessing."

As he watched the diminutive Fr. Bouvier placing his hands on the bowed head of Canon Towman with its strong, tousled, wavy, grey hair, Fr. Thomas became conscious of the intense presence of God's spirit in the room. His own heart was filled with that spirit too and he experienced intensely, its warmth and comfort and peace and goodness in a way that could never be experienced by hearts that are hardened and by minds that are closed against it.

Thirty Two

Fr. Thomas was troubled about the misinformation and misunderstandings that so many of the citizens of Cooley Park had regarding the Church and about their belief that the priests were distant from them.

"There's a major disconnect between the Church and the people of Harlem, Calcutta and the First Estate," he stated at a meeting of the priests in the sacristy.

"They are living within the parish," answered Fr. Bouvier, "in that way they are already connected."

"Theoretically, they are an integral part of the parish Catholic community, but in reality they do not perceive themselves as esteemed participants in Church life within the parish," answered Thomas.

"There's a chapel here for them, it is open from dawn to dusk but they will not make the effort to come to it," said Fr. Bouvier.

"Even in terms of distance," said Thomas, "they are actually a long way physically from the chapel, more than a mile away I would say."

"Their ancestors walked three or five or six miles to come to Mass," answered Fr. Bouvier "and often did so having fasted from midnight. I'm afraid I do not share your concern about their distance from the church."

"I think there are challenges here to be confronted," interjected Canon Towman. "New thinking and approaches will be necessary."

"I agree," said Thomas "and the establishment of some sort of tangible and permanent presence among them should be a top priority."

During the course of one of Fr. Thomas' occasional visits to our house, the conversation turned to his work in Lonerton parish and in particular to the task of reconnecting the disconnected residents of Cooley Park with Church life in the parish.
"It is good that you are spending so much time there and engaging with the people," I affirmed.
"It might be good," said Thomas, "but it is not enough. I need to establish a semi-permanent base there, some place in which I can establish an office and maybe have a facility for small groups to meet or to pray or to engage in adoration of the blessed sacrament - a place in which we could occasionally celebrate Mass."
"Is there any vacant house there that the parish could rent?" I asked.
"There is. There are certainly one or two that are boarded up."
"Couldn't you get one of them?" I asked.
"It is a good idea, but I would need a house in each of the three estates."
"What you need is a house with wheels under it, that you could move from one estate to the next," I laughed.
"Exactly," answered Thomas "and I suppose that houses with wheels haven't been invented yet."
"I suppose not," laughed my wife Hannah but she quickly turned serious and said:
"Oh! Hold on a minute. They have been invented and I know where there is one that is ideally suited to your needs. It is very near to us - just out there at the gable of

the house."

When our children were in their early teenage years, I bought a large second hand library van from the County Council. It was more akin to a small lorry than a van and it had been used as a mobile library visiting villages throughout the county. I converted it into a camper, complete with cooking facilities, bunk beds, washing and toilet facilities and we were able to go on holidays, tie the bikes onto the back of it and travel around the country during the summer holidays. It was quite a sizeable truck and the children liked the crunchy sound of the diesel engine. We had great fun travelling to faraway places and using the bicycles to explore the smaller country roads.

Time moves on and the children grew up and went their own way. For a while, my wife and I went on holidays but the van was too big for us and after that it was just parked there at the side of the house, becoming a bit of an eyesore and doing no good to anyone. We often thought of selling it but for some reason we didn't - perhaps in the belief that it might be of some use to someone some time and so indeed it was, because it became the first mobile chapel in all of Ireland in modern times and it helped transform the lives and environment of the citizens of the three estates of Cooley Park - The First Estate, Harlem and Calcutta.

Fr. Thomas asked me to set about converting it to serve as a mobile office and a mini mobile chapel and while this work was in progress, he outlined his plan to the Canon Towman and Fr. Bouvier who was openly hostile to the idea:

"I think it cheapens the Church and gives the wrong signal," stated Fr. Bouvier. "Do you propose to keep the Blessed Sacrament in this van?"
"That is part of the long term plan," said Thomas.
"I think a van is no fit place for the Eucharist to be kept, it would be disrespectful if not downright sacrilegious and I would be opposed to it."
The canon was sympathetic to the idea but reluctant to go along with something as drastic as using an old library van as a mobile chapel. He was concerned about how it would be viewed by the bishop and by priests in other parishes and indeed by the people of the parish:
"I am reluctant to approve such a radically new departure," he said.
"I am disappointed about that," answered Thomas. "I think it is an ideal mechanism for establishing links with these people and reconnecting them with Church life in the parish."
"Maybe you are right," said the canon, "but a van is just a van and I find it hard to see how it could be regarded as suitable for religious purposes."
"It is much bigger than a van, indeed it is more like a small lorry," said Thomas.
"It is still an unsuitable location for the blessed sacrament," declared Fr. Bouvier. "I think you should not proceed with it."
"But the conversion work is in progress," said Thomas.
"I think it is better to suspend that work for a while," said the canon. "I need more time to consider all of the implications of the proposal."

Thomas was disappointed that his proposal had not been

better received and he asked me to suspend the conversion work, but I refused.
"The difficulty that you have encountered," I said, "is not a difficulty with a van or with the people of Cooley Park. The problem is with your superiors and colleagues."
"It is better all the same to stop the work of modifying the van," said Thomas. "We will wait for a time and I will refloat my proposal with Canon Towman at a later stage."
I was angry at this.
"I want to remind you that this is still my van," I said "and I intend to continue converting it for use for the disconnected citizens of Cooley Park."
"Fair enough," said Fr. Thomas. "Go ahead and we will leave the final outcome to God."
"That's a good decision," I affirmed.

It did turn out to be a good decision because two significant events would bring about a change in the attitudes of Canon Towman and of Fr. Bouvier. The first of these significant events was Eddie Whiston's ongoing weekly protest at the chapel gate and the other was a fatal shooting involving local drug dealer Shawny Scrahill and his friend Johnny Doh Doohan by 'a party or parties unknown.'

Thirty Three

At the precise time that Fr. Bouvier was giving his blessing and sacramental forgiveness to Canon Towman, the spirit of all that is good was stirring the conscience of a wealthy, seventy two year old, overweight, amputee patient, as he lay hooked up to tubes and drips and unable to sleep, in his hospital bed in the Canadian city of Calgary.

Oil baron, Pedro Rodriguez, president of Mid Western Oils was on the flat of his back, looking at the ceiling of his private room. He was intent on contemplating his future but was unable to do so because of persistent flashbacks from the distant past and the weight of secrets that he had kept hidden for so long. His left leg had been amputated just above the knee, in order to prevent the spread of gangrene - brought on by diabetes, that got rapidly worse as a consequence of ageing and of his own reckless indiscipline and blatant disregard for the advice of his doctors and consultants.

As he struggled with ghost pains in his non-existent toes and simultaneously considered the use of prosthesis, he began, for the first time in his life, to seriously contemplate his own mortality. While in that frame of mind, his conscience disturbed him persistently and the pressure to reveal his secret past became progressively more intense. He had no peace of mind and he knew he never would, until he came clean and revealed all to those who loved him.

"Not too many of those around," he mused to himself. "Just Gabriela - no one else. I have much to tell and few to tell it to."

Pedro Rodriguez had done well since he left Brazil thirty eight years earlier, bringing with him the title deeds and exploration rights for the wasteland in mid western Canada, formerly owned by Petroleum Canada Oil and Gas. It was all of three years before he had acquired sufficient financial backing to commence in-depth exploration and another two before drilling commenced under the auspices of the newly formed Mid Western Oils Plc. The first exploratory well confirmed the presence of oil and gas in commercial quantities and subsequent development wells made Pedro Rodriguez a very wealthy man.

He had struck it rich and fulfilled a long held ambition. He was richer than he ever dreamed but having realised his dream, he came to understand that it did not guarantee happiness.
"Money can't buy happiness," he mused. "I can vouch for that."
He kept a low profile and shunned all kinds of personal publicity for a time but soon the twin demons of alcohol and his attraction for women burrowed their way into his mind and became a potent force, that impelled him on a path of physical and emotional deterioration, spiralling ever downwards. Then he met Andreina a tall, beautiful Venezuelan who was less than half his age. She married him, brought stability and affection to his life and gave birth to Gabriela - their greatest treasure.

Happiness reigned in the home of Pedro and Andreina for some years and Pedro achieved mastery over his life again and assured himself that he had annihilated his destructive demons for once and for all. He was wrong of course, for old demons are difficult to defeat. They can be weakened but rarely defeated and a constant state of war exists between them and the spirit of God, within the human mind and heart, for dominance and for the furtherance of their respective spirits of good or evil.

Pedro retained his youthful zest well into his fifties. The white Stetson hat that he customarily wore covered his shiny bald head, gave him a dashing appearance and made him seem younger that he really was.
Some women are attracted to powerful, wealthy men and it was with such a woman in the city of Medicine Hat, that Pedro Rodriguez was first unfaithful to his beautiful, kind and loving Andreina. Thus began a cycle of downfalls, regrets, lies, deceit and reconciliations that recurred again and again until Andreina left, filed for divorce and custody of Gabriela and moved back to Venezuela.

Now as he twisted and turned in his hospital bed trying to find a pain-free position, his mind recalled his wayward actions during that period of his life. For a few years after the divorce he became more disciplined and focused his full attention on his role as C.E.O. of Mid Western Oils. The company profits and his own personal wealth grew handsomely but he was not happy. His life was empty and devoid of real challenges. His old twin demons worked their persuasive powers on his mind anew and he reverted

yet again to his innate weaknesses, continuing his involvements with women and drowning his guilt with alcohol until he drifted into occasional bouts of depression. He began to disappear for days at a time, sometimes returning dishevelled, unshaven and unwashed.
"I am wealthy but abandoned by my own," he would say sometimes. "What could I expect because it is what I did in the past to my good and decent wife and my two and a half year old son. The evil has returned to the evildoer and I am paid back with my own coin."

Thereafter during spells of sobriety, he would work with concentration and be back to his old self for a period of time and then disappear again. It was rumoured among company personnel that during these bouts, he would sleep rough in the barns on his ranch - neither washing nor shaving nor changing clothes and leaving the place littered with empty alcohol bottles and filth. The rumours must have been true because it was in the barn of his ranch that his daughter Gabriela found him after she turned twenty one and came to the U.S.A. to reconcile with her father.

Now ten years later, Pedro thought of all those things as he drifted in and out of sleep in his hospital bed.
"Gabriela saved my life," he mused, "and my spirit and my soul as well. She cleaned me up, helped me get control of myself and become a good C.E.O. again but most important of all she became my best friend."
Gabriela did become her father's best friend. She commenced work with the company, worked closely with him and learned from him. She was tall like her mother and beautiful as well. She learned quickly and was very

competent. Two years before his hospitalisation, she had succeeded him as C.E.O. and he took on the newly created and more leisurely post of company president.

Thirty Four

Johnny Doh and Shawny Scrahill were the best of friends although Shawny was more greedy for money than Johnny, whose real name was Jonathan Doohan. They had grown up together, went to school together, fought for each other and fought against each other. They had shared common views on life and shared secrets and were closer than many brothers are.

It was Shawny who first introduced Johnny to the drinking parties that took place on the bank of the river on the sloping ground that falls away from the Calcutta section of Cooley Park. There was plenty of cover there, in the form of groves and clumps of bushes, should they wish to remain hidden but usually they drank openly. Generally their activities were harmless enough and the group was considerate enough to collect the empty cans into a plastic bag which they tied neatly and left there.

As time went on, they began to buy bottles of wine from the supermarket to augment the beer and later still bottles of spirits - usually tequila or vodka and then some of them were not so tidy. Under the influence of strong liquor, they often broke the bottles and walked away. In due course it was inevitable I suppose, that someone would get the bright idea to bring drugs for them to try and this was exactly what happened and the very small amount available was mixed with tobacco and rolled into a cigarette and passed around.

Very soon afterwards it became evident to Shawny that there was a demand for a steady supply of cannabis and he began to act as a go between - initially between a supplier and the group. In this way he was transformed from an occasional user to a supplier and he quickly realised that he could make a little profit for himself. There were risks for him if he should ever be caught but luck was with him and he began to make a nice little income.

As always, Shawny was anxious to include his good friend Johnny Doh in the business and see him share some of the rewards, but Johnny would not have anything to do with the dealing nor would he partake of drugs whereas Shawny was more reckless in regard to both. Shawny's business expanded steadily. He branched into harder drugs and in due course other people began to take supplies from him, which they would then sell to other groups or individuals locally and elsewhere, even in smaller villages within a ten to twenty kilometre radius of Lonerton. This was a very satisfactory arrangement for Shawny and he began to make a lot of money, while others took the risks and he himself was careful to keep aloof from them and remain unconnected, to avoid being caught.
After a time problems emerged with the collection of money. Some of the dealers were unable to collect money owed to them by some users and other dealers who did collect began to withhold some of it instead of paying to Shawny what they owed him. This in turn put Shawny into the bad books of his suppliers, who were not very nice people and not very patient with those who owed them money.

Around that time of difficulty, Shawny got what he considered to be a lucky break in the form of an offer from Bowzer Diggins who visited him after dark one night. He came directly to the point:
"I hear you're having trouble mate," he said.
"Trouble!" repeated Shawny. " What kind of trouble?"
"You're having trouble collecting money owed to you," said Bowzer.
"That's my business," retorted Shawny.
"Look mate, I won't beat around the bush," said Bowzer.
"I'm listening," declared Shawny.
"Your biggest problem," said Bowzer, "is a lack of discipline and control. You are unable to discipline those who work for you and that means you can't control them."
"That is a problem," admitted Shawny.
"If you cannot control them, they will begin to do what they like."
"And that's what some of them *are* doing - what they bloody well like," said Shawny.
"So, what are you going to do about it?" asked Bowzer.
"I must impose discipline and control, just like you say," answered Shawny.
"You must instil fear in them," said Bowzer "and that's the heart of your problem."
"What do you mean?" asked Shawny.
"You are incapable of instilling fear into anyone," declared Bowzer. "If you can't instil fear, they will walk all over you. Fear is what will make them show respect."
"I suppose you're right," said Shawny, "but I am the way I am, so what can I do?"
"Look mate, you need someone to enforce discipline,

someone who can instil fear and make them show you respect. I can do that for you mate."
"What are you proposing?" asked Shawny.
"I will be your enforcer," said Bowzer. "You sell the stuff to me. I will distribute, twist arms, make them pay, collect the money and then pay you."
"What's in it for you?" asked Shawny.
"Money," answered Bowzer. "I will expand into more rural areas, into more remote villages and into more schools."
"You have big plans," said Shawny.
"The more money I make, the more money you make," said Bowzer. "What do you say mate?"
"I'll think about it," said Shawny.

Shawny did think about it. Bowzer was one of the most feared thugs in Calcutta and Harlem and indeed in the entire Cooley Park - definitely not a nice guy. He was selfish, bullying domineering and totally without empathy for anyone other than himself. He had the strength and build and intimidating appearance to force his will on others, particularly on the weak and vulnerable.
"He will be well able to instil fear into those dealers that owe me money," Shawny explained to his friend Johnny Doh.
"I wouldn't trust Bowzer as far as I could throw him," said Johnny.
"What can go wrong?" asked Shawny. "He needs me to supply him and I need him to collect the cash. It's a 'win win' situation."
"I'm telling you to have nothing at all to do with him," warned Johnny.
"I have no choice," said Shawny. "I have no other option

at all."

Within a relatively short time, Shawny was back in the money and back in the good books of his suppliers, having repaid all his debts to them. The doubts he had about Bowzer disappeared and he began to trust him and congratulate himself on his choice of partner in crime.

Thirty Five

A meeting between the priests and Eddie Whiston took place in the home of Canon Towman the parish priest, in the parlour where the big table was. Those in attendance along with Whispy and his daughter Tessie, were Canon Towman, Fr Bouvier, whose pre-Vatican Two outlook moved him to ban Tessie from Holy Communion, and Fr. Thomas who was very much a product of post Vatican Two times and very much given to mercy and understanding for the failings and circumstances of others. Canon Towman invited Eddie and Tessie to take a seat at the table but Whispy refused the offer:
"If my daughter is not good enough to be allowed by you to meet wit Jesus in Holy Communion at de table of de Lord at Mass, I don't tink dat we can be good enough to sit at de same table as you any other day either. So tanks for the offer, but we'll stay standing."
"Tessie, will you at least take a seat?" asked the canon.
"No thanks," said Tessie. "I will stand with my father, just as he is standing up for me."
"Very well," said the canon.

Thus was the scene set for the meeting - the large polished, oak boardroom table, Canon Towman seated in a carver at the top, Fr. Thomas seated at the side of the table on his left, Fr. Bouvier at the right, some empty chairs on each side and Eddie Whispy and his very lovely daughter Tessie, standing dignified and respectful some distance away from the bottom of the table.

"Welcome Tessie and welcome Eddie," said the canon. "I want to welcome you officially. I am very glad that you came to see us."
"We're glad to be here to talk to you," said Whispy.
"We thank you for meeting us," said Tessie.
"Well, Eddie," said the canon, "you have been protesting every Sunday for the past six weeks across from the chapel gate and it has been a problem for us and I'm sure a problem for you as well."
"I know it is a problem," said Whispy "and I wish to God dat I didn't have to be dere at all wit my placard."
"The news media have taken up this issue with enthusiasm," said Fr. Bouvier, "and many of them are hostile to the Church. They use your kind of protest to condemn the Church."
"I know dat," said Whispy, "but I can't help it if dey are hostile to de Church."
"Your protest has caused a lot division in the parish," stated Fr. Bouvier. "Some people are supportive of what you are doing and other people are against what you are doing."
"Fr. Bouvier is right," said Canon Towman, "some people who support you want to gather signatures in support of you and some people who are not supportive of you want to gather signatures against you and want to have the protest stopped."
"I know dat," said Eddie, "but I never asked anyone to collect signatures or make petitions."
"Of course you didn't," replied the canon. "I know you long enough and I know that you wouldn't do that, but we must try to find a resolution to this issue and so to begin with, I would like you to outline for us, what the major

problem is - as you see it. I know that you are concerned about Tessie and I know that you have always been supportive and very helpful to the Church and that you are a really great Christian man and a really great helper in the parish. You do a lot of work cleaning the monuments and keeping the shrubs and hedges and all the rest of it. So I am very anxious to help and I called this meeting with the sincere hope of solving your problem."

"I tank you for dat," said Whispy.

"And so do I," said Tessie.

"Good," said Canon Towman. "Now we would like you tell us whatever it is that you want to say to us and we will see what we can do, to try to find a resolution to the problem."

"Well, de problem," began Whispy, "is not really my problem at all. It is your problem. My daughter Tessie is a good-living Christian girl. She has always been dat. She has been a good and faithful daughter to her mother and to me. She got married at a young age and de man she married wasn't suitable for her but she loved him and had tree children wit him and den he went off wit another young woman, leaving Tessie wit de tree children to rear on her own. Throughout all dat time she continued to go to Mass and receive Holy Communion. And den after a few years of being on her own, rearing her children, she met Dan Hayley. Dan was a single man and dey fell in love and dey wanted to get married - just de same as other people who fall in love."

"We wanted to get married in the Catholic Church, but the Church would not allow us to do that," said Tessie, "and I understand why this is so."

"You would not be allowed to marry in the Catholic

Church, because you got divorced," explained Fr. Bouvier. "If you had got an annulment, you would be free to marry. Why did you not chose to go down that route instead of getting a divorce?"
"Maybe," said Tessie, "that you think my former husband Max Delown was a caring and honourable man like you, but he was less than honourable and not very caring. He would not cooperate with the application for an annulment and I had to get the divorce to protect my rights to my home and to my children."
"So you see," said Whispy, "dey could not get married in de Church as you know, and so, dey got married outside of de Church and now dey are man and wife according to de law of de land, but not according to de law of de Church and because of dat, she is now banned from Holy Communion."
"I accept that for a while after I got married in the civil ceremony, you Canon always gave me Holy Communion. It wasn't until your new senior curate Fr. Bouvier arrived and began to impose his idea of things, that I was told that I could not receive Holy Communion in a Catholic Church," Tessie stated.
"Dat's right, she's right dere." agreed Eddie.
"I have to follow the plan of God the Father for life and for the family," Fr. Bouvier replied.
"Dat's alright for you to say," said Whispy, "but I am her father and I would not refuse her anything, let alone prevent her meeting wit Jesus the Son of God. Now if dat is my position, I who am just a human father, how can any of you tink dat God, her heavenly father wouldn't allow her to meet wit His Blessed Son in Holy Communion. Dat's what you're doing, you're stopping her from meeting

wit Jesus."
At this juncture Fr. Bouvier interrupted Whispy's flow of speech.
"If I may Mr. Whiston, I want to say to you that it is not I who is refusing Holy Communion to your daughter. I know you love your daughter, of course, naturally enough, but I am simply upholding the rules of the Church and the teaching of the Church. I know you say that God is merciful, and I accept that but the Church is responsible for teaching the will of God on earth."
"Well, I tink dere's someting wrong wit dat teaching," said Whispy. "It is not good to stop anyone from meeting wit Jesus."
"The teaching of the Church is approved by the *magisterium,* that group of experienced and holy people in Rome, who are very highly qualified and are guided in their decisions by the Holy Spirit and since the Holy Spirit cannot be wrong, the decisions of the *magisterium* cannot be wrong."

Whispy was getting angry because he mistakenly thought that Fr. Bouvier was using big words and talking down to him and he kind of 'lost his cool' and said more than he had ever intended - something he regretted later.
"How do you mean dat dey can't be wrong?" he asked testily, "everyone can be wrong."
"Because, as I said, they are guided by the Holy Spirit and the Holy Spirit cannot be wrong in telling them what to do," explained Fr. Bouvier.
"Maybe dey are misunderstanding what de Holy Spirit is telling dem. 'Tis easy to misunderstand. We all know dat"
"Dad," said Tessie, who wanted her father to calm down a

little.
Fr Thomas intervened at this point and said:
"I think we should look on this in the way that Eddie is looking at it. He says that he as a human father would not prevent his daughter from meeting Jesus, and if God the heavenly father loves us beyond measure, surely he would not want to stop Eddie's daughter from receiving Holy Communion and meeting Jesus in her genuinely complex circumstances."
"Dat's exactly de point I'm making," said Whispy.
"But that is exactly not the point," replied Fr. Bouvier, "because the Church through its *magisterium* teaches differently. Anyone who was married in a Catholic Church who subsequently divorced and remarried outside the Catholic Church, is prohibited from receiving Holy Communion in the Catholic Church. That is the point."
"I tink dat is right wrong altogether and I don't agree wit it," stated Whispy, very firmly.
"Leave it Dad," said Tessie, but Whispy was on a roll and he couldn't stop even if he wanted to:
"I can't read or write, as I already said, but I can hear what is preached at Mass and I have gone to Mass every Sunday of my life and I've heard all de gospels and de letters of St Paul and de Apocalypse but I never heard about dis *magisterium*."
"The *magisterium* is the teaching authority of the Church and it is established in Rome in the Vatican," explained Fr. Bouvier.
"Dad," said Tessie, "we don't know about these things."
"But what about all de stories I heard in de gospel at mass over de years," asked Whispy. "Dere's the story of the woman who was caught in adultery and dey brought her to

Jesus and dey were going to stone her but Jesus didn't see anything wrong wit her anymore dan themselves and he didn't condemn her. Jesus had no problem about meeting dat poor woman and dat's all my daughter Tessie wants to do when she comes to Mass, just to meet Jesus in Holy Communion, but you're stopping her."

"It is not like that at all. It is the teaching of the Church that's prohibiting her from receiving Jesus in Holy Communion," explained Fr. Bouvier. "I notice Mr. Whiston that you omitted to mention that Jesus instructed her to turn away from sin."

"I know he said dat alright," said Whispy, "but he didn't refuse to meet her, dough did he?"

"No he didn't," said Canon Towman, "because he was merciful and understanding."

"Leave it Dad," said Tessie again, but Whispy was in full flow and there was no stopping him now:

"And den dere was a woman who came wit a jar of expensive ointment and she washed de feet of Jesus wit her tears, and she dried them wit her hair and she put de ointment on his feet and de other people were complaining dat Jesus was associating wit sinners, but he put dem in dere place and he was very happy to meet her. I tink he would be very happy to meet my daughter Tessie also in Holy Communion and I'm sure he would too except for one reason - you are stopping him."

"But we're not stopping him," said Fr. Bouvier.

"Oh yes you are," said Whispy.

"That's not technically correct," said Fr. Bouvier.

"Well 'tis actually correct anyway," countered Whispy, "because my daughter must turn away from de altar and go back down to her seat witout meeting Jesus and be

embarrassed and ashamed in front of everyone. I tink dat don't square at all wit de stories dat I heard read at Mass from de gospels."
"I did not refuse her at the altar," said Fr. Bouvier.
"You're right dere," said Whispy, "but you said you would refuse her if she came up again."
"She could come to the altar with her hands crossed to each shoulder and she would receive a blessing," explained Fr. Bouvier.

Canon Towman felt bad that the discussion had turned so testy and he cleared his throat before saying:
"The problem," he said "is that the teaching outlined by Fr. Bouvier is the official teaching of the Church and it is part of the Church's teaching in order to protect the sanctity of the family. Now since Fr. Bouvier has made an issue of it, we cannot go against it - well not generally and confrontationally anyway. At the same time we must always be careful not to withhold God's goodness and mercy from anyone."
"Dat's what I want you to show to Tessie - God's goodness and mercy," said Whispy.
"I would like to hear what Fr. Thomas thinks," said Tessie.
"Life is often complex," said Fr. Thomas "and the lives of some are more complicated than others. I know that from the experience of my own life. I must make allowances for good living Christian people who are in complicated situations, for which they cannot be blamed. I think there are exceptions to every rule."
"If you relax the rule, it will weaken and collapse it," said Fr. Bouvier.
"I disagree with you," Fr. Thomas replied. "Holy

Communion should not be perceived as a reward given exclusively to those who are being good. No! Holy Communion is for everyone - particularly those who are struggling and overburdened."

"The prohibition on receiving Holy Communion applies to a lot of other people as well," stated Fr. Bouvier.

"I tink dat some people takes no notice of it," said Whispy angrily.

Fr. Bouvier spoke again:

"That is precisely the problem, Mr. Whiston. People are not living in full accordance with the teaching of the Church and the teaching of the *magisterium.* They are picking and choosing the bits that suit their desires and deciding - we will live by this rule but not by that rule because we don't want to. This is causing major problems for the Church and is leading to insubordination on a large scale and widespread disrespect for the teaching of the Church."

"I tink dat you are too much altogether about rules and regulations," said Whispy, "

"Well, that is your opinion," said Fr. Bouvier.

"Dere is a lot more to being a good Christian dan just keeping rules and regulations. Tessie here is always helping everyone, raising funds for de needy causes and she is raising her children and raising dem well, baking buns for cake sales and coffee mornings and I tink dat is what being a Christian is all about. I tink she is a far better Christian dan someone who keeps de rules only because dey want to save dere own soul and still you won't give Holy Communion to Tessie."

"We must adhere to the teaching of Christ as interpreted by the Church through the *magisterium,*" repeated Fr.

Bouvier, who was becoming quite exasperated at this point in the discussion.

"Are you telling me so?" asked Whispy, "dat my daughter, who does so much good and who is always helping everyone, is less worthy to receive Holy Communion dan de miserable person who never tinks about anyone's welfare only dere own?"

"Anyone who is living with someone else in an illicit relationship," said Fr. Bouvier, "is not in a fit state of grace and cannot therefore receive Jesus."

This remark by Fr. Bouvier caused Tessie to blush a deep crimson and after an audible sharp intake of breath she responded sharply:

"I see that you have judged me to be living in sin. If I were a murderer, who had killed a hundred people, all I would need do is go to confession, confess my sins and I would be fully entitled to receive Holy Communion, but I who have not harmed anyone am banned for life from receiving Holy Communion because, after my divorce I got married in a civil ceremony - something I just had to do."

"I am only a simple man and I know that I'm a bit innocent at times," said Whispy "and de canon and most other people know dat I never learned to read or write only my name but I tink Tessie is right in what she says."

"It is very difficult to judge who is in a state of grace and who is not," commented Fr. Thomas. "I find it hard to disagree with Tessie."

"So do I," said Canon Towman and rising from his chair and extending his hand to Tessie he said in his honest and kindly voice:

"Thanks very sincerely Tessie and Eddie for coming to talk to us. Eddie, you have given witness this evening in this room, to the abiding love of a father for his daughter and Tessie has given witness to the trust and love of a daughter for her father. I believe that I must trust in the goodness of God. Do you agree, Fr. Thomas?"

"I do agree. Tessie has suffered a lot due to being abandoned by her husband and she did what she thought best for her children and herself. We must remember that she is not excommunicated. We must be wise and discern what is right from her circumstances. We must be respectful. It will not weaken the teaching if we apply the love and mercy of God to Tessie. I think we should leave the decision to Jesus himself."

"Tank you Fr. Thomas," said Whispy. "I know you listened to us and I know dat Canon Towman listened to us, but I doubt very much dat Fr. Bouvier listened to us."

"Eddie," said the Canon, "I have one favour to ask of you - will you suspend your protest while we try to get a solution to the problem of your daughter receiving Holy Communion?"

"I can't promise dat," said Whispy. "I will discuss it wit Tessie. I'll tink about it and let you know."

As they walked home Whispy noticed that Tessie was quieter than usual, in fact she scarcely spoke at all.

"You're very quiet Tess," said Whispy.

"I'm furious," said Tessie.

"Furious about what?" asked Whispy.

"About what," she exclaimed? "About that Fr. Bouvier. Didn't you hear him say I was living in sin. Living in sin!"

"You're wrong dere Tessie. He didn't say dat at all, he only said dat you were not in a fit state of grace."

"Same thing," she answered.

"Don't be too hard on him," Tess.
"He is the cause of all the trouble.," said Tessie. "There was no problem until he began imposing his view of the rules - preaching love and at the same time excluding people and showing no mercy to them. He doesn't seem to understand that you can't love someone and exclude them at the same time."
"He is young and inexperienced. Life will teach him not to be so hard on people wit his rules and regulations," said Whispy.
"I can't wait that long," said Tessie. "I think he should start learning now and I intend to help with that."
"How will you do dat Tess?" asked Whispy.
"I will do exactly what you would do in such circumstances, I will picket his house."
"Tess, I'd rather you wouldn't do dat. I wouldn't like to picket the priest's house. But do you know what you can do, you can join me on de protest next Sunday."
"Very well so," said Tessie, "I suppose you are right as always. I'll do as you ask."
"Dat's great," said Whispy, "de newspapers will have a new headline next week."
"What will that be?" asked Tessie.
"Church gate protest doubles," said Whispy.

Thirty Six

Shawny Scrahill soon learned that his trust in Bowzer Diggins was misplaced. The period of running a smooth profitable operation did not last more than a few months. As time went by Bowzer began to hand over less money to Shawny and to keep more and more for himself. Matters got progressively worse for Shawny until eventually he found himself in financial trouble once again - only deeper this time. When he spoke to Bowzer about the matter, he protested that the dealers were not repaying him. He promised on several occasions that he would get tough with the defaulters, but the end result was the same - less money was coming in for Shawny and his debts were increasing.

Shawny was getting into deeper trouble and he began to feel the wrath of the city based heavies who were employed by his suppliers. Hostilities were small enough to begin with - a broken windscreen in his car, then a brick through his mother's sitting room window, but then it became more threatening and intimidating. All the windows in his car were broken and some weeks later a petrol bomb was thrown against the wall of his mother's house, just beside the front door. This did not do any damage and it was not intended to. It was just a warning. Shawny knew that and he understood.

The biggest trouble that Shawny had was that he simply did not have the funds to pay off his debts and he was

faced with the stark reality that he would be badly beaten or seriously injured. In desperation he approached Bowzer who suggested that he himself would talk to the city boys and ask for more time and he reported back in due course.
"They want €3,000 immediately," said Bowzer, bluntly.
"Immediately," repeated Shawny. "How soon is that?"
"Three days from now," stated Bowzer. "They will meet with you after that to discuss payment of the outstanding debt."
"When will the meeting take place?"
"Three nights from now," said Bowzer.
"Am I to hand over the €3,000 at the meeting?" asked Shawny.
"No!" explained Bowzer. "I will take €3,000 to them in the city. Then they will give instructions about the meeting, time and place etc."

Shawny was desperate and fearful for his life and he set about getting as much money as he could by any means. He explained his predicament to Eddie Whiston who gave him a few hundred and he also called to Fr. Thomas who also helped with whatever money he had to spare at that time. Johnny Doh helped and Shawny stole a few hundred from his mother to make up the balance.
"I'm worried that it is Bowzer who is delivering the money to the city boys," said Johnny Doh.
"I'm worried about that myself, but what other choice do I have?" said Shawny.
"I wouldn't trust Bowzer as far as I could throw him," Johnny declared again for the umpteenth time.
They were reassured when Bowzer reported back to Shawny that he had handed over the money to the city

boys and gave details of the time and place of the rendezvous, for the discussions about paying the remainder of the debt.

"You are to park your car at this isolated rural lay-by and wait there until you are contacted," explained Bowzer. "A vehicle will pull alongside and you will be asked:

'Is this the road to Killarney?' to which you will reply:

'Yes, but it is not the best road to Killarney.' You can have your discussions with them after that - *Comprende*?"

"*Comprendo*!" answered Shawny.

In the afternoon of the agreed date for the rendezvous, another petrol bomb was thrown against the side of Shawny's car setting it on fire. Shawny was so distressed about this that Johnny Doh insisted that he would drive Shawny to the meeting place himself.

They were fearful as they headed north to the rendezvous.

"I never realised until now that fear has a smell," said Johnny as he negotiated the twists and turns of the unfamiliar road.

"Are you afraid?" asked Shawny.

"Petrified," answered Johnny "but I'm not as scared as you."

"How do you know that I'm scared?" asked Shawny.

"I know, because I can smell the fear off of you," answered Johnny.

Almost everything turned out as they had been told. The car arrived, pulled alongside and the driver asked if this was the road to Killarney. Johnny Doh rolled down his window and gave the agreed response and immediately muffled shots rang out and the car sped away leaving

Johnny and Shawny slumped in their seats. Some miles away the assassin set fire to his car, was collected by a third party and successfully made his escape.

Unknown to anyone there was a witness, who for his own illicit reasons was in that vicinity and he immediately but anonymously alerted the emergency services and the gardai. He approached the car but there was so much blood everywhere that he did not attempt to attend to the two young men who appeared to him to be dead.

The incident dominated the news in the print media and on radio and television on the following morning.
"Two young men have been shot, in what is believed to be a drugs related assassination attempt," the newsreader announced. "One has died and the other is seriously wounded. The Gardai are investigating and appealing for witnesses to come forward. The names of the victims are being withheld until their families have been notified."

This tragic story which was in the news for a few days, was then superseded by new and different stories and quickly faded from the minds of people everywhere - except of course from the minds of the parents and loved ones of the victims, whose lives were changed irrevocably and forever.

Thirty Seven

Tessie did not join her father in his protest as she had planned, following the meeting with the priests. Instead she followed the advice of her husband Dan Hayley and thought better of it.
"Joining your father in the protest would only be drawing unwelcome attention to yourself and to the children and to me as well," advised Dan. "Leave it to your father. He will grow weary of it in due course and life will get back to normal for all of us."
And so it transpired.

On the seventh Sunday of his protest, Fr. Thomas was on his way to celebrate Mass and seeing Whispy with his placard, crossed the street for a friendly chat. After the usual pleasantries, Fr. Thomas said in a confidential but respectful tone:
"I wanted to explain privately about the Church's teaching on the family."
"I know de family is very important," said Whispy. "I know dat alright. We all know dat - Nora and Tessie and Dan Hayley and de children knows it. But what has dat got to do wit refusing Holy Communion to Tessie?"
"The rule that prohibits people such as Tessie from receiving Holy Communion, is only a sort of sub-rule for supporting a far more important rule for the family."
"And what rule is dat?" asked Whispy.

"In simple terms, the Church teaches that the family is the

original cell of society. It is the best place for children to learn to care and share and to learn relationships. It is the best place for them to learn love and affection and to learn their rights and responsibilities as well."

"I agree wit dat," said Whispy, "every word of it".

"Ideally," explained Fr. Thomas, "the parents would have a loving relationship with each other and ideally too, the family would pray together and try to live their lives according to the ten commandments."

"Dat's exactly what Tessie and Dan and the children are doing," said Whispy. "Dey are good people and dey prays together every night of the year."

"The rule about Holy Communion is more for people, who completely disregard the essence of family life," said Fr. Thomas.

"I can understand dat," said Whispy, "but Tessie and Dan are not like dat and still an' all, she is barred from meeting Jesus in Holy Communion."

"The good Christian family is a great builder of character and a good character makes a good building block for society," stated Fr. Thomas. "Good Christian families, combined together, make a good society and work to make the world a better place."

"I know dat," answered Whispy, "but Tessie and Dan's family is very Christian in every way, except for de fact dat she was divorced and dey married outside de Church."

"I agree with you," said Fr. Thomas "and I think I have a solution to the problem."

"Dat would be great altogether," answered Whispy. "I'm getting tired of all dis protesting."

"I'll explain my plan to you and maybe that would encourage you to give up the protest. Now here is what we will do...."

Before he had time to finish, the sacristan who was agitatedly pointing at his watch, called to Fr. Thomas from the chapel gate across the road.
"It's nearly time for mass," he shouted.
"Think about the family unit," said Fr. Thomas as he parted from Whispy and hurried into the chapel yard.

Shortly afterwards Whispy was approached by three members of a latter day hippie colony from the other side of the mountain - two men and a woman, all with their hair in dreadlocks and untidy clothes and smelling strongly of something or other. They explained that they wished to join his protest.
"We're here to support you man," said one.
"I don't need support," responded Whispy.
"We are from the movement for free love," explained another.
"Dis is a respectable one-man protest," declared Whispy in his strong clear voice, "and derefore I will not give permission to anyone to hijack my protest. Now be gone with ye and I don't tink much of yerself and yer movement for free love."

They left without complaint but nonetheless their intrusion upset him. He began to think that he had made his point and done enough, especially considering everything that Fr. Thomas had just explained to him about the importance of the Christian family and all that.

While he was considering whether or not to cease his

protest, he was approached by a clean cut cameraman from a national television network and a youthful looking, slightly unkempt, ginger-bearded journalist who asked to interview him. It soon became clear to Whispy that this young man had an agenda of his own:
"Do you condemn the Catholic Church for its treatment of your daughter?" he asked rather self-righteously.
"I do not indeed condemn de Catholic Church," said Whispy.
"Are you saying that the Church can mistreat your daughter and you won't condemn it for that?"
"The Church is not mistreating my daughter - I never said dat and I'm not condemning de Church either," said Whispy.
"Isn't that rather surprising, considering that you have been here protesting for several weeks?"

Eddie Whispy was a man who had spent very little time in school due to difficult family circumstances, but he was educated in the school of life, he was wise in the ways of people and he understood immediately that this young man was trying to use him to condemn the Church. Besides he was still distressed over the arrival of the hippie folk and he began to get angry.
"Now you listen to me," said Whispy. "I know exactly what you are getting at. You want me to say dat I condemn de Church and I won't do dat."
"Even after what they have done to your daughter?" asked the journalist in feigned amazement.
"Dis is a local issue," said Whispy "and I will not condemn de whole Church because of dis one issue."
"Why not?"

"Why not? Why not? Because dat would be right wrong altogether. De Church is helping de poor and de sick and de helpless and de prisoners and it is doing dat every minute of every day - all over de world in de hills and in de valleys, in de deserts and in de jungles, in de lowlands and in de islands, in de cities and in de villages and in de missions everywhere."

"Would you agree that the missionaries are damaging the culture of these native peoples?"

"Damaging de culture of de native people? Dey are curing de sick and sinking wells for water for de tirsty and teaching de children to read and to write. Many of dem are putting dere own lives in danger so dat dey can help others - which is a damn sight more than you and your equals are doing."

"All right, Mr. Whiston, we'll leave it at that. Would you like to make any further comments about your protest before we conclude the interview?"

"No further comment," Whispy replied vehemently and having said that, he put his placard on his shoulder and walked briskly home, put his placard in the shed and went in to Nora his wife.

"I tink I have done enough protesting," he said.

"I think so too," said Nora and she put her arms around her beloved, innocent, open honest man and told him how much she loved him.

"Everything will be alright," she said.

"I know dat," answered Whispy. "We'll trust in God and leave it all to Him. Dat's de best ting to do now."

Thirty Eight

The shooting dead of Johnny Doh was the most traumatic event in the history of Cooley Park and left most of the residents in a state of dismay. He was born in Harlem, was reared in Harlem and lived in Harlem with his parents and two sisters, decent, friendly people all. He was the innocent victim of drug dealers, with whom he had no involvement whatsoever and he was murdered because of his lifelong, loyal friendship with small time, local drug dealer Shawny Scrahill.

He was laid out in his coffin - the best that his parents could afford, in the small sitting room of their terrace house, at the tender age of twenty three. The hundreds who attended his wake and funeral were sombre, pale faced and tight lipped. It was the sheer silence of the occasion that was so striking and reflective of the shock, that his death caused to all who knew him and to his parents and sisters who loved and admired him. People just filed in, sympathised with the relatives, stopped and stared at the open coffin and moved on silently, sombre-faced and perturbed.

The parish chapel was full to capacity and Cooley Park was almost deserted during the funeral mass. Fr. Thomas, the chief celebrant, used the occasion to address directly the issue of drugs in their community to a silent congregation:
"We are here today mourning the tragic death of a good, decent, good humoured and honourable young man, shot to death by the evil force that drives and encourages

involvement with drugs - and it is an evil force - have no doubt about that."
"This evil places itself between the body and the spirit and ultimately destroys both body and soul. This evil encourages the use of drugs for a short-lived, physical high, which is inevitably followed by depressive coming down, depression in the spirit and injury in the soul."
"This evil cannot be overcome by government legislation alone. It can only be defeated by prevention - namely when every individual in the community agrees to never get involved with drugs, because the evil lies not in the drugs but in their misuse by individuals, for soul destroying pleasure and more sinisterly, for financial gain. That is what must be done and it demands action from everyone, not just from one or two or three but from everyone. The sooner everyone accepts this responsibility, the sooner the problem will be solved."
"My sincere and heartfelt prayer today, is that everyone would accept *that* responsibility, so that never again need we gather to mourn the loss of a bright young man, who was murdered long before his time to die had come. May he rest in peace."

After that traumatic event there was little clerical opposition to the idea of a mobile chapel for Cooley Park. As soon as I had finished converting the camper, I gave it a complete overhaul, serviced the engine, paid the road tax and insurance, drove it to the lower Calcutta section of Cooley Park and parked it at the edge of the green area.

Initially the van was divided into two main sections - one section for the members of the public who would come in and the other was partitioned off by a counter and a glass panel. This would enable the priest or whoever it was that was staffing the office, to converse with the visitor without being in physical contact with them - and there were good reasons for this type of prudence.

We hadn't planned any formal ceremony to mark the occasion, but it appears that Fr. Thomas had spread the news and about thirty people gathered round to inspect the new office and they insisted that I should be photographed with the community as I handed over the keys to Fr. Thomas.
"I want to thank my brother for donating this mobile office to the community of Cooley Park. I thank him for converting it and for making it ready for use among the good people of this community. It will be necessary to make plans for how best we can use this facility and I will be consulting with you all in this regard as soon as possible. Meanwhile it will be a base for me in Cooley Park and I hope you will come and visit me there to chat and to make plans."
Then he sprinkled it generously with holy water from a little bottle that Eddie Whiston handed to him.
"I ask God our Father to bless this office. May it help connect the citizens of Cooley Park with the Church, may it be of service to the people of the community and may it bring them many benefits and blessings. I now declare the new Church office officially opened."

Initially Thomas probably expected that more people would come to consult and meet him in the office, but those who did come were small in number. After the funeral of Johnny Doh he bought a tabernacle and having got approval from Canon Towman, he was able to keep the consecrated hosts there. He made a little altar there and so it became a place of prayer. At times he would expose the Blessed Sacrament - usually for a few hours each day and he would say his priestly office there.

During these times some people began to come, generally older folk at first but more and more young people came as time went by. They would pray or sit quietly in front of the blessed sacrament and gradually more and more began to use the office either for prayer or to discuss personal or community issues.

In the summertime he organised the recitation of a few communal prayers, first on one evening a week and then three evenings a week and finally every evening. It was parked in rotation in the open areas of Calcutta, Harlem and The First Estate and so it became a mobile chapel in a very real and practical sense.

Thirty Nine

Gretel Bernhart Bouvier was at Sunday Mass in the little church in Puerto Del Carmen, a few weeks after her trip to Timanfaya with the girl guide leaders. When she turned round with outstretched hand to give the 'sign of peace' to those in the seat behind her, she was surprised to see the smiling face of the man with whom she had shared the camel ride:
"Peace be with you," he said.
"And also with you," she smilingly responded.
They chatted briefly after Mass and went their separate ways.

Later that week they met in the *Supermercado* and this became a regular occurrence in the weeks that followed. A pleasant friendship developed between them and they often remained chatting, long after they had finished their coffee and got to know a lot about each other.

Jack Donoughue, who really was a perfect gentleman, regularly took Gretel's purchases to her car and she commented on this one day while they were having a coffee together.
"You bring the groceries to my car every time we meet, but you never have groceries for yourself. Don't you buy any?"
"No! I get everything I need at the hotel where I live."
"Why then do you come here to the *Supermercado?"*
"To meet you of course," he said. "I thought you had

guessed that by now."
"I made that assumption, weeks ago," replied Gretel.
"And you still kept coming."
"So did you," she answered, and they both laughed together.

Gretel was still a good looking woman, medium height, attractive medium build and as she became happier she dressed better and paid more attention to her hair and make-up. There was a new pep in her step and a sense of living life again in contrast to the aimless, lethargic lifestyle she had experienced since her mother Ericka died.
Jack Donoughue was a tall strong man, handsome in a rugged sort of way, with a fine head of slightly greying hair which was always combed and in place. His tanned sculpted face reflected a lifetime of outdoor activity and manual work.

Each knew early on that there was a physical attraction between them but they did not discuss it. It was growing stronger as time went by and they were comfortable together. Their relationship developed quickly and regular lengthy chats over the telephone became a daily occurrence. Jack learned a lot about Gretel's past and what she learned about Jack, confirmed her initial assessment that she had indeed met an extraordinary man.

Jack Donoughue had been a building contractor in Killarney in Ireland for most of his adult life and he had a reputation for honesty and good workmanship. He was the father of two adult children and had been married for twenty eight years before his beloved Maura died from

cancer.
In addition to being a good builder, he had an innate instinct for identifying properties which would be suited to development for resale or for rent and he had amassed an impressive portfolio of properties - many of which were rented as business premises, apartments or a combination of both. The aggregated rental income was substantial and more than enough to live on and when Maura became ill he sold the contracting business and devoted himself totally to caring for her until she died two years later.

He was deeply affected by the death of his beloved Maura but he was consoled by the fact that he had done everything humanly possible for her during her long illness. They had grown closer during the years of her illness and their love had deepened. Their son and daughter were both doctors engaged in research - the son in Vancouver, Canada and his daughter nearer home in London. Each was married, had their own home and both were committed to their work and careers.

He was kept busy for a time after the funeral tidying up his wife's affairs, erecting a headstone and doing many other related tasks but after awhile he was at a loss for something useful to do and began to lose interest in life.
"I need to be productive every day," he explained. "Being unproductive equates to being useless and I don't want to be useless."
He visited his son and his daughter and while each of them was brilliant in providing for his needs, they had their work and careers to mind. He eventually returned home, dissatisfied in himself and so obviously unsettled in the

dark evenings and in the cold and rain of early winter, that his friends recommended a long winter holiday in the sunshine.
"Go to Lanzarote," advised one of his neighbours - a lady who was a regular visitor to the island. "I think you will like it there."

Jack took the advice. He loved the climate and settled in very contentedly. He developed a routine of alternately walking along the sea front or sitting in his balcony to read during the day or at evening time to see the boats return to port. In the evening time too he liked to watch the agile seagulls dip and dive and with extended wings float on rising air currents in an impressive exhibition of aerial acrobatics, before returning to their nests for the night. He was so contented that he began to consider building a small villa for himself, if he could find a suitable location.

One day while walking his attention was drawn to a big *Se Vende* sign on a large rock strewn, rubble littered site. The sign was faded and the long grasses and weeds suggested that the site had been for sale for a long time. His enquiry to the estate agent confirmed that opinion, but it also ended any hope he had of building a villa there.
"That entire site is earmarked for commercial development namely the construction of a hotel, comprising fifty two *apartamentos,* two swimming pools, restaurant and *supermercado* to cater for every need of the holidaymakers," the estate agent explained. "No one can build a private villa there senor."
The vendor, who was the sole investor had become a victim of the deep recession, which at that time engulfed

Spain and its islands and he urgently needed to offload the site which was a costly millstone around his neck. The detailed, approved plans, surveyors' reports and actuarially projected costs were available as part of the deal and would be very useful to a prospective developer. It was the kind of project that Jack would have loved to tackle once upon a time, with energy and enthusiasm and organisational ability. But he was younger then and those days were long gone.

Forty

Thomas did not use the tea-making facilities in the mobile chapel in the beginning and very often he was invited to homes for a cuppa and on other occasions one or more of the women would bring tea and scones or a sandwich to him. On those occasions they would sit and chat while he was having the tea or maybe share and discuss personal, family or community issues.

Soon they began to make tea and coffee using the facilities in the mobile chapel and this quickly became a regular feature of each day. Topics discussed varied widely and could include: the weather, recent deaths, the cost of living, the local schools, some issues local and national but the discussion invariably turned to the problems of drugs and alcohol abuse among the young people in Cooley Park.

"The greatest worry I have is that my children would turn to drugs," said one mother very earnestly.

"It is the worry of all of us," said another, "but how can we prevent them from getting involved? The drugs are easily accessed and there is pressure from some peers to get involved."

"We can advise them regarding the damage and destruction drugs cause to people's lives," said another.

"Advice doesn't always work. Look at Teveena Scrahill and how hard she tried to rear Shawny and to rear him good and despite all that, look at the destruction he brought on himself and on poor Johnny Doh and on many more as well."

"Advice will work for some, but it is not enough in all cases."
"What more can we do? We are helpless to do anymore."
"You're right. We can't stand up to intimidation from the likes of Bowzer Diggins. We haven't a chance. If the young people make the choice to get involved with drugs, there is nothing we can do. It is their choice and that's the bottom line."
"I agree that it is their choice - in the same way that we all have a choice between good and evil," interjected Fr. Thomas, "but we can try to guide them to the right choice and support them in that."
"How can we do that?"
"I don't know yet, but I will think on it," said Fr. Thomas.

He continued to strive to establish links with the people and his greatest success in that task was with the women and a few homemaker men. Gradually relationships were built up and the people repeatedly stressed how bad the drugs problem had become since the killing of Johnny Doh and the wounding of Shawny Scrahill.
It has been said that good can come from evil and while some would dispute the veracity of that statement, the reaction of the citizens of Cooley Park to the killing of Johnny Doh resulted in a communal determination to stamp out the evil that had brought about his death.
"The best way to prevent suffering and pain from excess alcohol and drugs is to convince young people not to start in the first place," stated one mother.
"The problem can only be defeated by quiet, persistent individual action by everyone," said another.
"What do you mean by persistent action?"

"I mean that it must be ongoing continuously. One protest march or something like that would soon be forgotten and have no long term effect."
"But the young people will be under peer pressure. You can't counter that."
"You can if you are supported by the whole community - young and old."
"Each family should work with their own young ones and discuss with them. That way there will be a common approach," said one young woman.
"Maybe we could lay out a common approach for them - a sort of template," said another.
"I think it is a good way," said Fr. Thomas, "the family unit is the key to success but the community should support the families."

After weeks and weeks of discussion and hundreds of cups of tea and scones that strategy was agreed. Every family would encourage the young simply to choose not to take part in the drinking parties and not to get involved with drugs.

Fr. Thomas arranged a series of lectures explaining the extraordinary harm that drugs were doing and eventually, slowly bit by bit, the new idea began to get a grip and the young people, encouraged by their parents, began to pledge themselves to choose right and say 'No' to drugs and excess alcohol.

Some families drew up a family charter - a set of rules by which their own family members would live. This imposed restrictions on the older people who drank to excess.

Gradually the idea spread and more and more families adopted the charter. But all did not go smoothly.
There were attempts at intimidation by some of Bowzer's lackeys and this was brought up for discussion in the mobile chapel on another 'tea and scones' occasion.
"The children could be subjected to intimidation once the family has signed the charter," said one mother.
"Worse than that," said another "their windows could be broken or graffiti sprayed on the walls or maybe their house burned down."
"A bottle with petrol and a wick was left outside my door," said another "and I'm frightened."
"My family won't sign any charter if that is the outcome," said another. "We can't go on with that strategy or some of us could be intimidated or burned to death in our homes."
"It is very serious, Fr. Thomas," said another. "We will have to stop the family charters."
"It is an awful worry," said another.
"No one will sign a charter if their house could be burned down."

Eddie Whispy who had heard about the intimidation arrived and joined in the discussion.
"We can't give up dis easily," he stated.
"That's alright for you to say," declared one woman. "You have no children in your house. It is very scary for families with children."
"De family should sign de charter in secret. Tell no one about it. Keep it to demselves. Den dey won't be intimidated," suggested Eddie Whispy.
"I think that could be the answer," declared Fr. Thomas.
"You need a committee to organise dat," said Whispy,

"made up of people who won't scare easily."
"So to be clear," said one of the women, "the family will sign the charter in private. They will tell no one. Is that it?"
"Dey should tell one of de committee confidentially, once de committee is formed," said Whispy. "Dat will be a support for dem."
"You won't get anyone to go on that committee?" stated one mother emphatically. "If a parent is on the committee, their children could be intimidated."
"I think we have a consensus," stated Fr. Thomas. "I will set up a committee over the next few days. I will see to it that there are no parents on it who have children at home and we will work very much in secret."
"Like a secret underground movement," said Whispy humorously.
"Eddie," said Fr. Thomas, "you're brilliant. You've just given me a very bright idea. I will ask Alessandra Ozolins to join the committee. She will know exactly what we should do."

The newly formed Cooley Park Community Committee or the CPCC was absolutely determined to stamp out anti-social behaviour, drug dealing and intimidation. Fr. Thomas was chairman and Pauline Doohan, mother of the late Johnny, was secretary. Eddie Whiston and Alessandra Ozolins were charged with establishing secret and confidential lines of communication with the families.

Alessandra was brilliant in this role. She designed a standardised Family Charter for good behaviour, and within a matter of months a majority of families had signed up. She insisted on secrecy and confidentiality until a solid community consensus was achieved, so no one spoke of it, no one boasted, no one revealed anything. They just signed the charter, abided by it and remained silent about it.

Later on, the family charters were combined into a community charter and this added more strength and support and things began to improve in Cooley Park. Gradually a united movement grew and the more it grew the greater the drop in the numbers using drugs and the greater the drop in the income that Bowzer Diggins was taking in from his sale and supply business.

It was all becoming too problematic for Bowzer. He had become accustomed to living a high lifestyle and the serious fall in income adversely affected him and made him very unhappy. He discussed the issue with his lackeys, some of whom were also suffering a loss in income.
"It is all the fault of the priest," he stated to some of his lackeys one night, "the priest and his bloody caravan chapel."
"What can we do?" asked one.
"Call in a shooter," suggested another.
"Too risky," said Bowzer.
"Is there another way?" inquired someone else.
"Targeting the mobile chapel is the best way for weakening the influence of the priest," said Bowzer. "That bloody caravan will have to go. That's the best way to ensure that he's not around the place. He's destroying our business."

Bowzer's initial moves were basic enough. In the dark of night his lackeys painted graffiti on the door of the mobile

chapel, just two words - "BE WARNED."
The citizens were perturbed at this. Fr. Thomas let it be known that he himself would not clean the graffiti and eventually some brave local people, led by Eddie Whispy cleaned and repainted the door, an action that made Bowzer even more unhappy. He thought long and hard again and his cunning brain hit upon a more insidious strategy.

He had inadvertently acquired information about the circumstances of the deaths of Thomas' wife Mary and of his son Indie. He immediately saw that this could be used to turn the people against the priest.
"It is a cunning plan," he thought to himself. "I'm cunning as the fox."

Forty One

The first move in Bowzer's cunning plan was more graffiti and the people were taken aback one morning to see "OUT WITH THE ABUSER" sprayed in large letters on the side of the mobile chapel.
"Did you see the graffiti on the mobile chapel?"
"I did. Isn't it awful?"
"Is someone accusing Fr. Thomas of abusing someone or what?"
"I don't know but I hope it is not true."
"Of course it is not true. That good and holy man wouldn't abuse anyone."
"Still you would wonder why someone would write that."

Later on that day and during subsequent days, Bowzer's lackeys relentlessly spread rumours around about Fr. Thomas. Out of the deep and painful long ago came the resurrected and twisted tale:
"He caused the death of his wife."
"He neglected to protect his son which resulted in his death by drowning."
This caused a lot of confusion and distress among the people of Cooley Park. Around town, the pubs were full of the news and it was discussed by shoppers, in homes and over garden walls.
"There's no smoke without fire," some were saying.
Incredibly, some believed the worst while more began to have serious doubts evolving in their minds about their priest.

Despite all of this, Fr. Thomas would not be diverted from his strategy for the defeat of the evil of drugs and he had the full support of the CPCC.
"I see the hand of Bowzer Diggins in this," said Pauline Doohan.
"So do I," said Eddie Whispy. "It is de work of de diggle himself."
The committee agreed. They understood its purpose and knew it was nothing short of evil in action.

Some people are fickle and will believe anything. Amazingly some began to think that maybe Bowzer Diggins was right and actually trying to do good for the community. This news was conveyed to Bowzer via his lackeys and it was this that emboldened him to organise a protest meeting outside the little mobile chapel.

The meeting was well publicised and well organised with good quality amplification and stewarding, performed by Bowzer's lackeys and some other gullible locals, all wearing high visibility vests and armbands, while his chief lackey acted as master of ceremonies.

Trotsky Moran, wearing his wire rimmed glasses was the opening speaker and his objection to the presence of the mobile chapel - which he insultingly dubbed 'the caravan'- was on ideological grounds. He had dreamed of an occasion like this in which he could help enlighten the people.
"The presence of this caravan here in this estate of working class people, is not for the good of the people,

but for the good of the parish priests and bishops, who are in league with the bourgeoisie wealthy classes."
He had a good clear voice and was a competent public speaker.
"The presence of this Catholic caravan is to coerce the proletariat and frighten them into submission with threats of hell's fire and eternal damnation, for the benefit of the billionaire and millionaire classes."
"The presence of this church caravan with its superstition, is misleading our young people and our children and I say this caravan of superstition must go for the sake of our children. Out with it I say! Out with it."

There was a small spattering of applause from two of Bowzer's lackeys, who were to the front of the crowd, but the residents in general who knew Trotsky Moran of old did not applaud or acknowledge his contribution. One or two who were in an advanced state of inebriation did shout encouragingly:
"Up with the working classes Trotsky. All the way boy!"

Bowzer Diggins, who was the keynote speaker was far more crafty and persuasive in the words that he used.
"Ladies and gentlemen, friends and neighbours, you all know me and know that I keep a low profile and mind my own business without troubling no one, but I am pleased to be here tonight to speak on behalf of many people in this park and community."
"This meeting is not about me or you or the working classes or bourgeoisie but about the children - the innocent children in this community. The people in this community are worried that their young little children would be

visiting the priest's van on their own. Now that might be o.k. if everything was alright, but it appears that everything is not alright. Sadly, there are rumours that are troubling to many of you."

"Feelings about the safety of children are running high in the community and despite my best efforts for a peaceful approach, there are some who would be capable of burning this caravan if it is not taken out of the estate."

His words were greeted by load applause from his lackeys and from the few drunken spectators.

"That's the spirit Bowzer."

.

Fr. Thomas was elsewhere at the very time that this protest was in progress but it was astounding that some of the people, even some of those with whom Fr. Thomas had connected fairly well, were swayed by the arguments of Bowzer Diggins who again called for the mobile chapel to be taken from the estate.

"I am solemnly of the view," said Bowzer, "that despite my own best efforts to protect it, this van will be petrol bombed, if it isn't taken away very soon. I will do my best to prevent this, but there is only so much I can do to help."

There was applause again from his lackeys and two of them raised bottles, apparently filled with fuel and they had wick tops on them.

Alessandra who was dressed in slim fitting black slacks and jacket was prominently positioned to the front of the crowd of about sixty and she had no illusion about what was happening here. She saw Bowzer Diggins exactly for

what he was - an intimidating bully. She had experienced such individuals in the underground struggles against the totalitarian regime in her homeland. Diggins was an evil influence in the community and she had seen his likes before. Gradually a deep anger simmered within her and when she saw the molotov cocktails held aloft, she sprang forward and vaulted onto the rostrum. She grabbed the microphone from Bowzer Diggins and a sudden hush fell upon the crowd as she addressed them in strongly accented words:
"Good people, do not be svayed by ze crooked vords of a bully! I have seen bullies who ver a lot vorse and dictators and I have dealt vit zem. Do not give in to ze thug. Do not be fooled by him. Ze pryist is a good man, ze pryist has brought ze carawan chapel here to help you and to be a force for good for us here in Cooley Park. Ze pryist has suffered much in his own life. All that he loved vas taken from him, his vife and his childs. His heart should be broken but instead he has come here. Ze pryist is doing much good and ze good he is doing is harming ze drug dealers - ze dealers of death. Ze dealers of death vant him out of Cooley Park and that is ze real reason for zis meeting."

Bowzer stepped forward, grabbed the microphone.
"Don't listen to the words of this two bit prostitute," he growled stepping to centre stage once more, and then turning to his lackeys he ordered:
"Remove that slut from here!"
Many in the crowd observed the state of coiled physical alertness that Alessandra adopted, the tension that pervaded her and the intense manner in which she focused

on Bowzer's two lackeys, something that alerted them to impending danger and stopped them in their tracks. She addressed them and her voice was cold and menacing:
"Do you zink that you vill remove me from ze stage? I who fought in ze underground for ze freedom of my country from despotic dictators? Do you zink that any of you quislings vould be able to remove me? I do not vish to demean myself vit you, you vile lackeys. You serve a bully because you are veak and afraid of him, but I have no fear of your master Bowzer Diggins."
"Get the slut off the rostrum," shouted Bowzer and the two lackeys charged together followed closely by Bowzer himself.
After that everything happened with lightening speed. Alessandra sent the two lackeys tumbling into the crowd. Then she turned swiftly and with one lightning blow to the head, knocked Bowzer senseless and prostrate on the rostrum.
"I think you killed him," shouted one of the lackeys.
"If I had vished to kill him, he vould be dead, but I did not vant to kill him zis time. Next time I vill not be so kind. As for you, spineless lackeys I admonish you not to interfere vit ze pryist and ze mobile chapel again and if you do, I vill demolish you vit pleasure."

Eddie Whiston, always courageous, always ready to fight injustice came on to the stage and taking the microphone in his hands shouted aloud:
"I propose dat de camper van stays in Cooley Park."
"I second ze proposal," said Alessandra.
"And I propose that we name it Cooley Park's Mobile Chapel" said Whispy.

"All in favour raise your hands," said Alessandra.
The response, was instant and affirmed with a roar of approval.
"Anyone against?" she asked.
No one, not even Bowzer's lackeys or stewards raised a hand.

Bowzer was still out cold while all this took place. It may be that he hit his head when he fell but he remained unconscious until the ambulance arrived and he was removed to hospital.

The gardai came and questioned the people and the lackeys unsurprisingly, said that Alessandra had hit Bowzer a false blow with a baseball bat. The guards inquired among the people but they all gave the same answer: "We saw nothing," they said. "We saw Bowzer and his lackeys charging at Alessandra and the next thing we saw was Bowzer lying on the ground. There was no baseball bat and we did not see Alessandra hit him."
"Are you saying that she didn't hit him?" they were asked.
"We are not saying that. We are telling you that we didn't see her hit him."

Life had taken a turn for the worse for Bowzer Diggins. His clientele had fallen in number and he was finding it harder to get anyone to travel to the outer villages to deliver the goods and collect the money from the local contacts. It was clear that the family charters and the support of the Cooley Park Community Committee was working successfully. Bowzer was no longer able to

engender fear into people in the way that he had before. People were not prepared to give way to him and his bullies and occasionally somebody would threaten that they would tell Alessandra, if he didn't stop his bullying.
The fact that Alessandra was a woman and that she had felled him so easily was a major blow to his ego and diminished his ability to intimidate and cause fear to people. In general he became the object of silent contempt. He knew it and his hatred for Fr. Thomas festered and grew enormously.
"I'll make him suffer," he declared to himself, "and make him suffer hard."
People developed great respect for Alessandra and accepted that she had indeed been a highly trained operative of the underground movement in her homeland. Some said that her husband had died at the hands of the secret police. No one knew why - but she had resolved that she would never marry another. Clearly she had been well trained in combat and clearly she had retained impressive combat skills. She had humiliated Bowzer Diggins in public and weakened his power.

Forty Two

No matter how hard he tried, Jack Donoughue was unable to get thoughts of that Lanzarote development site out of his head, in the days and weeks that followed his visit to the estate agent. He considered it in all its aspects - good location, readymade plans and projected costs.
"Those were boom time costs," he mused, "they would come in at least thirty to forty per cent lower at this time."
"All the building workers have left the island to work elsewhere," the estate agent had told him.
"All of them?" queried Jack.
"All except those who are prepared to work for low wages," was the reply, "and all the cranes and machinery are lying idle and getting rusty all the time."
Jack had seen that for himself.
"No one here has the kind of money needed for a project of that magnitude," the estate agent had said. "No one has that kind of cash or if they have they are not prepared to risk it with a project like that at this time."
"You could be wrong there," mused Jack silently. "I have the cash and it is a risk, but I might be inclined to take a gamble."

As time went by, thoughts of the development persistently encroached on his mind. No matter how often he banished them, they kept returning and he could not stop himself becoming excited about the possibilities that the site presented - area, location, availability of low cost skilled labour, cranes and other machinery that could be bought for knock-down prices, fully completed planning permission. No sooner would he have concluded consideration of one aspect of the project than some other aspect would come into his mind. It would be by far his biggest ever challenge but challenges had always injected excitement and energy into his life. He had sufficient funds but if things went wrong he could lose everything - that was the gamble, the chance he had to take.

He awoke one night weeks later, tossing and turning, with all of those thoughts churning around in his head. He remained still for awhile, surrendered to sleeplessness, got out of bed, went to his balcony and looked out at the vastness of the great Atlantic Ocean:
"Columbus sailed from here westward into the unknown across that vast ocean that lies out there before me," he said half aloud to himself. "He must have been a man of great courage and of faith too perhaps. Building a hotel is not half as daunting a task as that - except that I don't have the courage."
He did not know how long he spent there on the balcony, lost in thought and lost in time but after awhile a sense of purpose and excitement took hold of him and he said aloud:
"I will build that hotel. It is a big challenge but it can be done and I'm going to do it. I am going to meet that challenge head on. - if God will spare me my health and my strength."
He returned to bed and was very soon sleeping a sound, untroubled sleep.

By the time he met Gretel, his greatest project - which he

named Hotel Donomaur - was completed, comprising a large reception area, lounge, restaurants, bar, poolside bars, fifty two *apartamentos*, two swimming pools and shopping facilities. The colour on the exterior was predominantly white but a narrow band of green and yellow was painted around windows and external doors, in a token tribute to the flag of his native land. The name Donomaur was composed of abbreviations of 'Donoughue' - his own surname and of 'Maura' the Christian name of his late beloved wife.

The hotel was generating a good profit and Jack lived in one of the penthouse *apartamentos*. He lived humbly and apart from the workers, very few knew he was the owner and most assumed that he was just another foreigner who had retired and come to live in the Donomaur. He had divested himself of all his Killarney based rental properties, when prices were high, before the recession, and this enabled him to fund the project without resorting to substantial borrowing - in essence his vision had been realised and his dream had come true.

In the second year of operation the Hotel Donomaur had generated enough profit to allow work to begin on Jack's own pet project - the construction of an underground chapel carved out of the great sloping mound of volcanic rock adjacent to the hotel, in which people of all Christian denominations could come together for Mass or services. Prior to that, holidaymakers in all that area would have to travel to Puerto Del Carmen for Mass. The chapel was the only addition that Jack made to the original plans and he was humbly gratified to see it full to capacity for weekend

Masses and services.

At the end of the third year of operation Jack established The Donomaur Better World Fund to which ten percent of the hotel profits were paid each month and which allocated funds to emergencies or areas of greatest need.

The relationship between Jack and Gretel strengthened and grew more comfortable with kindness, humour and laughter as its hallmarks. He continued to live in the Donomaur although he did occasionally stay in the guest room of Gretel's villa.

The physical attraction between them became stronger and more apparent but while neither of them wanted to cross that line, each knew, deep in their own hearts, that it was probably only a matter of time. When Gretel became ill, he stayed with her until she had recovered fully. After that, Gretel took an initiative that raised their relationship to a different level.
"You don't have to return to the hotel, you know," she said to Jack one evening.
"Do you mean that I would stay here on a full time basis?" asked Jack.
"Yes," said Gretel. "I am lonely here when I am on my own. Paul my only son has, as you know, committed his life to the serving God's people as a priest and I cannot be part of that. I reflected a lot during my illness and I realised how happy I was that you were here with me."
"It was happy for me also," answered Jack, "and I have to admit that I am also a little lonely at times at the hotel, despite having so many people around."

"I would miss you too much if you returned to live at the hotel," she said.

Their fervent wish was to marry within the Catholic Church, but that was not an option in their circumstances. While both were committed, practising Catholics, they were ineligible to marry in accordance with the rules of the Catholic Church, because Gretel was divorced and was unable to establish, whether her former husband, Pierre Bouvier - whom she hadn't seen for more than thirty years, was dead or alive.

Jack and Gretel were married by a registrar in a civil ceremony in the presence of two of their friends who acted as witnesses. The marriage remained a closely guarded secret and they decided that they would not inform their own families for some time.
"It is better not to tell Fr. Paul, that we are married - for the time being at least," suggested Gretel.
"That is a wise course," agreed Jack, "especially in view of his trenchant opposition to marriages such as ours."
"He is so straight laced and rigid but still so good and holy in his heart," said Gretel. "That protest in his parish, that was publicised all over the world, was caused by his refusal to let some woman receive Holy Communion - a woman in a situation similar to ours. It would be better to let some more time elapse, before we tell him our news. It will be upsetting for him I think."
"Will you write and tell him or speak to him on the telephone?" asked Jack.
"Neither of those is a good way to do it. It is best to wait until he comes to visit. That will give him some time to

reflect and adjust to it before he goes back to his work in Ireland."

"Do you wish to break the news to him on your own?" asked Jack.

"No!" she answered. "We're together now, and we will speak to him together."

Forty Three

Fr. Thomas was worn-out, dog-tired exhausted on a night in late August when he was awakened at from a deep sleep at 1.30am by the persistent ringing of the telephone.
"Please come quickly," the male caller said, "my elderly neighbour is dying. Can you come to anoint him, as soon as possible please."
"I will go immediately," answered Fr. Thomas. "Just give me directions on how to get to the house."
Thomas repeated the directions as he wrote them on a sheet of paper:
"Come as far as Callaghan's Cross, turn left, drive on for another mile and go straight through the next cross roads. Just beyond the cross, there's a forestry gate on the right and I will be waiting there to show you the way."

Thomas prayed as he drove along:
"God our Father, I ask you to send your Holy Spirit to help me so that my words will be comforting and helpful for this sick man and for those who love him."

He was a few miles into the journey when he realised that he had left the written directions at home, but he had pictured them carefully in his mind and he knew that the sick person's home was in one of the most remote, hilly parts of the parish.
The journey seemed long, as is often the case when you travel unfamiliar roads, especially small rural roads in the dark of night. You have to carefully follow the spots of the

car headlights on the ditch, as you round unfamiliar turns, not knowing what lies ahead.

When he finally reached the forestry gate, he pulled in just in front of the waiting car and rolled down the window. A man approached from behind and put a revolver to the side of his head:

"Out of the car. Get out," he commanded.

"But I am on my way to a sick call," stated Fr. Thomas.

"There is no sick call," said another voice, "get out and you will not be hurt. Now open the door."

They bound him hand and foot, put a gag in his mouth, a blindfold over his eyes and bundled him into the boot of their car.

He prayed as they drove along. Soon the ride became rougher and he knew they were on twisty potholed roads. Later on, he felt that they had changed to a gravelled surface and the car finally crunched to a halt after travelling for what he estimated to be the most of an hour.

They untied his legs and manhandled him roughly from the boot. Tying a length of rope around his neck, they led him, still blindfolded, through twisting paths that varied from firm, to gravelly, to downright soft and soggy and he slipped frequently and fell a few times along the way.

They finally stopped, stripped him of his coat and shirt and vest, made him stand against a tree - still gagged and still blindfolded, bound his ankles together and tied him to its sturdy trunk. They were about to throw the rope across an overhead branch when the forestry clearing was invaded by at least two litters of strong pups loudly yelping and barking. Shining the flashlight on them the abductors saw that the pups were accompanied by two nursing

bitches - a collie sheepdog and a beagle whose deep howling would carry a great distance in the stillness of the night.
"Throw the rope over the branch," said one.
"There's no time," said his friend. "We have to get out of here before those bloody dogs draw the whole country on us with their barking. Come on! Let's make a run for it and get the hell out of here."

The barking subsided and the dogs spent some time sniffing around Fr. Thomas, but the night was cold and a cold, dank fog covered hills and woodland and having satisfied themselves that there was no threat to them, the dogs went back to their nearby beds to curl up cosily and to sleep.

Stripped to the waist, tied to the tree and unable to move, Thomas suffered severely in the cold of that awful, miserable night. The freezing fog condensed forming droplets on his nose and all through the night he was breathing the dank cold air into his lungs. The gag was severely uncomfortable and caused painful dryness in his mouth and tongue, and sometimes he feared that he would suffocate or even choke, if he involuntarily swallowed a piece of the cloth. Icy coldness seeped quickly through from the damp ground to his feet and ankles. He wished that he could move his legs a little but the binding made this almost impossible and the best he could do was press the toes of one foot hard against the ground and pull upwards with the other leg. This did help a little but the rope was grinding against his ankle and after awhile the skin got raw and began to bleed. The rest of his body suffered too from restricted movement and he suffered severe pain when tendons groaned and muscles went into spasm from being locked for so long in the one spot. The ropes bit hard into his body and the very act of breathing exacerbated his pain.

He prayed mentally and continuously - rosary after rosary, and lines from his favourite psalm:
He leads me on the path of right,
He's true and faithful to his name.
And should I walk the valley's night,
Its evils will not frighten me,
For with his crook and staff nearby,
He keeps me safe and comforts me.

His clothes were wet and soggy with mucky peat from all the times he had fallen and he thought of the night so long ago, that he had soiled his clothes when he fell drunkenly into the flower garden at Rossa Lee's house.
It was a long night and he suffered intensely, placed himself in the hands of the Lord and he was comforted.
"Being tied like this gives me a better understanding of the awful suffering of Jesus on the cross," he thought. "I join my sufferings with His for the good of all humanity."

It seemed like an eternity before he could see the faint light of dawn underneath the edges of the blindfold and he twisted his nose and jaw in an effort to loosen it, but it was no use. It was a grey and dreary dawn and there was no chorus of birdsong because neither thrush nor blackbird nor robin sang their notes of welcome for so dull a day. He mentally recited the prayers of the morning Mass. In the prayers after the consecration he offered his life to God and declared his willingness to accept this cruel death if it was to be his fate.

"I offer my life to you Heavenly Father and unite it with the sacrifice of Jesus on the cross. If I'm to die here, I will accept my fate with humility for the love of God, who is the source of all that is good and holy. I pray for those who have brought this suffering upon me and I forgive them from deep within my heart."

On the very night that Fr. Thomas was suffering great physical pain tied to a tree in a forestry clearing, Shawny Scrahill was enduring another night of mental anguish as he tossed and turned on the bed of anguish that he had made for himself.

Shawny had never managed to get the killing of his good friend Johnny Doh out of his mind nor did he ever cease blaming himself for his death. Johnny was the original 'good guy,' who consistently refused to have anything to do with drug dealing. He was Shawny's friend from childhood but Shawny knew in his heart that it was he who unintentionally led him to the *rendezvous,* where his life was ended in a hail of bullets.
"It is just the same as pulling the trigger myself," he often said to himself.

Shawny bore the marks of the wounds in his shoulders and in his cheeks where bullets had entered and exited. They

didn't pain him anymore, unlike the mental scars that festered and grew. He became more withdrawn into himself, spending a lot of time alone in his room pacing the floor and talking aloud to himself as he walked.
"Bowzer, the bastard was pocketing a lot of the money from the outer areas," he mused. "How could I have been so stupid? I should never have trusted him. I was so stupid, stupid, stupid. It is because of him that I could not pay my debts to the city boys."

Shawny understood the rules of the city boys - you paid the money or else. The rules were clear: first you were given a warning, beaten up or your car burned or your house damaged. If you arranged a meeting to pay the money, all threats were suspended until that meeting was over. If the debts were paid, you were in the clear. The city boys had always stuck to their side of the bargain in the past so why did they do differently this time? This was the question that he couldn't get out of his mind.
"They had got the €3,000 that I gave to Bowzer. The meeting was arranged to discuss paying the remainder."
According to the rules, all other actions would be deferred.
"Why did they petrol bomb my car when they knew that I was sending Bowzer to hand over the money to them? Why did they try to kill me when they knew I was planning to pay the remainder of the debt? Why? Why? Why?"
That question perplexed him and the unfairness of it all came to dominate his thinking so much, that he would sometimes become blind to his surroundings and loose all sense of time and place.
"Why had the city boys done this? They knew they would

get the money so why did they break their own rules? It is a mystery to me."

The solution to the mystery came to Shawny in a moment of great mental clarity as he was lying awake in his bed in the middle of the night - and he sat bolt upright shouting:
"It was Bowzer the bastard. Sweet Lord God, how could I have been so stupid? Bowzer was behind it all. It was Bowzer and not the City Boys who arranged the rendezvous. Oh the crooked, double-crossing bastard. He never paid them the money. That's what happened. He probably used it to pay the shooter to kill me, paid him with my own money. Oh Lord God, could anything be more stupid than that. I'm the thickest, dumbest, most stupid fool in the universe."

He jumped out of bed and ran downstairs when he realised the enormity of the betrayal that Bowzer Diggins had perpetrated on him and how cleverly he had done it:
"The cunning bastard," exploded Shawny, "the cunning double-crossing bastard."
He kept repeating these words over and over: "the cunning bastard, the cunning double crossing bastard."
After awhile, the tension that pressured his brain almost to bursting point subsided and he began a new mantra:
"Bowzer will pay for this. By Christ he will pay!"

Then, when he grew tired of repeating the mantra, and as the pale light of the breaking dawn was overcoming the darkness of the night, he knelt on his two knees on the tiled kitchen floor and swore a solemn oath:
"I swear by almighty God, that Bowzer Diggins will pay

with his life for the murder and double-cross that he has done. That is my solemn oath and I will keep it. I swear it. I swear it by almighty God. I swear it."

Forty Four

When Fr. Thomas failed to arrive to celebrate the 9.30am Mass in the main parish church, the sacristan tried to contact him by telephone and when that failed he drove to his house. He noticed that the car was not there but apart from that, everything else was as it should be.

Another hour passed before they contacted the gardai and word spread like wildfire around the parish that Fr. Thomas was missing. The gardaí discovered the handwritten note with the directions on the table and this gave them a good lead to follow. About mid-day his car was located near Callaghan's Cross - following a report from an observant forestry worker. A search party was organised to search the large forestry plantation but no trace of him was found - leading the gardai to correctly suspect that he was taken to another location.

Earlier on, Fr. Bouvier had contacted me to tell me the distressing news about my brother but I was in school and there was nothing I could do, other than to ask the children to pray for his safe return. I informed Nora and Rose and promised to keep them updated on developments.

As the morning progressed and hour followed hour, Fr. Thomas felt himself growing steadily weaker and his head kept falling low on his chest. He began to groan deep in his throat and he thought that it helped to relieve the excruciating pain.

The news of his suspected abduction featured prominently on radio and television news bulletins and there were many calls for information and witnesses who might have seen something unusual. Parishioners discussed the news in the shops, in the street, on the telephone and wherever conversations were held. Others gravitated to the church and rosaries and prayers were recited for his safe return.

Around mid-morning he prayed Lauds - the morning prayer of the Church and as soon as he had finished, the family of strong collie pups came again sniffing around him but not barking so loudly this time. Their mother, a wise old black collie was with them but she did not bark. She had come to this isolated place to give birth and protect her pups because her previous litters had been disposed of by the farmer who owned her. There were six pups in the litter and she reared them all here until they were strong enough to look after themselves.
Having seen Thomas tied to the tree, the black collie sensed instinctively that something was wrong and she hastily made her way to her owner's farmyard where she stood barking agitatedly outside the front door but unfortunately, there was no one in the house at that particular time. When she failed to get any response she went back to her pups and fed them.
In the early afternoon the black collie sniffed around Fr. Thomas again and ran back once more to bark at the farmhouse door but there was still nobody there to take notice or respond to her frantic barking.

The discovery of a burnt out car fourteen miles north of Callaghan's Cross brought the garda search closer to the location where Fr. Thomas was still tied to a tree, still gagged, still blindfolded and still suffering enormously. They began to concentrate their search on that locality but they still had not located him by mid-afternoon.

The sheep farmer and his wife were both in the farmhouse eating their dinner and discussing the abduction of Fr. Thomas when the faithful collie paid her third frantic visit for help in the late afternoon. When the farmer eventually opened the door, she ran to the end of the yard and stopping there, continued to bark with urgency.
"There's something wrong with the dog," his wife said. "She's very agitated. I think she wants us to follow her."
"I'll follow her and find out what is wrong," he answered. "I'll finish the dinner when I return."

The farmer quickly followed the faithful collie on his quad - not even waiting to unhitch the trailer - and was astounded to find Fr. Thomas, blindfolded and gagged, tied to a tree in the forestry clearing. He quickly cut the ropes with the blades of his shears but Fr. Thomas was unable to walk or even stand upright at first. Eventually, after much effort the farmer managed to load him into the trailer of the quad bike and bring him carefully to the farmyard. Thomas had lacerations to his legs, arms, neck, body and damage to his tongue and mouth from the gag and he would later develop a heavy chest infection from being exposed for so long half-naked to the cold night air.

The farmer made a cup of strong hot tea with lots of sugar which Fr. Thomas sipped gratefully, while the farmer's wife, who was a nurse tended to his wounds. The gardai and ambulance arrived and he was taken to hospital where he was detained for almost a week.

It was widely reported in the news media that the abduction was linked to Fr. Thomas' efforts to stamp out anti-social behaviour and drug dealing in his parish, but the gardai refused to comment on this claim. They continued their investigations and appealed repeatedly for information from the public.
He soon ceased to be an item of interest for the news media who instead turned their attention to the farmer who had rescued him and to the clever collie dog on whom they conferred heroic status.

A few weeks after Fr. Thomas returned to Lonerton after his ordeal, Shawny Scrahill's mother Teveena came to him in the mobile chapel in a distressed state.
"Fr. Thomas," she said, "I'm worried to distraction about Shawny. I think he is planning to kill Bowzer Diggins. He blames him for the death of his good friend Johnny Doh and I found out that he has got a gun - some kind of handgun - a revolver or something like that. I know he plans to use it to kill Bowzer Diggins. Shawny has no care for his own life any more. He is filled with remorse over the death of his friend and I think he will blame himself forever. To be truthful, Fr. Thomas, I don't think he will survive for long because his grief and sense of guilt is so great and I'm sure he knows that himself. But the course

he's bent upon now is to kill Bowzer Diggins. I'm sure of that."

She took out her handkerchief and wiped the tears from her reddened eyes and face.

"Shawny was involved in something that was very wrong and now he is bent on doing something that is far worse. He was getting the drugs and selling them himself but he wasn't getting the money that was owed to him and so in an effort to improve things he accepted the offer of Bowzer Diggins to act as collector for him. Far from sorting out his troubles, they became a lot worse as Bowzer began to pocket more and more of the money for himself and he knew full well that Shawny would be in trouble with the suppliers. The bullets that killed poor Johnny Doh were meant for Shawny and Shawny wants to avenge his death. He's sorry in his heart that those bullets didn't kill himself."

"I see," said Fr. Thomas. "So now Shawny has a gun and wants to kill Bowzer."

"That's why I'm here Father. I want you to stop him from killing anyone. Will you talk to him Father Thomas, because I don't want any more bloodshed?"

It took Fr. Thomas many sessions of talking, over many days, to get Shawny to defer his plans to kill Bowzer Diggins.

"But I swore a solemn oath to kill him," said Shawny. "I can't break a solemn oath."

"I would agree with you if it was an oath about doing something good, but your oath is to kill a man," said Fr. Thomas.

"Killing Bowzer would be doing something good, in my book," said Shawny. "I understand what you are saying, but nothing, bar my own death will stop me from keeping my oath."

Some days later Fr. Thomas tried again.
"Shawny, I know you won't break your oath."
"Definitely not."
"Alright, I'll accept that but I am asking you to defer it."
"To defer it. What does that mean?"
"To delay it for a while."
"For how long?"
"Long enough to see Bowzer stripped of all his wealth and sent to jail."
"How can that be done? You make it sound so simple."
"There is a law in the country, which could be applied to Bowzer, which would effectively strip him of the wealth he had gathered illegally. It is called the Criminal Assets Act," Fr. Thomas explained.
"No one will give evidence against him in court," argued Shawny. "They will be afraid because he will intimidate them or kill them or someone belonging to them."
"The Criminal Assets Bureau will be giving the evidence - all about his lifestyle, bank accounts, cars and the rest of it."
"So no locals would be giving evidence?"
"No," said Fr. Thomas, "it would not be necessary. However if they could get a credible witness to connect him to the drug trade, he would face other charges, but that witness would be putting himself at risk, maybe in danger of being killed."
"I'm willing to be that witness," answered Shawny.

"You will be incriminating yourself, do you realise that?"
"I know that full well. I know I will be jailed. It is what I deserve."
"Your life may be in danger."
"I know, but I caused the death of my best friend and took him from his family. I am dead already - dead in my heart and in my spirit and my soul."
"Will you agree to defer carrying out your oath?"
"I agree. I can wait."
"Thanks be to God," said Fr. Thomas. "Now here's what you must do..."

Shawny made a statement to the gardai outlining his new found belief that it was Bowzer Diggins and not the City Gang who was responsible for the death of Johnny Doh. The local detective who took down the statement, had reached a similar conclusion earlier on in the investigation, but he was unable to prove anything until Shawny made his statement and incriminated himself as a drug dealer. The statement helped a lot but the gardai needed more before they could bring a successful prosecution against Bowzer as the investigating detective explained to Fr. Thomas:
"Defence counsel will probably claim that this statement was concocted by Shawny for the sole purpose of getting revenge on his enemy Bowzer Diggins. They will claim that there was not a shred of evidence to connect Bowzer with the killing of Johnny Doh."
"That's a disappointing setback," Fr. Thomas declared.
"Don't be too discouraged. We're still working on the case and something might come up."

The breakthrough that the gardai needed came sooner than they had expected. The anonymous witness to the shooting who was waiting in the wooded path to meet a woman who was not his wife, gave information to the gardai that led to the arrest of Patrick Joseph Hearne generally known as Weedy Joe, for the murder of Jonathan (Doh) Doohan.

As part of an unofficial plea bargain, Weedy Joe revealed the name of the man who hired him to do the killing and shortly afterwards the police arrested Bowzer Diggins. He was charged with the murder of Johnny Doh and the attempted murder of Shawny Scrahill - offences, for which he was subsequently found guilty and jailed for life.

Forty Five

A sense of peace and calm had settled over Cooley Park. Some would go so far as to say that a good community spirit had taken hold.
Fr Thomas was playing the violin in the public section of the mobile chapel one evening in early June. It was a lovely evening and the weather was fine and the blackbird and robin and thrush were singing their melodies on the higher branches of the trees. Canon Towman came to visit.
"You're a good musician," stated the canon.
"Yes! I'll accept that," said Fr. Thomas.
"You have a national reputation."
"Only to a limited extent," said Fr. Thomas, "although I have played with some of the top musicians in the country."
"Tell me," said the canon, "are there any musicians there who might be described as one tune musicians?"
"Yes there are," replied Fr. Thomas. "I suppose everyone of us was a one tune musician at some time or other."
"I recall," said the canon, "a man in my home area and he never played only the one tune over and over again. He practised it again and again and whenever he was asked to play, he played that tune, and even if he wasn't asked to play, he would arrange for himself to play it by asking someone:
"Have you heard this tune?" or "Do you know this one?" - and there he would go again, without waiting for an answer, playing his one and only. Now he did become very good at playing that tune. He played it so much and

introduced so many different variations into it, that it was difficult for other musicians to play with him and because of this, he usually played it solo. One might say that he was committed to that tune and focused solely on it."

"Yes I knew such people," said Thomas. "I think we all were a bit like that in the beginning but we gradually picked up new tunes and learned new styles, studied the craft a bit more, learned a bit more and gradually built up a broad repertoire."

"I was thinking," said the canon, "that our good and holy, diminutive senior curate Fr. Paul Bernhart Bouvier is a little bit like that - in a theological sense of course."

"I think that too," said Fr. Thomas. "Too much of his focus seems to revolve around the area of the technicalities of Church regulations. His entire focus is narrow I think - a bit like the musician with the one tune - and I do not mean to be offensive when I say that, for he really is a very holy and committed priest."

"I agree," said the canon. "The trouble that I have now this evening, is that the bishop wants to make changes in the diocese and he wants me to recommend Fr. Bouvier for some particular role."

"Why won't the bishop do that himself," asked Fr. Thomas.

"He is finding it difficult to find a position to which he would be suited because his focus is so much on one specific aspect of Catholicism - like the musician who is always playing the one tune."

"Yea. I see," said Fr. Thomas, "but a musician with one tune can become a great musician by going to the trouble of learning a few more tunes. I think P.B. Bouvier is a brilliant man and he means well and is motivated by the

very best of reasons. Why doesn't the bishop ask him to broaden his focus and cast his net wider - on the other side of the boat - like the apostles did on the advice of Jesus?"
"Good idea," said the canon. "I'll make that recommendation to the bishop. Now play another tune before I go."

Thomas did as he was asked and closed his eyes to better savour the music in his soul. On his way out, unnoticed by Fr. Thomas, the canon switched on the public address system and the neighbourhood was filled with very fine music - reels and jigs and hornpipes and the occasional waltz and slow air. Very soon people gathered round outside and some clapped hands and some just listened and others danced on the tarmac. Some even came up and sang songs and everyone joined in. It was all very pleasant and a clear demonstration that Thomas had succeeded in his mission to Cooley Park. There was happiness in the air.

Canon Towman, acting on Fr. Thomas' advice, recommended that Fr. Bouvier would be required to broaden his theological focus. The bishop accepted the advice and Fr. Bouvier was appointed to the bishop's office as assistant secretary and assigned to engage in research and study. Bishop Tranton who was a quiet and deeply humble man, was specific regarding the areas in which he required Fr Bouvier to focus his attention:
"I want you do a study on the instruction of Jesus to St. Peter to feed his lambs and feed his sheep. Are you willing to take on that assignment?"
"I am willing," said Fr. Bouvier.
"Good," said the bishop, "I would like if you would place

the study within the context of the proclamation of the Kingdom of God, as announced by Jesus in the Synagogue in Nazareth."

"To bring the good news to the poor, to bring freedom to the prisoner and sight to the blind," answered Fr. Bouvier.

"Specifically", continued the bishop, "I am asking you to investigate whether the Church's practice of restricting Holy Communion is in keeping with the direct command of Jesus."

"I will be happy to take on that assignment," answered Fr. Paul.

"Good," repeated the bishop. "I propose that you would have that document published for the enlightenment of others as soon as it is completed. Now may I ask if your mother is well?"

"She is well, thank you," answered Fr. Bouvier. "She has had much turbulence in her life in recent years, with the deaths of both of her parents and the sale of the company and the sale of her parental home."

"And the ordination of her only son to the priesthood," interjected the bishop.

"You are aware that she now lives permanently in Lanzarote," stated Fr. Bouvier. "She has her own villa there."

"Is she on her own?"

"Yes, unfortunately, since her mother died. It is something that I worry about sometimes."

"Does she have any friends?" asked the bishop.

"Only a retired Irishman who lives some miles away in a hotel."

"Take a week off to visit her - in a few months time when you have settled in here to your new role."

"Thank you, bishop. I will do that. I haven't seen her now for more than a year. She will be delighted to see me I'm sure."

Forty Six

When Fr. Paul Bernhart Bouvier did eventually come to visit Lanzarote, he instinctively sensed a change in the relationship between his mother Gretel and Jack Donoughue, whom he had met on previous occasions. There was an evident shared understanding and familiarity in their behaviour towards each other and both looked healthy and happy together.
"You two seem to be familiar friends," he remarked, as he looked across at them, standing side by side at the kitchen sink, on the evening of his arrival.
"Our circumstances have changed," said Jack.
"Your circumstances have changed," repeated Fr. Paul, looking somewhat puzzled. "In what way?"
"Our circumstances have changed," stated Gretel firmly, "because we are married."
"Mar - mar- married," gasped Fr. Paul. "How could you be married when my father, who is your husband may still be alive?"
"You know that your father divorced me when you were only a child. I still have the divorce papers."
"But you are still married in the eyes of the Church."
"Married," answered Gretel sharply, "how could I be married to a man whom I have not seen for more than thirty years?"
"You were married, until death you do part," stated Fr. Paul. "That is the clear, unambiguous teaching of the Church."
"Yes, we know and that is why Jack and I were married in

a civil ceremony," answered Gretel.
"How could you do that? How could you?" asked Fr. Paul, who was so shocked that he was breathing in short, sharp breaths.
"We dearly wanted to be married in the Church but the Church prohibits this, as you rightly pointed out," said Jack.
"Well then you have abandoned the teaching of the Church, a teaching which I have fervently devoted all my priestly life to protecting."
There was a brief pause while everyone contemplated all that had been said.
"The table is set," said Jack. "Let us all sit and have something to eat and relax a little."
"Yes," agreed Gretel. "Let us all sit down together for dinner. You must be hungry by now Paul."
"I'm sorry," said Fr. Paul. "I just could not eat anything. I am too sick in my stomach at what I've just been told."
"Why don't you go to your room and rest a little," suggested Gretel. "You are tired. I'm sure you will feel better after awhile."
"I will not stay in this house," he answered. "I am a priest. My mother married outside the Church. I cannot stay here in these circumstances."
"Where else can you stay?" asked Gretel. It is now after dark and it will not be easy to get accommodation."
"I can go to the airport and sleep there if necessary." he responded dejectedly.
"That won't be necessary," said Jack. "I'll arrange accommodation at Hotel Donomaur. I'm sure you will like it there."
"Thank you," said Fr. Paul.

"Will you be offering Mass as usual, in our little chapel tomorrow?" asked Gretel.
"Yes. That is my intention. I have celebrated Mass every single day since my ordination."
"We will arrange for a taxi to bring you here for morning Mass as usual," said Gretel.
"Will you be attending the Mass?" he asked.
"Yes," said Gretel, "both Jack and I will be attending the Mass."
"The teaching of the Church is clear regarding the right of couples in illicit relationships to receive Holy Communion and I am duty bound to ask you not to approach the altar to receive the Eucharist. I am duty bound to refuse to give you the Holy Eucharist, because you are living in an adulterous relationship," proclaimed Fr. Paul.
"An adulterous relationship," exclaimed Gretel, "that is harsh language from a son to his mother."
"Harsh, but true in the eyes of the Church," answered Fr. Paul.
"Is it permissible to approach the altar for a blessing at Communion time?" asked Jack, trying to act as normal and as amicable as possible.
"Of course," said Fr. Paul, "approach with your hands crossed to each shoulder and I will bless you with all my heart."

After the Mass on the following day Gretel and Jack and Fr. Paul had an open-air breakfast in a cliff-side restaurant overlooking the harbour of Puerto Del Carmen. It was late November and the broad sea lolled gently in a benevolent breeze beyond the long, curved wall that sheltered boats of many colours, shapes and sizes at anchor in the harbour just inside.

The trio had finished their meal and they gazed in silence for awhile at the beauty that stretched before them. A solitary boat moved imperceptibly on the outer edges of a broad swath of sea, that glistened like shimmering silk in the sloping rays of the half-risen southern sun. Overhead the sky was soft and blue and decorated with patches of woolly, white cloud with deep, dark, serrated edges and a grey blue haze partially obscured the many peaked landscapes in the west. All was peaceful and the peace permeated them and the atmosphere around them and they absorbed it for a long while before Gretel spoke quietly but firmly to her son:
"You were young when you left home to live and study at the seminary."
"Yes!. Seventeen years and five months. I remember. I was young, but I stayed the course."
"Did you know, that I had to sign giving my permission for you to go?"
"Yes, I did know at the time but I had forgotten it."
"It was hard for me to consent to your going, did you know that?"
"I did not think very much about that at the time. I knew you would miss me and I would miss you and Granddad Wilhelm and Nana Ericka."
"Granddad Wilhelm had hoped that you would take over the business when you were a little older. Did you know that?"
"Yes! I suppose. He had mentioned it to me occasionally, but I had to travel my own road and follow my own dream."

"He had a dream too, a dream that you would both work together for a few years and when he had taught you all he knew he would hand over the company to you. It broke his spirit when you left. He had no dreams left to cling to."
"I would not wish to hurt him, but I had to answer a different call, the call of God."
"It was very hard for me too. You were my only son and my hope. It involved many sacrifices for me to let my son go to work for God, when I needed him so badly at home."
"Mother, why are you talking like this to me and telling me all this now - so many years later?"
"Because today, I attended Mass celebrated by that same son, who is now a reverend priest and he refused to let me meet Jesus in Holy Communion. Is that the law of the God for whom I made such difficult sacrifice?"
"We must always remember that God loves us and that in his great mercy, he will show us forgiveness," Fr. Paul responded.
"Forgiveness! Forgiveness for what? For not continuing to live as I had lived for more than thirty years without the comfort and love of a kind and caring man in my life - yes more than thirty years, since my husband - your father walked out and left me."
Fr. Paul put his head down but he did not answer and Gretel continued:
"Or, is it because I adhered to the teaching of the Church regarding my relationship with my husband and created a problem that he couldn't live with? Is this the gratitude of the God who loves us, to prevent Jesus from meeting with me?"
Fr. Paul did not respond. This was not the time nor the

place for this discussion he felt and he kept his head down, staring at the tips of his fingers and at the near empty glass on his table. Jack Donoughue held his silence but Gretel was in the grip of her old rash impetuousness and it compelled her to continue without regard to etiquette or restraint despite her own better judgement:
"Have I not been good and decent and honest all through my life and in all my dealings? Have I not been holy and prayed fervently and attended Mass and met personally with Jesus all my life? Is that not true, Reverend Fr. Paul my son? Don't hide your head but answer me! Is that the truth?"
"It is the truth," said Fr. Paul without lifting up his head.
"And now, after all of my good life and all of my sacrifices, I am prevented from meeting Jesus in Holy Communion, because I was lonely and alone, and afraid sometimes and I wanted to share the rest of my life with an extraordinary man who treats me with respect and who brought much happiness into my life - and because we were married in a civil ceremony. This is my crime and my punishment is harsh indeed - is this not the truth my reverend son?"

People were walking by on the cliff path as she spoke, but were too occupied by their own conversations to notice anything that Gretel was saying. It was only when the waiter showed a young couple to a nearby table that Jack intervened to end the unhappy discussion.
"Look out there at the orange parachute," he said "a little to the left and almost as far as where the sea meets the sky. If you look closely, you will see the small motor boat that is towing it. I cannot see the person in the glider's seat."
"Neither can I," said Gretel, who was glad to have been

distracted from her rant.
"I see them," said Fr. Paul, "There are two of them, a man and woman I think. I can see them clearly."
"It is thus with many things in life," remarked Jack, "some people can see things very clearly that others cannot see at all."
Then he turned to Fr. Paul:
"Would you like to come back to the villa with us?" he asked.
"Not today," answered Fr. Paul. "I will walk back to the Hotel Donomaur. I will reflect on all that has been said this morning, as I go along the way."

Forty Seven

Cooley Park progressed quickly after the jailing of Bowzer Diggins. The Family Charters were signed by almost everyone, even by some of Bowzer's former lackeys.
The Community Charter was adopted at community level, under the guidance and encouragement of the Cooley Park Community Committee. This was simply an expanded version of the Family Charter - the main difference being that it required all residents to help with the physical appearance of the estate and to act *in loco parentis* in order to encourage good conduct.
"What's de meaning of *in loco parentis?*" enquired Eddie Whispy from Fr. Thomas.
"It means to act in the place of a parent," explained Fr. Thomas. "So if an adult saw a young person misbehaving or doing something dangerous they would be entitled to tell him to stop."
"Dere's nothing new in dat," said Whispy. "We were all corrected by adults when I was a youngster. Sometimes I was told I would have my backside kicked if I didn't behave."

In the summer of the year of Bowzer's conviction, the Calcutta community decided to paint all houses in the estate and to follow up with minor landscaping around each house and in the wider area. This inspired a similar initiative in Harlem and latterly in the First Estate. By the end of September of that year all three estates had been transformed with matching coloured houses and shrubs and flowers. The owners of the scrapped cars removed them, fences were repaired, muddied areas re-seeded and dogs were no longer allowed to roam freely around. It was a magnificent community achievement and they were rightly proud.

Although the work had progressed satisfactorily, Fr. Thomas began to feel restless. He had an instinctive feeling that his work here was done. Around that time, the bishop announced his retirement and Canon Towman had informed Fr. Thomas that he would most likely be moved to another parish, maybe even be made a parish priest. Thomas thought this was unlikely due to his relative lack of experience in priestly life and besides, Fr. Bouvier was senior to him and would have prior claim to any such promotion.

Ever since his abduction, Fr. Thomas had been receiving positive media publicity, not just locally but nationally for his approach to solving the problems of Cooley Park and reconnecting the people with the Church. The effectiveness of his strategy of using the natural strength and cohesion of the family unit, coupled with community consensus, for stamping out drugs and anti-social behaviour was the subject of much discussion. The mobile chapel also generated a lot of interest and was the subject of a documentary on national television.
He had managed to defuse the dispute involving Eddie Whispy and his daughter's fight to receive Holy Communion. He invoked the example of Jesus ever reaching out to those who were marginalised and gave Holy Communion to Tessie whenever she attended Mass

in the mobile chapel.

Some weeks later Fr. Thomas was visited by a three person deputation who challenged his decision to allow Tessie to receive Holy Communion.
"Tessie is as fundamentally good and Christian a person as you would ever find," explained Fr. Thomas. Although she is trapped in circumstances that are not of her own making, she is loyal to the commandments, in so far as is possible for her. Her selfless giving of her time to the community and to fundraising and other charitable works sets her apart as an exemplary Christian."
"But she is a divorcee and is living with a man who is not her husband in the eyes of God," argued one member of the deputation.
"The law of God prohibits her from receiving Holy Communion," stated the second.
"And the law of God must be obeyed," argued the third.
"Agreed," answered Fr. Thomas, "but we must be sure that it is God's law we are enforcing and not some human version of it."
"Please explain."
"Written law, may have some imperfection in so far as it may be unreasonable in some exceptional circumstances," explained Fr. Thomas.
"Are you not being a heretic here?" they ask accusingly.
"No, because we must ask if it is within the spirit and intention of God, that a genuinely good and holy young woman like Tessie Hayley, should be deprived of the opportunity of meeting with Jesus in Holy Communion - all because of circumstances outside her control," explained Fr. Thomas.

"Are you saying that God's law is imperfect?"
"No! I'm saying that the human interpretation and implementation of God's law may be imperfect in some instances."
"Would clarify that for us?"
"The teaching about the sanctity of marriage and of the family is soundly based and good in itself - however using this teaching to prevent a good Christian woman from meeting Jesus in Holy Communion, may not be in accordance with the spirit and intention of God, the supreme lawmaker."
"So what are we supposed to do?" they asked, "give Holy Communion to every Tom, Dick and Harry, who has no regard for the laws of God or man?"
"You misrepresent what I am saying," said Thomas. It is reasonable - even essential in some circumstances to decline to give Holy Communion."
"But, you can't have it both ways. Either you apply the law or you don't."
"You are not correct in your understanding," said Fr. Thomas. "I have been trying to explain to you that in some cases, such as that of Tessie Hayley, it would be unreasonable to refuse to let her meet Jesus in Holy Communion."
"You are inventing an opt-out clause all of your own," they declared.
"No, it is not an 'opt-out' clause and I am not inventing it. It is already there. The ancient Greeks had a mechanism for this called *epikeia."*
"What is *epikeia*?"
"The word means reasonableness. The virtue of *epikeia* allows that any law would not be applied, in circumstances

that would breach the intentions or spirit of the lawmaker."

"So you are asking if it is reasonable to think that God the loving Father, wants to prevent Tessie Hayley from meeting with Jesus in Holy Communion?"

"That is what I am asking," said Fr. Thomas.

"And you believe that God the Father would not want to bar her from Holy Communion - is that so?"

"I could not believe otherwise - for the reasons that I have outlined."

"Aren't you being arrogant by implying that you know the mind of God?"

"I didn't say I knew the mind of God. I referred to the intention that God had - as is evident in the invitation issued by Jesus Himself to Tessie and everyone else like her."

"To what invitation are you referring?"

"The invitation of the Lord to those that are weary and bearing heavy loads. He invited them to come to him for help and rest - Is that correct?".

"Yes, it is."

"So if the Lord invited them, who are we to inhibit or obstruct them from meeting him?" argued Fr. Thomas.

"Well, we can't disagree with that," they replied. "Maybe we should look into things more deeply and be less judgemental in future about people like Tessie - people whose life circumstances are outside of their control."

"*Epikeia* also prohibits the application of a law in circumstances in which it would do more harm than good," said Fr. Thomas.

"For example?"

"Refusing Holy Communion to Tessie would be harmful

to such a good and genuinely holy person. It would also be likely to turn her children against the Church and maybe even her friends as well," explained Fr. Thomas.
"Looking at it from that perspective, *epikeia* is a good mechanism. It has the potential to solve many delicate problems," they agreed.

They were good people - the members of that deputation, good prayerful people. They were reasonable and recognised the wisdom of the explanation that Fr. Thomas had given to them and they were more at peace with themselves as they returned to their respective homes.

Canon Towman had established a custom of regularly inviting Fr. Bouvier and Fr. Thomas to share the supper with him one evening each week. It was always a very basic supper.
"Plain food for plain country men," the canon used to say.

On one such occasion, long after Fr. Bouvier had left the parish, the table was set for three people. For a minute Thomas thought that the canon was slipping up a little bit and that habit had prevailed upon him to have three places - forgetting that Fr. Bouvier was no longer with them. The canon seeing the look on Fr. Thomas's face said:
"We will be joined by another guest in a minute or two, someone who wants to talk to you and who has a proposition for you."

Just then exactly on cue the papal nuncio entered the room and Fr. Thomas recognised him instantly. The canon did the introductions and both Thomas and the nuncio

acknowledged that each had a good knowledge of the other. The trio had a lively discussion on issues of current interest in the Church. When they had finished their humble supper, Canon Towman looked directly at Fr. Thomas and addressed him as follows:
"The nuncio has a proposition that he wishes to put to you. It is a proposition that I fear you would want to refuse and this is also the view of the nuncio and it is for that reason that it is being put to you at this table and in my presence."

Forty Eight

At one point along the cliff path west of Gretel's Lanzarote villa, one can sit and view the broad ocean in its vastness and the distant hills in a sweeping panorama, unencumbered by any glimpse of nearby towns or harbours or houses. If you are there when all is calm and quiet, you can hear the mild waves lapping softly as they gently kiss the base of the volcanic, black rocked cliff.

Jack Donoughue came regularly to this place, usually in the early morning, to reflect on life, on past adventures and on future challenges looming into view - knowing well that with his strong faith, everything would work out alright in the end.
"Everything will be alright," he said, "because it always is anyway. I know that because life has taught it to me."

It was early on the morning of the day after their restaurant meal with Fr. Paul and as usual Jack was walking briskly on the cliff path, his mind pondering on the discussion they had the previous day and on the surprisingly trenchant stance that Gretel had taken over the refusal of Fr. Paul to give her Holy Communion.
"I think she was right," he mused, "I really think she was right and fair and balanced in everything she said."

The sun had not yet risen in the east to chase away the grey light of dawn and drive the feather-light, grey-white clouds from the sky. He rarely ever saw anyone out and

about at that early hour and so he was surprised to see a hunched figure, sitting on his favourite cliff-side seat - elbows resting on the knees and the head bowed low and resting on upturned palms.
"Someone thinking deeply," mused Jack "or someone resting under a heavy weight of worry."
He walked more noisily as he approached the solitary figure, so that his shoes crunched more loudly on the gravelly path. He coughed aloud to warn of his impending arrival but the hunched figure, whom he now discerned to be a man, remained motionless.
"Perhaps he is not well," thought Jack so he came nearer:
"*Buenos Dias, senor,*" he said aloud.
The man slowly raised his head from his hands, his face looking tired and haggard and dreadfully weary and Jack recognised him instantly:
"Ah, Fr. Paul," he said exuberantly, "you have come to savour the view and the peace."
"Not exactly," replied Fr. Paul. "I came to reflect and to try to clear my brain of the turmoil that your civil marriage to my mother has brought to it."
"Of course," said Jack. "I know it has not been easy for you."
"It is a hard thing to refuse Holy Communion to my own mother," said Fr. Paul, his face distorted with grief, "but I have to be faithful to God's law."
"I understand fully why the Church seeks to maintain the sanctity of marriage and I agree that it is fundamental to the wellbeing of all human life and society," said Jack, "but I think that refusing Holy Communion for such reasons excludes too many."
"It is the teaching of the *magisterium* of the Church," replied

Fr. Paul "and I agree with it. I am bound by it and I must enforce it without exception."
"Even if that exception is your own mother," exclaimed Jack.
"Mother or brother or sister," answered Fr. Paul, "the rules apply to all without exception."
"Isn't there also the rule which states that the things you bind on earth, will also be bound in heaven - or something like that?" asked Jack.
"Yes, of course," said Fr. Paul.
"It follows therefore," said Jack "that if you refuse to let your mother meet with Jesus here on earth, then she will be similarly refused in heaven, for all eternity of course."
Fr. Paul remained silent for awhile.
"I will need to reflect some more," he replied. "We will meet later on after mass."

In the evening of that same day, in Lonerton Canon Towman and his guests were still seated at the dining room table when the papal nuncio revealed the purpose of his visit:
"Fr. Thomas," he began "I have been in contact with the Holy Father and he is familiar with your work and with your background and with your life. The Holy Father desires that some people who have had experience of life outside of religious life, would be appointed to positions of authority in the Church. The Holy Father is also familiar with the work that you have been doing and with your approach and success in Cooley Park. It is for those reasons that he has authorised me to ask if you would

accept responsibility for the diocese, as bishop of Killeenreagh - in succession to Bishop Tranton, who has announced his retirement - as you already know."
"I am a little astounded," declared Thomas. "Does the Holy Father know that I am just a junior curate?"
"Yes!" answered the nuncio.
"And is he aware that I was married and aware of the circumstances in which my wife died and of the circumstances in which my son died?"
Despite himself, the mention of his wife and son caused the words to catch in his throat and so he had to repeat them to properly pronounce them and with sufficient strength.
"Does he also know that some would blame me for the death of my wife and drowning of my son?"
"The pope is well informed. He is aware of all of that," replied the nuncio.
"Is the pope aware that I descended down to the depths, to the borderline of alcoholism and the very gutter and dregs of life?"
"The Holy Father knows that these experiences did not take from your goodness. He sees them as experiences, that prepared you for dealing with the problems, which you handled so well in the poorer housing estates of this parish and helped you to cope with the abduction that you suffered. He is even aware of how well you handled the protest of that man Mr. Whiston about the refusal to give Holy Communion to his daughter. The Holy Father sees you as a man, strengthened by those experiences. They are part of what helped you in your work in the parish and they will help you in the more onerous responsibilities that face you, should you accept - and I do hope you will

accept, the role as bishop of Killeenreagh."
"I would like some time to think about it," said Fr. Thomas. "How soon do you need to know my answer?"
"We will not pressurise you for time, but we would like to know sooner rather than later."
"Is it O.K. if I go and pray by myself?" asked Fr. Thomas.
"Of course," said the Canon. "Would you like to use the little oratory in my house?"
"Thanks, but I would rather not," said Thomas. "I will go to the mobile chapel in Cooley Park. I think it is where my heart is."

It was there in that mobile chapel, which was then parked in the Calcutta section of Cooley Park that he knelt and bowed low in front of the tabernacle. He prayed deep and heartfelt prayers and thought back to his beloved Mary, to his beloved Indie and how he felt for so long that he had failed them and been a coward and he prayed:
"Dearest God, you know the depths of my heart and you know that I blamed myself for many years and branded myself a coward because I failed my wife and child. You know that deep in my heart I promised that never again would I show a lack of courage in any circumstance, no matter how difficult. It seems to me that today, you my Lord and my God are putting that resolve to the test. My Lord and my God, I have sworn that I will never be a coward again and I will do as I have been asked this day. I only ask that you will be with me and help me in all of my work."

He remained in kneeling position bowed low and prayed, and there and then he made the decision to accept the role and responsibility as bishop of Killeenreagh. Immediately he felt a great peace as his soul was filled with the Holy Spirit of God, the spirit of all that is good and kind and decent and holy and it was a spirit that was wonderful.

"God my father, you are now and ever have been, the great force and power of good that permeates all things. You are 'good' itself and I know that I share that good also. I have felt your goodness at times when I was pure in heart and clean of hands. I can truly say at this point in the journey of my life, that I love you in my heart and I commit myself to do all that is required of me."

He prayed some more and the response that formulated in his mind, was the response he gave to the papal nuncio when he returned to the canon's house some hours later:
"The things that were most precious in life to me were all taken from me - my wife and my children. I do not blame anyone for that and I do not wallow in sorrow and self-pity. I have sunk down to my own personal hell and been saved from that and been raised up again. Having been saved by a higher power, I have cast myself upon the tide of God's will, content to float to whatsoever destination that tide will take me. So far, it has brought me to this parish and now it is leading me elsewhere and so, placing all my trust in God, I am happy to go where it will lead me. Praise God. Praise God. Praise God."

Forty Nine

Fr. Paul came to the villa for lunch for the first time, on the day before his return to Ireland. He had meditated deeply on his refusal to allow Holy Communion for his mother and Jack Donoughue and thought it best to come as a gesture of reconciliation. He also had some other news which was a source of great excitement for him:
"The manager of Hotel Donomaur has invited me to celebrate morning Mass in their chapel tomorrow. My flight is an evening flight, so I accepted the invitation. Will you be able to attend the Mass?"
"Yes, we'll be there," said Gretel. "Attending Mass is always a privilege and a necessary part of life for all Christians who work for good."
"It is a most unusual and interesting chapel named La Capilla De San Pedro La Roca - the Chapel of Saint Peter The Rock," explained Fr. Paul. "It is carved out of a rocky slope and is not visible from a distance. It may be difficult to locate."
Gretel glanced sideways at Jack, drew in her breath and was about to speak but he intervened:
"We will be able to find it," he said. "I am familiar with the area."
"I was given a guided tour by the hotel manager," said Fr. Paul enthusiastically. "It is a truly amazing building, almost completely hidden. It is essentially a broad based dome, carved out of the rock and natural light enters via a large heptagon-shaped tower directly over the altar in the centre of the circular floor. I was told that the seven sided shape

represents the seven sacraments. Different coloured stained glass is used and it splashes varied colour on the altar and on the floor below. Even though the tower protrudes slightly above the surface of the slope, it blends in well with the shrubs that grow there."
"La Capilla De San Pedro La Roca is well known to us," said Gretel but Fr. Paul in his excitement, continued as if he hadn't heard:
"The facade is in the traditional Spanish style but it is not visible from a distance because of the tall date palms and coconuts palms with their ringed trunks, that grow around the front. Vines and a fig tree also grow closer in, and there's a mustard seed in a glass case just inside the door."
"You like it," commented Jack.
"Yes, it certainly was a surprise - something so beautiful underneath the surface of the rock, and yet one could easily pass by without ever noticing it," said Fr. Paul.
"Maybe there are many beautiful truths that lie just beneath the surface," said Jack "but they remain hidden because no one probes deeply enough to reveal them."
"Such as?" asked Fr. Paul.
"Such as the boundless, all-encompassing mercy of God," answered Jack, "as evidenced by Jesus who reached out to meet sinners and by his ever readiness to forgive. He did not allow apostles or Pharisees or anyone else to prevent him from meeting the sinners."
"What precise point are you making?" asked Fr. Paul.
"I'm saying that good people are approaching the altar with outstretched hands to meet with Jesus in the Eucharist, but you are preventing Jesus from going to them."
"But they may not be worthy because of their lifestyle,"

said Fr. Paul.
"They may or they may not. Who am I to judge them? Who are you to judge?
"But if we know they are unworthy," argued Fr. Paul.
"We do not know that. No one is worthy," said Jack. "Everyone declares their unworthiness before receiving the Holy Eucharist."

Later, long after he had left, Gretel and Jack were sitting on their balcony and chatting about their lunch with Fr. Paul and the discussion they had with him.
"Why didn't you tell him that it was you who built and owns La Capilla De San Pedro La Roca?" she asked.
"Because it might influence him to allow us have Holy Communion," answered Jack.
"Isn't that what we want - not to be refused Holy Communion?"
"It would be better if he made that decision on the basis of mercy and not on the basis of additional good works that we might have done."
"I think he should be told. It is unfair to keep it from him."
"He will be told. I have arranged it."
"When?"
"Tomorrow, immediately after mass. He will be told gently."
"You are very considerate to him. I'm not sure that I would be that charitable," said Gretel.
"I try to be what the Christian must be," said Jack. "It is best that way."

The celebration of mass was joyous with some singing and

readings by residents of the hotel and of the neighbourhood. Fr. Paul made forgiveness the theme of his short homily and he seemed serene and at peace in himself.

Jack and Gretel approached the altar at Holy Communion time with arms crossed as they had done for the past six days, to receive a blessing from a solemn faced Fr. Paul, but today there was joy in his face and reverence in his voice as he clearly proclaimed:

" *El Cuerpo De* Cristo!"

"Amen," they answered and stretched out their open hands to receive the Eucharist and meet with Jesus deeply within body and soul and mind and spirit. It was a joyous moment for mother and son and Jack was happy for them both.

Later as Fr. Paul was disrobing, the low-sized, slightly rotund, neatly dressed, very talkative sacristan asked:

"You like our underground capilla, Padre Pablo?"

"Yes, I like it very much," answered Fr. Paul.

"It was constructed by the owner of the Hotel Donomaur," declared the sacristan.

"It is a fine facility and available for services by all faiths, I believe," said Fr. Paul, who clearly was impressed by La Capillo De San Pedro La Roca.

"And you have seen the fig tree at the front beside the door, yes?"

"Not today but I saw it yesterday," responded Fr. Paul.

"The fig tree and the vines were planted by the owner as a reminder that we must all bear good fruit in our lives. The mustard seed encased in glass in the entrance is a reminder that a little bit of faith can spread far beyond ourselves and

grow enormously."
"He must be a very good man that owns the Hotel Donomaur," commented Fr. Paul. "I would like to meet him sometime."
"But you did meet him Padre Pablo," replied the sacristan. "He received the Eucharist from you today - he and his wife Gretel."

Fr. Paul felt his head reel and he sat down heavily on the nearest chair. This revelation was akin to the flash of lightning that knocked Saul from his horse on the road to Damascus.

"And to think that I refused Holy Communion to that good man for the last six days. Oh my God! How stupid I have been but you have led me here Lord so that my eyes might be opened to the boundless fullness of your mercy."
"Are you unwell Padre Pablo?" asked the sacristan. "Here, have a little water. Perhaps you are dehydrated and need a drink."
Fr. Paul closed his eyes for a little while after he had drunk the cool refreshing water and then looking directly at the sacristan he mused aloud:
"I am shocked by the lesson I have been taught here this day."
"May I ask what that lesson is, Padre Pablo?" asked the sacristan.
"That you cannot love someone and be merciless to them at the same time."
"Si, Padre Pablo," said the sacristan "there can be no love without mercy - it is not possible."

Jack and Gretel said goodbye to Fr. Paul at Arrecife Airport later that afternoon.
"God bless you my son," said Gretel as she hugged and kissed him.
"God bless you too," said Jack, "I think you have the potential to do great things for God."
"Thanks," said Fr. Paul. "May God bless you mother and you Jack and may God bless you both together."
He turned to watch them and they were holding hands as they walked away - the Irishman that looked like a Spaniard and his German born, Irish reared mother from whom he had inherited so many of his ways and characteristics.
After awhile, Jack put his arm around her shoulder and she looked up at him and smiled a happy smile.
"They certainly are a happy couple," mused Fr. Paul and he turned and headed for the departure lounge.

On the flight home he felt a peace like he had never known in all his years of swimming against the tide with his hard judgements and lack of mercy.
"Sometimes, maybe you have to be far away from home to be able to see things as they really should be seen," he thought. "I have learned much on this trip. Thanks be to God."

He settled contentedly into his seat and slept peacefully until a memory from the past jolted him wide awake:
"Oh my God," he said, "Eddie Whispy's daughter Tessie Hayley to whom I refused Holy Communion. I must make amends - publicly if possible, because it became a very public issue. Oh my God, I am so heartily sorry. I will

make amends, I promise and I pray to you to help me keep that promise."

Fifty

The ordination of my brother Thomas as bishop of Killeenreagh took place in the Cathedral in the town of Deisne. The usual protocols were observed in relation to invitations: the standard number of people were invited from each parish - priests, public representatives etc. There was room for family members also but on the day, the dignitaries and invited politicians were accommodated on the left hand side towards the top of the Cathedral and the people that Fr Thomas had invited to attend, along with his own family were standing at the back of the cathedral just to the right of the main door. Amongst them were people from Cill Gobnait - the parish where he taught, including Packie and the McMahon family, as well as people from The First Estate, Harlem and Calcutta - Eddie Whispy, Pauline Doohan, Alessandra and others.

Just before the ordination mass commenced, they were conveyed in full view of everybody to the seats that had been allocated to them in the very front at the right hand side. This was done under instructions from Fr. Thomas. It was his way of saying to them how highly he valued them.

At the reception after the ordination, Bishop Thomas had his picture taken with many dignitaries and with many others including Nora, Rose and myself but the picture that most pleased him was the one taken with Eddie Whispy, his daughter Tessie Hayley and his friends from

Cooley Park.

The wheel of life had turned a neat trick on Fr Paul Bernhart Bouvier. He had gone from being senior curate to Fr. Thomas in Lonerton, to being his lowly assistant secretary in the diocesan office.
He was with Bishop Thomas in the great big house that served as bishop's residence one bright summer evening two years into Thomas' service as bishop of Killeenreagh. Both were in a slightly sad and sombre mood, having just returned from the funeral of their former parish priest, the big hearted Canon Towman, who had died suddenly while cutting grass outside his house on a warm and beautiful sunny day in May.

They sipped cups of green tea from mugs and looked around at the tall wooden bookshelves and at the many volumes of Canon Law and Church literature thereon. In silence they observed the huge, weighty, old, frayed window drapes and examined their faded colours and the detail of their design - all the while dealing with flitting memories of their time with the late canon in the parish of Lonerton. When their gaze reverted back to the large fireplace with its marble and slate inserts, they had recovered sufficiently to begin their chat.

"I'll miss the canon," said Thomas. "He was a fine man in every respect. I learned a lot from him."
"So did I," replied Fr. Bouvier, "but regrettably for me and for others, the lessons did not sink in until I had moved away from Lonerton."
"But you did learn the lessons and applied them and

spread them through your subsequent life and especially through the learned discussion papers you have produced," said Bishop Thomas. "Your paper *Body be Active - or Die* has been influential."
"I based that paper on your approach to the challenges you faced in Cooley Park," replied Fr. Bouvier. "There you applied the gospel through a call to Christian responsibility for each individual, for each family and for each local community. It worked well and the fruits of it are there to be seen today in a model estate of model citizens."
"I suspect," said Bishop Thomas, "that your recently published paper *Banned From The Fold* has its roots in Lonerton parish and in your refusal to give Holy Communion to Tessie Hayley - Eddie Whiston's daughter."
"Correct," answered Fr. Bouvier. "It deals with the blanket ban on individuals from receiving Holy Communion. I now see we must consider individual circumstances and actions and look again at this issue."
"You have learned the value of mercy too I see," said Thomas.
"It was taught to me during my last visit to Lanzarote when I found out that my mother - who was divorced by my father as you know, had secretly married her friend, widower Jack Donoughue in a civil ceremony. In my merciless zeal for adhering to the teaching of the Church, I refused them Holy Communion for six days of the seven that I spent there."
"That was a difficult situation for you," said Thomas.
"It was difficult until I realised how much like the biblical Pharisees and the Sadducees I was."
"My mother used to say that we understand everything

better when it comes to our own door," said Bishop Thomas.

"And how right she was," said Fr. Bouvier. I am deeply regretful that I banned good and decent people from receiving Holy Communion."

"The important thing is that you have learned to better understand and to be empathetic," said Bishop Thomas.

"It troubles me even more that I refused Holy Communion to that decent, good living Tessie Hayley - and all because she had been divorced and remarried in a civil ceremony."

"Don't let that trouble you. I'm sure that Tessie has long since forgiven you. It is what she would want to do because that is her nature."

"But it does trouble me. I think that it should. I believe that we have to repair and make up for damage we have done in our lives."

"You think you need to talk to her?"

"I fully intend to do that, but what I did was very public and I think that I should deal with it in public."

""I believe that I can help you with that," said Thomas, - "you see I need to appoint a parish priest in Lonerton to replace our dear departed friend Canon Towman."

On the night that he was to be installed as parish priest by Bishop Thomas, Fr. Bouvier addressed the congregation in the following words:

"When I first came to this parish some years ago, as a curate and as a younger man than I am now, my understanding of the Church had been very narrow and I focused too much on rules and regulations. I'm afraid that my attitude, while it was sincerely held, caused pain and distress to some people. I am now very remorseful for any hurt that I caused to anybody arising from that attitude. I would like you to reflect very carefully on the words of the *confiteor* because as I speak them at this Mass this night, I will be confessing my failures to you - and I ask you to forgive me."

I think that the *confiteor* was recited with exceptional reverence and volume in the parish chapel that evening.
"Now, we have finished the c*onfiteor*, I ask you again to forgive me and to pray for me but I also ask if there is anyone who does not forgive me to say so now, for if there is, I cannot proceed with being inducted as parish priest - until that forgiveness is forthcoming."
There was a prolonged silence, a silence that was eventually broken by the strong clear voice of Eddie Whiston.
"Dere is nothing to forgive. All dat is past and gone. We will not look back like de ploughman in de gospel. We will look ahead of us and plough a straight furrow. We cannot go forward if we are always looking back."
There was sustained applause and a visibly emotional Fr. Bouvier proceeded to prostrate himself at the foot of the altar and was ordained parish priest by his former junior curate, Bishop Thomas Kendley.

There was a particularly heart-warming moment in the Mass when Eddie Whiston, his wife Nora, their daughter Tessie, her second husband Dan Hayley and one of their children who had just received her First Holy Communion lined up in the queue where Fr. Bouvier was distributing the Eucharist. He was deeply touched - as were Eddie and Tessie. Big soft tears rolled slowly down her kindly face as she came away from the altar having received the Eucharist from him and those members of the congregation who saw her were touched in their hearts too. It was a deeply spiritual experience for her and for many others as well.

With regard to the mobile chapel, which he had once so strongly opposed, he stated:
"I will do all in my power to ensure that it will continue to be used for prayer, for Eucharistic adoration and for the custom of daily, community tea and scones, for many a year to come."

Fifty One

Thomas' tenure as bishop of Killeenreagh was very much focused on the call to Christian responsibility and 'Spirit' inspired action.

His first pastoral letter outlined his priorities and the mechanisms which would be required to achieve them. He wanted parishes and everyone in them to be to be actively Christian - promoting the need for Christian activism at individual, family and collective community levels. The pastoral letter gained some media attention, including balanced coverage from radio and television stations from which the following interview extract is taken:

Reporter: Your pastoral letter places a lot of emphasis on consensus and responsibility of families and of communities. Which comes first - responsibility or consensus?

Bishop Thomas: Responsibility comes first but consensus, especially family consensus and community consensus support and help the individual to be responsible and actively Christian.

Reporter: Which has the primary role - the family or the community?

Bishop Thomas: Individual responsibility comes first - then the collective family responsibility which should affirm and support the individual. The aim is to enable families and local communities to achieve consensus on the rightful standards and responsibilities by which they should live.

Reporter: A protest in Lonerton - your former parish - over

banning a woman from Holy Communion received widespread publicity. What's your view on banning people from Holy Communion?
Bishop Thomas: The Church's teaching on marriage is well intentioned and designed to uphold marriage and the family - as desirable and essential to the wellbeing of society as a whole. I support that teaching. However there are exceptions to every rule and some people find themselves in less ideal situations that are not of their own making.
Reporter: And is banning those people from receiving the Eucharist the answer?
Bishop Thomas: What would Jesus do?
Reporter: You're the bishop. You tell me what would Jesus do?
Bishop Thomas: I believe that Jesus would welcome everyone, including those whose lives are complicated by circumstances outside their control - circumstances which they neither sought nor wanted.

Bishop Thomas had great support in this reforming work from his one time nemesis and former colleague Fr. Paul Bernhart Bouvier. Since his road to Damascus conversion on the island of Lanzarote, Fr. Bouvier had broadened the extent of his knowledge of Christianity with a particular focus on the inexhaustible fount of God's infinite mercy. Bishop Thomas had appointed him diocesan coordinator, to ensure that each parish was doing what the bishop had suggested and to ensure, that there was sufficient help there among the Catholic community.

Fr Bouvier continued to broaden his own horizons and the

bigger the challenge he faced, the more his intellectual brilliance shone through in the many discussion documents and papers that he published. He applied himself to learning other languages. In that regard he began with Italian and generally holidayed in Italy or specifically in Rome each year. He also learned Spanish and the slightly similar Portuguese language. He was already fluent in German and had a good knowledge of French and could speak Irish very well.

During subsequent years Parish Christian Action Committees were established and expanded their remit to include issues of the wider world such as hunger and justice. A new clause was added to all charters stating unequivocally that each individual is unique and special and has a unique contribution to make to the world. Gradually Bishop Thomas' vision of "Active Christian Parishes - Active Christian People" took hold and began to develop into an Active Christian Diocese.

Two years after his appointment Bishop Thomas returned to Lonerton to humbly assist the parish priest Fr. Bouvier at the funeral Mass for Shawny Scrahill who had been found dead on the floor of his bedroom by his loving, heartbroken mother Teveena. It was a dull and dreary November day with continuous drizzling rain. The attendance at the Mass was small - maybe because people remembered that Shawny had been a drug dealer and that Johnny Doh Doohan was shot because of him. Shawny was twenty eight years old at the time of his death.
"What a waste," declared Bishop Thomas, "what a waste of a young life. The evil one is forever prowling around and we must always be on the alert so that we are not

taken by surprise and led along the path of ruination and destruction."

After Easter of the following year Bishop Thomas was back again in Lonerton for the official naming of Harlem and Calcutta.
"Praise the Lord," he exclaimed as he surveyed well painted houses in a matching colour scheme, landscaped green areas and floral colour provided by an extensive array of hanging baskets, window boxes and cultivated flower beds. He was particularly touched in his heart when he was blessing the impressive, new, flower-adorned limestone slabs - one at the entrance to Harlem and the other at the entrance to the lower Calcutta, estate:
"My heart is glad," said Bishop Thomas, "to see this, so called Harlem estate renamed *Jonathan Doohan Park,* in memory of a loyal and upright young man, shot to death by evil forces in the early, pulsing prime of his life. I myself am also honoured to see that the insultingly nicknamed Calcutta estate will henceforth be known to all and sundry as *Bishop Kendley Place.*"

The diocese developed steadily as an active Christian diocese and it was featured in some Catholic newspapers as an example of a diocese infused with the spirit of Christian action. Much credit was given to Bishop Thomas but an equal measure of credit was given to Fr. Paul Bernhart Bouvier - the diocesan coordinator whose commitment and tireless energy were essential and effective. Neither of them sought or wanted any credit for themselves.
"The credit belonged to the people," they said "and to the

spirit of God that inspired and motivated them."

In May 2001, when Bishop Thomas was fifty five years old, he was called to Rome to serve in a newly formed *Pontifical Council for the Pastoral Care of the Members of the Body of Christ on Earth*. It was widely anticipated that Paul Bernhart Bouvier, who had built up a national reputation for his theological writings, would be appointed to succeed him as bishop of Killeenreagh but it was not to be.

Fifty Two

Bishop Thomas' doctoral thesis - *An Examination of the Scriptural Basis for Restrictions on Reception of the Eucharist,* dovetailed neatly with the work of the pontifical council of which he was a member.

He had received much assistance from Fr. Bouvier and it was through their cooperation on the thesis, that the former rigid traditionalist and the more moderate Fr. Thomas became soul mates dedicated to a common cause, namely to help make the Catholic Church a welcoming, nourishing place for all, especially for the excluded, the marginalised and the disconnected.

Promoting this ideal became a central focus for both of these good men. More significantly it became a central aim of the pontifical council and it was generally in tune with the thinking of the Holy Father at that time.

Back in Ireland, Fr. Paul Bernhart Bouvier experienced a rapid rise through the hierarchical structure. Two years after Bishop Thomas had left for Rome, Fr. Paul was appointed Archbishop of Relbehenny and three years later he was elevated to the position of Cardinal - a promotion that was in accordance with tradition in that archdiocese. He continued to write learned letters and discussion papers, some of which were given careful and positive consideration by the pontifical commission of which Bishop Thomas had become chairman.

Drawing heavily on the scriptures which showed Jesus reaching out to those who were alienated and in the margins, Bishop Thomas Kendley and Archbishop Paul Bernhart Bouvier continued to propose that the Eucharist was a sustenance and healing balm most especially for those that needed it and that they should not be deprived of it. They cautioned against judgement without mercy and warned that those who judged without mercy would themselves face a similar fate.

Jack and Gretel Bernhart Donoughue fitted into each other's lives like favourite gloves fit on the hands and they were completely comfortable and at ease in each other's company.

"I like being with you," Jack would often say.

"And I like being with you too," Gretel would reply.

Generally, they lived in her villa and Jack was out and about each morning walking the cliffs as he loved to do. Each evening they would sit on the balcony, talking together, listening to the sound of the waves and the call of the gulls or reading and always praying the rosary together. Gretel became involved with *The Donomaur Better World Fund* and her business experience and acumen made her a valuable addition to the management committee.

They stayed at Hotel Donomaur too sometimes to enable Jack to keep a watchful eye on the business or to 'keep his hand in' as he himself liked to say and to maintain familiarity and good relationships with management and staff.

They did not travel abroad, apart from a few trips to Ireland and to London to visit Jack's daughter. A planned trip to Vancouver to visit his son had to be deferred because it clashed with the planned elevation of Paul to the position of Cardinal. They did promise however, that they would visit within a year thereafter. Jack was eager to see them all again and was particularly looking forward to holding his first and only grandchild in his arms.

They were the principal guests in Rome for the ordination of Cardinal Paul Bernhart Bouvier. Five other cardinals were ordained on the same day. It was a joyous day for Gretel and it seemed that her decision all those years ago to name him after St. Paul - the great missionary, was inspired by a higher power.
"I am humbly proud," she said to Jack, "although I know that sounds contradictory."
"It makes perfect sense to me," said Jack. "I think it explains your feelings very well but maybe you could add the word 'grateful' to the list."
"Yes, you are right," said Gretel. "I'm humbly proud and very grateful to God. I think that explains it better."

There was the usual frenetic clicking and flashing of cameras as well as the official photographic sessions, which were very well organised and oriented towards family and friends. Gretel insisted that Jack posed alongside herself.
"You are here with me because you are my husband," she said, as she smiled up at him. "Nothing can change that."

They were accorded primary position for the first blessings of the newly appointed cardinal. It was a deeply touching, emotional moment and one which they and Cardinal Bouvier would treasure in their hearts. Another heart-warming emotional jolt was to follow immediately because the couple who were accorded second place in line for his blessing were his former parishioners from Lonerton, Tessie and Dan Hayley, whom the cardinal had specifically invited.
"God my Father," the cardinal prayed, "I am grateful that you have chosen me to be your servant and work for you," and he blessed them and hugged them both.

Gretel and Jack did not stay on in Rome after the customary celebratory meal but promised to return for a longer holiday at another time.
"Throw a coin into Fontana di Trevi, to make sure that you do return," admonished a smiling and happy Cardinal Bouvier.
"No time for that now," grinned Jack, "although we do know the legend."
"We will do it on our next visit," promised Gretel.

A feeling of holiness and peace, that can only come from the spirit of God, had infused them while they were in the Vatican and it still remained with them on the homeward flight. They spoke but little and each seemed to be content to dwell on their own individual reveries - Jack thinking about his dearly departed Maura and Gretel reflecting on Rome and on her parents Wilhelm and Ericka and reflecting too on Pierre Bouvier, the man who walked out on her and on their son Paul when he was at the tender age of two and a half years old.

"I often wonder if Pierre is still alive," she said "and if he is, I wonder if he knows that his son is now a cardinal?"

"What does your instinct tell you?" asked Jack.

"My instinct tells me that he is alive and if he is still alive, he knows that his son, whom he used to call Peaboy, is now Cardinal Paul Bernhart Bouvier."

"If that is your instinct, then you are probably right," affirmed Jack.

Fifty Three

Gretel's instinct was entirely accurate. Pierre Bouvier was indeed alive and was back in hospital in Calgary, for follow-up surgery on his amputated leg some months after his son Archbishop Paul Bernhart Bouvier had been ordained a cardinal. His hospital records showed that he was aged seventy two, that he was a citizen of Brazil and that his name was Pedro Rodriguez - which indeed it was, for he had used no other since he acquired that name and that identity in Rio De Janeiro thirty eight years earlier. At that time, he also acquired company shares from his former self and never again used the name Pierre Bouvier. He had become Pedro Rodriguez and that is the way it would be, without deviation in his life thereafter.

Gabriela Rodriguez, sat patiently in a chair watching her father in a restless sleep unsuccessfully trying to shift the weight of his body from its 'lying on the back' position. The heavy medication was adversely affecting him and he frequently uttered incoherent mumblings in his sleep. Sometimes he called out her own name and that of her mother Andreina and other names as well. Sometimes too, in the minutes before he awoke from his drug induced sleep, he uttered coherent phrases or short sentences.
Today, Gabriela watched her father's eyelashes flicker rapidly and tried to make sense of the disjointed words and phrases that he uttered:
"Shirley... .. wrote it...the letter to Gretel...had to be Shirley...she lied."

Then he became agitated and swinging his arms wildly from side to side he inadvertently disconnected the tubes that dripped the medicine into his veins.
"Jealous Shirley... treacherous bitch" he groaned and soon afterwards he was wide awake.
"I think I was talking in my sleep," he remarked to Gabriela later, after the tubes had been re-inserted and after he had settled peacefully once more.
"Yes you were," she replied. "You have talked a lot in your sleep since your surgery, mostly incoherent mumblings or calling out names."
"Names! What names?" he asked.
"Mother's name and mine of course and names of people we both know but there were other names too."
"Others?" he asked, "what others?"
"Someone named Shirley who was treacherous and lied in a letter - I think."
"Please continue," he said.
On other occasions you called out to someone named Gretel and most frequently to Paul or Peaboy - as if they were significant in your life. Were they significant in your life?"

He was silent and completely motionless for awhile and then he looked at his beloved daughter saying:
"Gabriela, your name means 'God with us' and the name fits you well - for you have saved me from self-destruction and restored my dignity, but today I must ask you not to judge me too harshly and not to abandon me because of the secret past that I must now reveal to you."
"You know I will not judge you too harshly and I certainly will not abandon you."

"You know me as Pedro Rodriguez," he began, "but that is not my real name..."

Gabriela sat unmoving, as her father revealed to her the part of his life that he had so carefully and craftily hidden for so long. When he was finished, she reached in over the protective bed-guard and hugged him.

"Thank you for telling me all of that. You have lived through some hard and interesting times," she said, "but everything is alright now. All things will come together for you. As for me, I am excited to have learned that I have a half-brother. I hope that I will someday soon get to meet him - the brother I never knew I had."

"I dearly would like to meet him too," replied her father, "but it is better that he would not know that I am still alive."

"Don't be silly," she said.

"I am not being silly. The news that the recently appointed Cardinal Bouvier had been contacted by his long lost father - who had remarried outside the Church after deserting his wife - the cardinal's mother - would be an embarrassment and a scandal."

"May I ask how you knew that your son - my brother had been ordained a cardinal?"

"I carefully followed his progress, almost since the night I left him and his mother Gretel - when he was but a child - only a two and a half year old. I am a wealthy man - it was not difficult for me to keep myself informed."

"You mean you spied on them?"

"No! I kept myself informed because he is my son. I wanted to be satisfied that neither he nor his mother were in need of any monetary assistance."

"And if they had been in need?"
"I would have given it to them - gladly."
"So why will you not now go to visit him?"
"Because it would be used by enemies of the Church and by hostile elements of the media to discredit Paul and the entire Catholic Church."
"I still think you are being silly," said Gabriela "but I will reluctantly accept your advice for now."

His recovery after the follow up surgery was slower than he had anticipated and he spent months in a rehabilitation centre. During that time he devoted a lot of thought to his past life and became preoccupied with devising ways and means for righting the wrongs that he had done. The words from the heart that he wrote to his ex-wife Andreina were but one step in trying to repair some of that damage and trying to bring healing and relief to own his wounded soul and to those whom he had hurt:

Dear Andreina,
Eloquence was always one of my most outstanding talents, but lying here, on the flat of my back in my hospital bed, I realise that even my most effusive words cannot adequately describe your loving goodness to me - the forty nine year old man whom you married when you were barely twenty three.

You came to me then in all your fresh young beauty, equipped in great measure with gifts of humility and good sense - acquired from your humble close-knit family of paltry means. You were gifted with a loving heart, nourished by parents and sibling brothers and sisters, whom you dearly loved and who loved you just as dearly in return.

All these gifts you brought to me and gave to me, but the greatest gift of all, was the foremost desire of your heart and mind and spirit, to be a good and caring and loving wife to me and a good and caring, loving mother to any children that God might send to us. You tried with all your mind and passion to fuse your loving heart with mine and to blend our spirits into one. (Oh, how is it that I can now so clearly see, that which I could not see then? But now it is too late, alas, much, much too late).

I remember still and never will forget, the giving love of your warm body, your warm palms pressed in comfort against my face, the strong embrace of your slender arms around me or the forceful warm power of your lips, and the relaxed contentment of our love as the two of us became one - together.

All that you were you gave to me, all that was you, all that was of you, all that was in you, to comfort and uphold, to guide and show me the way, to walk beside me and ease my burdens as I trod the many roads and varied pathways of my life.

I see it all so clearly now, but I did not see it then. Ah, how blind I was, how blind. I saw but some and did not see it all, for I was obsessed with the pursuit of wealth, too devoted to making money, too preoccupied to know and see that which really matters in life.

The gift of new life too you gave to me and from your maternity bed you handed me our own child, conceived in purest love, as if to say: 'this is my gift to you, take her gently in your arms.' You named her Gabriela. It means 'God with us,' you said. You named her well, for she is that, which her name implies.

We had happy years and your great love helped me clear wrong spirits from my mind, until I, like the biblical house was swept clean and my demon put outside. We were happy then, you and I and Gabriela, but then after some years - again like the biblical tale, the demon returned, bringing more demons with it - to occupy that place in my heart, where my love for you and the strong spirit of God should have been residing.

The rest you know all too well. You pretended at first not to notice my wrongdoings and betrayals - ignored them as if they didn't happen, forgave, forgave again and yet again and yet again until at last it became too obscene to forgive - and then you left.

I had given many gifts to you, worth thousands and hundreds of thousands and a million dollar diamond too, but these were gifts that money bought and they could not satisfy. All you ever wanted was the love of my heart, but it was not there for you because I was wasting it elsewhere, lost in the things of the world. All the gifts that I bought for you, were but trinkets compared to the selfless love that you gave to me. How could I have been so stupid, stupid? Stupid, stupid me.
Signed
Pedro - whom you used to love.

Fifty Four

Thomas lived in Trastevere in Rome, which was within walking distance of the Vatican. He loved Rome, loved its warmth, its historic buildings, its fountains and was deeply touched in his Christian heart by the catacombs - resting place of so many martyrs - victims of cruellest persecutions. He loved St Peter's Basilica, built on the site of the burial place of the first pope - the rock on whom Jesus promised to build his Church. Thomas could identify with Peter because, like himself, he made some pretty big mistakes.

The chains, in the Church of San Pietro in Vincoli, that once held Peter prisoner and which were made ineffective by the good angel of God, had a special meaning for Thomas. They reminded him that, like thousands of others, he and Alessandra and Jordana and Shawny Scrahill, had been held prisoner by chains of a different sort - the chains of self-blame, of guilt, of poor self-concept and self-esteem - chains from which they could be freed only by God's power and goodness manifested through the goodness of people such as Rossa Lee, Canon Towman and others. He liked to visit the Basilica of St Paul Outside The Walls, which was built to the memory of the great missionary after whom Rev. Paul Bouvier had been named by his mother Gretel. Thomas was content in the city of the seven hills.

After five years in Rome Thomas' health began to fail. The

respiratory problems, brought on by his abduction while he was curate in Lonerton, and by the long hours tied to a tree in the cold dank air, began to grow steadily worse, forcing him onto heavy medication and occasional use of oxygen. He was hospitalised for a lengthy period where he had continuous access to oxygen and he continued to prepare his final report as chairman of the Pontifical Council.

I visited him a few times along with my wife Hannah and our sisters Nora and Rose visited him as often as they could. He had many more visitors, once news of his illness and its severity spread to Lonerton and to Cill Gobnait - the school community where he had taught in his younger days.

On one occasion his reading of the holy office was interrupted by a distinctively familiar voice in the hospital corridor:
"Dat's de room dere - dat's de number of it dere look - 17. Dat is what we were told at reception - *uno sette* - one seven. The porter counted it out on his fingers so that we could understand"
"Praise God," said Thomas to himself, "that's Eddie Whiston, God bless his good and generous soul."
Thomas was delighted to see his old friends from Cooley Park - Eddie Whiston and his wife Nora, Pauline Doohan and Alessandra Ozolins and they had a wonderful visit talking of old times, old friends, old deeds done and challenges overcome.
"How are Tessie and Dan Hayley?" Thomas inquired.
"They are as happy as could be," replied Nora. "Tessie is

as good and helpful as ever and Dan as kindly and easygoing as always and of course their children are grown up now."

"And how are things in Cooley Park?" inquired Thomas.

"Very good," answered Pauline Doohan. "Very respectable and disciplined."

"De Cooley Park Community Committee is still active and influential," interjected Eddie Whiston, "although we miss you very much and we miss Alessandra too since she left to concentrate on her new security company."

"Is your company doing well," inquired Thomas, addressing Alessandra who was standing at the bottom of the bed.

"Ve are doing vury vell," answered Alesssandra, who still retained strong traces of her native accent. "Ve run a vury professional operation and I now employ twenty persons."

"That is wonderful news," declared Thomas, "such great news to hear."

"I have also met a vonderful man and ve vill be married next year."

"That news makes me so happy," said Thomas. "I'm delighted for you and I hope you will be very happy. By the way, do you know what became of Jordana?" he inquired.

"Yes I do know vat became of Jordana," Alessandra replied. "She died last vinter. She died alone. I do not know any more information of her."

"How did she manage after her course in the detoxification centre?"

"She did vell for a period of time and she tried hard, but vent back to her old habits. I vas vury sad ven I heard she had died."

Bishop Thomas was silent for awhile and his face became sad and distorted as if he were trying to stop himself from crying and control his emotions before he could respond.
"She was gentle and insecure in herself and had such a low opinion of herself. That is what destroyed her," he said, "her low opinion of herself."
"No," said Alessandra. "It vas that vermin boyfriend who destroyed her. Ze two of them passed me on ze street one day but pretended to not see me. He vas vearing expensive suit but it vas too small for him and vearing a bright coloured tie although his shirt buttons ver open. He vas holding her hand and I saw a scar on her left cheek just beside her nose. She did not look happy. I think maybe he vas taking her to a client, to some place she did not vant to go. Ze low life rat. I vould like to break some of his bones."
"The poor child," said Bishop Thomas, "the poor, poor child."
"Trotsky Moran died also," said Eddie Whiston.
"Did he?" responded Thomas. "The poor man was harmless enough."
"He was dead about three days before he was found," said Whispy.
"That shouldn't happen in a community," said Thomas.
"No it shouldn't," answered Pauline Doohan "but he was very contrary as you know and his nearest neighbour who normally kept an eye on him was away on holidays."

On another occasion a nurse entered his room accompanied by a young woman diplomat from the Irish Embassy who stood there looking smilingly at him. He switched off the oxygen supply and removed the mask

from his face before he spoke.
"*Buonasera signorina*," he said.
"You do not recognise me," she stated.
"I'm sorry but I don't," he replied.
"Look more closely. I'll give you a hint: You taught me in school once upon a time."
"I'm sorry, you will have to tell me your name, your first name at least," said Thomas.
"I will give you another hint," she said. "We had a picture in our house that you liked, a picture of a middle aged Holy Mary with a blood spatters on her clothes and hands and face."
"And a scratch on the side of her cheek," said Thomas. "I remember now. Rossa Lee was your mother and you must be Rose Anna. If I had met you on the street, I would not have recognised you. You look so distinguished and sophisticated."

They hugged then and she told him all about herself and all the news about his former friends and all about the Cill Gobnait and the school - the place that had once been so important in his life and where Indie had attended school:
"Her mother, yes, she was fine....Her dad died a few years ago....the McMahons were still playing music... yes Packie was still alive.. still loving everyone and loved by everyone in return.... Rose Anna herself - she had pursued her youthful ambition to be an ambassador for her country... no she hadn't made it yet, but she was confident.... she gave him her card...if he needed anything or any help from the embassy, just say the word and she would arrange it."

Fifty Five

Gretel Bernhart Donoughue's ex-husband Pierre Bouvier - alias Pedro Rodriguez was recovering well after a long sojourn in the rehabilitation centre. Although he was unsuccessful in adapting to use the prosthesis, he became adept at using the old fashioned long 'under-the-shoulder' wooden crutches.

Gabriela came to live with him and ensured that he adhered to the prescribed diabetic diet and medication. He reduced his weight, regained his strength and became quite strong and mobile again.

Father and daughter got on remarkably well and he generally referred to her as his best friend, but they disagreed sharply regarding initiating contact with her half-brother Cardinal Paul Bernhart Bouvier - the son he had deserted long ago.

"But he doesn't even know that he has a sister - he doesn't even know that I exist. We surely owe it to him to contact him and tell him. I think he has a right to be told," insisted Gabriela

"I won't contact him and I won't meet him," Pierre declared vehemently for the umpteenth time. "I disrupted his life when I deserted him long ago - I will not now disrupt his life again."

"But you promised him," complained Gabriela.

"I did not promise," asserted Pedro.

"But you did," insisted Gabriela. "Perhaps we will meet again somewhere, sometime - you said to him. They were the words you used."

"Those words amount to a vague aspiration, not a promise," said Pedro. "Now that he is a cardinal, it is impossible for me to meet him because it would disrupt and complicate his life."
"Why is it impossible? Surely everything is possible. You could meet him in secret."
"It could not be kept secret. I will not meet him. I will never meet him. It would be selfish of me to try. That's my final word on that issue."

Pedro enjoyed a long spell of good health and mobility. He was able to carry out his functions as president of Mid Western Oils Plc. albeit to a much reduced extent. He even met with his ex wife, Andreina. She thanked him for his letter and they agreed to restore a basic level of communication.

Age was catching up with Pedro. The years of excessive drinking had adversely affected his health and he eventually suffered a severe stroke. His ability to speak was greatly diminished as was his control over his arms and he was confined to a wheelchair. He was tough and he fought back and engaged fully with a strict rehabilitation regime.

He was still in the rehab centre on the day that Irish diplomat Rose Anna Lee visited Bishop Thomas in hospital in Rome, the exact same day that a plane carrying one hundred and forty two passengers, crashed into the Atlantic ocean - killing everyone on board.
The tragedy received widespread news coverage throughout the world. The following evening, Gabriela Rodriguez was watching the television news with her

father in his room in the rehabilitation centre, when it was announced that Gretel Bernhart Donoughue, mother of newly appointed Irish Cardinal Paul Bernhart Bouvier was among the casualties - as was her husband Jack Donoughue.

Pedro was visibly distressed and upset at the news. The death of his former wife in such awful circumstances seemed to affect him deeply. Perhaps it revived old and bitter memories in his mind but whatever the reason was, his condition worsened and his speech was reduced to monosyllables.

Gabriela was filled with empathy for her father and could only guess at the thoughts that were running through his mind. She felt a great sympathy too for her half brother Cardinal Paul Bernhart Bouvier, who had suffered the loss of his mother in such awful circumstances.
"It is a difficult time for your son," she said. "My heart is grieving for him. We should not leave him alone like an orphan at this awful time in his life. Common decency demands that we contact him and go to comfort him."

Some of the wreckage was subsequently recovered and some bodies, but the bodies of Jack and Gretel were not found.

One month after the air crash, Cardinal Bouvier presided over a memorial Mass for his mother Gretel and her husband Jack Donoughue in La Capilla De San Pedro La Roca - the chapel that Jack had carved out of the rock beside his Hotel Donomaur. The circular interior was full to capacity and a large crowd was gathered outside under the canopies which had been erected to provide shade from the heat of the sun, blazing down from a flawless, sky of azure blue.

Management and staff of Hotel Donomaur acted as ushers and ensured that everything was orderly and well organised - just as Jack Donoughue would have wanted. A large number of priests and some bishops concelebrated with Cardinal Bouvier and there was impressive participation by the locals and the hotel employees in the singing of hymns and in the responses to the prayers of the Mass.

After the Mass, Cardinal Paul Bernhart Bouvier stood at the foot of the altar to receive condolences and Jack Donoughue's son and daughter did likewise some distance away.

The last to approach the cardinal was an elderly man in a wheelchair pushed by a tall and beautiful young woman. While they were still some distance away, some strange instinct impelled the cardinal to go to meet them and as he approached he saw that this was a stroke victim, something that was evident from the sideways position of the mouth and the way in which the skin was pulled tightly over one cheek. As he drew nearer, he noticed the trousers tucked around the man's amputated left thigh.

The old man caught hold of the sleeve of the cardinal's cassock and he in turn stooped a little lower, so that he might better understand the words that the invalid was struggling to verbalise. Hard as he tried however, he could

not understand - although the man was repeating the same word over and over again, and so straightening himself up, the cardinal addressed the young woman:
"He keeps repeating a word that I can't understand. It sounds like peeb," he explained to the young woman. "Do you know what he is trying to say?"
"Yes, I do know," said the young woman. "The word is Peaboy and with that word he is trying to tell you that you are his son and that he is your father, who gave you that name when you were but a child."
Cardinal Bouvier knelt on both knees on the floor, placed his hands on the stroke-distorted face of his father and kissed his bowed head.
"How strange," he said, "that on this day of the memorial mass for my mother that she sent my father to console me. Blessed be God forever."

Fifty Six

Time was running out for my brother Bishop Thomas and he knew it. Although he was nearing journey's end, he was alert and talkative on the day that he was visited by his friend and former nemesis, Cardinal Paul Bernhart Bouvier, who was dressed as usual, in the drab tan coloured robes of a humble monk.

"No scarlet silk cloaks for me Thomas," he explained.

"You're as bad as myself," said Thomas weakly. "I never wore the bishop's mitre. Tall hats are too pompous for a humble man like me."

"Same here," said Cardinal Bouvier. "I wear the traditional small skull cap instead of my Cardinal's mitre. It is enough."

"Scarlet of course?"

"Yes, but only to show that if necessary, I am willing to die in defence of my Catholic faith."

"I am sorry about the loss of your mother," said Thomas. I have prayed much for her and for you and for her husband Jack Donoughue."

"Thank you," answered Cardinal Bouvier.

"I would have gone to Lanzarote for the memorial Mass if I had been able," said Thomas.

"I know you would. It was a beautiful ceremony and a fitting memorial to them. You know a big surprise awaited me after the Mass."

"A surprise?" prompted Thomas.

"Yes, a big, pleasant surprise - I met my long lost father

Pierre Bouvier."
"Oh it is wonderful news you bring," said Thomas. "Glory to God."
"He is not in good health. One leg has been amputated and his speech and limb movements are severely damaged due to stroke."
"Were you able to communicate with him?"
"His daughter Gabriela was with him and she helped us communicate both after the Mass and later when I met them in Jack Donoughue's Hotel Donomaur."
"Praise the Lord," said Bishop Thomas. "You have a sister as well - how wonderful that is - how wonderful!"
"Yes, her name is Gabriela Rodriguez. My father acquired a new name and a new identity in Brazil, where he went after he had left my mother and he has used Pedro Rodriguez as his official name ever since."
"I'm glad you met them both," said Thomas.
"I think my mother sent them both to me to console me on a very dark day in my life. I am truly grateful for that."

After a brief silence in which he struggled for breath, Thomas said:
"I am glad to have known and worked with you, Paul, although we came with opposing perspectives in the beginning."
"We came to a convergence via different paths," replied the cardinal. "We eventually became united as one in our desire, to promote a truly merciful and welcoming Church, for all members of the Body of Christ on earth."
"I am nearing the end of my journey," said Thomas, "ploughing the headlands as the countryman would say, and nearly finished. We may not meet again my friend."

"You tilled the field of your life real well and sowed good seeds," said the cardinal. "I can testify to that. Is there anything troubling you? Anything that you want to say to me or ask of me?"

Thomas lapsed into silence again. He seemed to deteriorate quite suddenly and struggled to draw his breath before continuing and pausing frequently for oxygen and for breath between sentences:
"The experiences of my life taught me .... that the Catholic Church ... is the greatest force for good on earth.....it has stood the test of time....but some teachings of the Church ..... could not be applied ..... in all circumstances..........The circumstances of ..... people's lives ....differ and vary...... I have reflected for ..... most of my life on this - in truth and honesty I hope ... and this led me .....to a vision .. ..which would allow.... every member of the Body .... of Christ on earth..... access to Holy Communion ....provided they lived good lives ...were genuine and .....genuinely sought.... and accepted.....its truth."
"Your work has come from your heart and this is one of the many fruits of your labour," answered the cardinal.
"Sometimes I worry...... that it may have ...have come from a shallow pride .... rather than.....from true .... humility....... If it is from pride......... it could..... lead many .... down a *cul de sac* ....and that would weigh ... heavily.... on my soul," reflected Thomas, struggling mightily for breath as he put on the oxygen mask once more.
"You need not worry, my old friend," said Cardinal Bouvier. "The tragedies of your life stripped you of any shred of pride and taught you humility most profound and true. The tragic death of my mother and the awful

circumstances of it, has given me some insight into the extent of your suffering."

"Thank you," said Thomas.

"You learned well and came to understand that your life does not belong to you alone. Your life is your individual, unique slot in the ongoing work of creation. You used it well and emptied yourself in the service of others."

"Thanks for that .... Paul..... I..... needed those ....reassuring ..... words."

"Don't worry anymore. Through your work and mine, a focus has been placed on a different pastoral vision for the nourishment of all members of the Body of Christ on earth. You are not the final arbiter. Others will expand the study and test it against the teaching of Jesus in the scriptures and I myself am committed to that."

"There are ma..ny different ho..mes in heaven," commented Bishop Thomas.

"So indeed there are," affirmed the cardinal.

"Before you .. go, Paul .... I ask for .... your blessing.... and the .... forgiveness ...of the sacrament of .... reconciliation .....for any .... residue that remains.... of the wrongs ... I have done .... in my life."

Paul Bernhart Bouvier, a cardinal of the Catholic Church took the confessional stole from the pocket of his humble robe and spoke the words of forgiveness with all the sincerity of his heart.

"Thank you my friend," gasped Thomas. "Now please pray ... with me ....for I am very...tired," and with his eyes tightly shut he began:

"Like as the shepherd to his sheep,
So is the Lord my God to me.

Attending to my ev'ry need,
A resting me in pastures green
Near waters still he leadeth me,
My weary spirit to make clean. "

He leads me on the path of right,
He's true and faithful to his name.
And should I walk the valley's night,
Its evils will not frighten me,
For with his crook and staff nearby,
He keeps me safe and comforts me.

Thomas' voice faded in and out as the prayer progressed and ceased completely at the lines:
"A feast he hath prepared for me,
Within the sight of sullen foes.
My head he did anoint with oil,
My very cup it overflows.

He quietly breathed his last just as Cardinal Bouvier finished final verse of that beautiful prayer:
Goodness for sure will follow me,
And kindness all my lifelong ways,
And I will dwell in God's own house,
Forever and for all my days."

"Good bye my good friend," said Cardinal Bouvier. "There are a hundred million saints in this world at any given time and you my friend were one of the greatest of them."

The cardinal joined his hands upon his lap, bowed his head and prayed in deep and silent prayer. He prayed for a long time and he felt a deep layer of peace resting above the ceiling and the sweet odour of sanctity filed room.

Fifty Seven

The death of his mother Gretel and of her husband Jack Donoughue took a heavy emotional toll on Cardinal Bouvier. The natural grief that one feels in such circumstances, was greatly exacerbated for him, by the awfulness of their deaths and the non-recovery of their bodies.

In the aftermath of a sudden death, the mind is often visited by varied scenarios, suppositions and imaginings of what might or might not have been. These inevitably become repeated reflections - some of which can be positive and bring healing and more of which bring pain and sadness and regrets. Paul Bouvier's most frequently recurring memory was his last glimpse of his mother walking away from the terminal of Lanzarote Airport, holding hands with Jack Donoughue. He remembered Jack putting his strong arm around her shoulder and was touched by the manner that she looked up at him and smiled.
"It is a good picture to remember them by," he soliloquised "and it brings comfort and peace to my mind."

He often thought of Jack Donoughue and of his wisdom and understanding:
"There is another rule," Jack had reminded him that morning long ago in Lanzarote, when he was agonising about whether he should or should not give the Holy

Eucharist to his mother Gretel - "whatever you restrict on earth will be restricted in heaven."
"How easily Jack exposed the narrowness of my focus," he mused. "My understanding was selective and narrow, while his was broad and comprehensive. He saw the fullness of the gospel whereas I only saw the part. Life had taught Jack - just as life had taught Bishop Thomas Kendley."

He often thought of Bishop Thomas and wondered what he would think of the thoughts and imaginings that were going through his mind since the tragedy.
"You cannot avoid these reflections," he would say. "They follow bereavement just as surely the ebb of the tide follows the flow - and just as the soaking and compacted sand is dried by the warming sun, so too will your drooping spirit be warmed and revived by the warmth of God's grace."
"Yes!" said Paul to himself, "that's just like what he would say."

Meeting his long lost father at the memorial Mass was a wonderful surprise. The encounter brought another cohort of memories and mixed emotions - as did the meeting with Gabriela, the half sister he never knew he had.

Despite all these reflections and imaginings, life has to go on - even if half the world had died. A cardinal has great responsibilities and Paul Bernhart Bouvier did not spare himself, as he discharged his many functions with competence and commitment - and with a great deal of empathy and merciful understanding.

He was very frugal in his lifestyle. His car was far from new and far from posh or fancy and he generally used public transport whenever this was practical.
A young man and a girl - both wearing earphones, were seated opposite him on the train to Cork one day. The girl seemed to be absorbed in listening through her earphones and the young man was trying without apparent success to get his iPod to function. When he eventually gave up, he wound the cable of the earphones around it, pushed it aside on the table, looked across at Cardinal Bouvier and smiled.
"It is not being cooperative," remarked the cardinal.
"No!" replied the young man, "the batteries need recharging."
"We all need to have our batteries recharged at times," remarked the cardinal smilingly.
"I suppose," said the young man, and then looking more closely across at the cardinal, just as the girl removed her earphones, he continued:
"Haven't I seen you before somewhere?"
"Perhaps you have. I'm Fr. Paul Bouvier."
"Are you the cardinal?" asked the girl.
"I have the responsibilities of a cardinal at this time."
"You don't look a bit like a cardinal," remarked the young man.
"What should a cardinal look like?"
"Ah, you know - wear high hats and scarlet clothes and all that."
"The high hats are called mitres and they are worn for ceremonial occasions only. I prefer to wear the small skull cap - called a zucchetto."

"I read somewhere that you wear the robe of a humble monk each day - is that true asked the girl?"
"Yes, it is true. It helps to keep me humble."
"I was so sad to hear of the death of your mother in that awful plane disaster," remarked the girl.
"Thank you," said the cardinal. "It was very sad for everybody."
"Oh! I saw that on the T.V." interjected the young man. "Her husband was killed too wasn't he?"
"Yes, he was," answered the cardinal.
"But he wasn't your father - or was .." commenced the young man, who then shut up - having been the recipient of a solid kick in the shin bone, under the table, from the girl.
"Oops! Sorry! I talk too much," he admitted.
"That's quite alright," answered Cardinal Bouvier. "My parents' marriage broke up when I was a child. My father left my mother and disappeared without a trace. Thirty five years later, my mother was living on her own in Lanzarote and it was there that she met and eventually married Jack Donoughue."
"Was that embarrassing for you? - your father and mother breaking...."
This time Cardinal Bouvier could actually hear the thud as the young man received another kick under the table.
"Oops! Sorry! I did it again," he said. "Sometimes I talk too much."
"That's alright," responded the cardinal. "At least you're open and honest. Was I embarrassed? Shocked would be a better word, but ultimately I came to understand and to accept. It taught me to understand better, to make allowances for people's circumstances and to be humble -

very humble."
"Does a cardinal have to be humble?" asked the girl.
"Yes! He must surrender himself to God and give all that is in him and all that he is to his role and responsibility under God."
"I'm a Catholic myself," declared the young man, "but I don't attend Mass very often anymore. I'm disillusioned with the Church."
"In what way are you disillusioned?" asked Cardinal Bouvier?
"The Church and the pope talk about the need to help the hungry while sitting on incalculable wealth in the Vatican. The pope should sell the art and sculptures and give the money to the poor and hungry. Just look at the Sistine Chapel and all that art worth countless millions."
"First of all," explained Cardinal Bouvier, "I want to say to you not to confuse cardinals and other clergy with God. Cardinals and clergy will make mistakes and maybe even do that which is wrong. This sometimes make us angry - but we should not go taking revenge on God for their errors by falling away from the Mass and the sacraments - that would be playing into the hands of the devil. It would be doing exactly what he wants."
"O.K. - I take that point," said the young man, "but what about selling the artistic riches in the Vatican and in the Sistine Chapel?"
"Well you can't sell the art which is painted on the walls and ceiling of the Sistine Chapel," replied the cardinal, "but I agree with the overall thrust of what you are saying."
"And do you think the pope should sell off some of the art and sculpture and give the money to the poor?" asked the girl.

"I think the whole question of the apparent wealth of the Vatican should be examined with a view to finding the best way in which it can be utilised for the poor and hungry - set up a committee with personnel from the world of business, charitable organisations and from the world of art and let them come up with proposals."
"Why do you need a committee? Why not auction them off and give the money to the poor?" asked the young man.
"Tourists pay to see these works in the Vatican Museum and generate an income for the Vatican - which needs money to survive. If they were sold off, they would be gone for good."
"O.K. but do they need them all? Could some be sold and leave enough for the tourists."
"I have been considering that very idea," replied the cardinal. "If there is a surplus, we must carefully examine how these works of art could best be used for the benefit of the poor on an ongoing basis."
"Why not sell them off and give the money to the poor straightaway?" asked the girl.
"Because it would be better if we could find a way to generate income for the poor on a continuous basis."
"Yes, that would be better," answered the girl, "but how could that be done?"
The train had slowed as it neared its destination and already some passengers were standing up to take their belongings from the overhead storage rack.
"Look, why don't you both think about how it could be done? Discuss it with friends, do a little research and prepare suggestions. There's my card. Send the proposals to me when you have prepared and considered them."

"Will you read them?" asked the young man.
"I will read them and promote them if they are practical - that's a promise."
"Will we shake on that?" asked the young man, extending his hand.
They shook hands then - the young man, the girl and the cardinal.
"Your research will probably reveal that the Church is already doing a huge amount for the poor," suggested Cardinal Bouvier. "Hundreds of Catholic agencies work with the poor worldwide."
"Really? I didn't know that," replied the young man.
"Ah, you do know," interjected the girl. "There's Trócaire the Irish Agency and Concern and many more. I presume you give some money to them."
"I don't really. The little bit that I could afford would make no difference."
"Every little helps," declared the girl.
"She's right," agreed Cardinal Bouvier, "the gospel story of the widow's mite illustrates that - and if I might add, helping the poor and hungry is the responsibility of every member of the Catholic Church."

They parted at the railway station and shook hands again.
"Thanks for discussing with us," said the girl.
"And for listening to us," said the young man. "I have learned a few things."
"And so have I from listening to you," replied the cardinal.

Fifty Eight

Pierre Bouvier - alias Pedro Rodriguez, lived a full year after the tragic death of his former wife Gretel. He died alone, but peacefully in the nursing home where he had spent the last months of his life - deteriorating progressively from cirrhosis of the liver - a condition caused by excessive drinking of alcohol and it was the condition that ultimately caused his death.

His funeral service was a private affair. He was laid to rest on elevated ground, adjacent to the corral on his ranch, near the foothills of the Rocky Mountains, having been reposing in the ranch house for a night and a day.
Former business acquaintances attended by invitation. Old stories were told, humorous anecdotes shared, adventures recalled and wild tales discussed - all relating to the man known in the oil industry as Pedro Rodriguez - the tall Brazilian.

Gabriela Rodriguez and Cardinal Bouvier were the chief mourners. Gabriela's mother Andreina was also there, bearing her own grief for the man she loved and simply had to leave. Her formal, black mourning attire was indicative of her status as a principal mourner and she was tall and dignified in her manner and in her bearing.

Mid Western Oils issued a brief statement to the press announcing the death of its founder and former chief executive officer, eighty three year old Pedro Rodriguez.

The statement contained the customary expressions of praise for his achievements and expressed condolences to his daughter Gabriela who had succeeded him as company C.E.O. some years previously.

Gabriela invited her brother, Cardinal Paul Bouvier, to go through their father's personal effects which included: a large collection of Stetson hats, two repeating rifles with telescopic sights, a collection of old Colt 45 six guns from the period of the old wild west, some items from the various native Indian tribes of the area and a well worn bible on a locker in his bedroom.
"Look Paul," exclaimed Gabriela - it's our father's bible and opening it she read the inscription on the inside:
'To Pierre, hoping that this bible will be a source of help to you throughout your life... From Ericka and Wilhelm.'
"They were my grandparents - my mother Gretel's parents," explained Paul as he took the bible and examined the inscription.
A faded picture fell from its pages and picking it up Gabriela exclaimed:
"Look Paul, there's a picture of a woman holding a baby in her arms. Do you know who she is?"
"That's my mother Gretel," he explained, "and the baby I think, has to be me."
"That is proof for you Paul, that all these years, he did not forget you or your mother," proclaimed Gabriela. "It makes me happy to know that."
"It is a great consolation for me to know that too," he said. "May God rest all their souls in the peace of heaven."
The duties of a cardinal are multiple, onerous and varied. In addition to the normal routine duties he had to deal

with the legacy and historic issue of the sexual abuse of children by priests.

He embarked upon a series of Consultative Meetings with the priests, where they could air their views and where he could listen to them with care. It was clear from these meetings that the sexual abuse of children by priests was a source of great and grievous heartbreak to them as one priest stated:

"The sexual abuse of children by a small minority of priests is our most painful heartache because it is the very antithesis of what priestly acts should be. It defiles the innocent and the vulnerable and the heartbreak has been exacerbated by the lack of enlightenment in the manner in which some religious leaders handled the matter."

"It pierces the heart of every priest," said another "and it bleeds the very soul of our collective priesthood - the holy priesthood that Christ entrusted to us."

"There is a great need for some public acts of penance," declared another.

"That might be interpreted as an act of penance for something that we ourselves have done - and that would not be right nor just," said another. "We must do something, and we are willing - but the question is what should we do?"

"My former parish priest, the late Canon Towman had the answer for your question," replied the cardinal. "Ask yourself what would Jesus do? So what did Jesus do? He took on the suffering of others - ours were the sufferings that he took on and he was humble - even allowing himself to be crucified on a cross."

"So we should try to take some of the suffering of the abused on ourselves and this should be reflected in

whatever we do - Is that what you are suggesting?"
"Yes, but we should involve all Catholics in this and not just priests and religious," declared the cardinal - and thus it was agreed.

Cardinal Bouvier and Gabriela developed a close and enduring friendship and maintained regular contact. They visited Poland together - meeting at Krakow and touring the salt mines and Auschwitz. Gabriela was shocked and deeply distressed by what they saw there and by what they learned about the appalling evil that was perpetrated there.
"How could this have happened?" she asked.
"The evil began with thoughts in the minds of a few individuals and developed into a wrong and evil spirit. This evil spirit motivated them and drove them on, influencing and infecting the minds of more and more people. Thus it grew and became bigger and bigger until it became a powerful ideological and philosophical force. It was promoted by slick propaganda and controlled media, accepted by many and eventually became a powerful, ideological, evil cooperative capable of effecting the appalling evil deeds of Auschwitz."
"Ah, I see - and the Nazi Party was the evil ideological cooperative."
"Precisely!"
"It is difficult to understand why so many people allowed themselves to be a part of this evil work," remarked Gabriela.
"They were tricked - fooled by slogans and lies into believing that what they were doing was actually right and that it would make life better for them," replied Paul.

"The slogan over the gate into Auschwitz 'Arbeit macht frei (work sets you free) is an example of their evil cynical lies," said Gabriela, "but surely everyone was not fooled - why did they not try to stop it?"
"Opponents were branded as enemies, put down or taken to the extermination camps. Those who were left were perhaps afraid or they were too occupied with their own lives or simply said - it is not my business, it doesn't concern me."

Auschwitz left an indelible impression that compelled them to silence for much of the journey back to Krakow, as they pondered the horrors and evil that still permeated the place.
Gabriella spoke after a long period of silence:
"I'm appalled and sickened at what I saw in Auschwitz," she stated.
"The key thing to remember," replied Paul, "is that evil has not gone away. It is as active today as it ever was, working away, implanting evil ideologies, promoting them with crooked propaganda, lies and using its influence over news media and broadcasting services. We must be on the alert to make sure that nothing like that ever happens again."

In contrast, Wadowice, the childhood home of St. Pope John Paul II was reflective of a spirit of holiness and goodness because it had been touched by long contact with the divine spirit of God through the person of Karol Wojtyla and his family. While Auschwitz reflected horror and revulsion, Wadowice inspired holiness and goodness. Gabriela and Paul were affected deeply by Wadowice and the goodness and holiness of their hearts was enhanced and affirmed.

The funeral service of Pope John Paul II, in which a strong gust of wind dislodged tall ceremonial hats and blew against the scarlet capes of some cardinals, left a lasting impression. It was like a blow to the chest of Cardinal Bouvier, because he saw it as confirmation of his own belief that such stylish, elaborate dress was not in keeping with a Church that is trying to reflect poverty and humility in a modern world.
"It surely was the wind of the Spirit of God," Paul remarked later to Gabriela.
"Did you notice how the wind blew so strongly against the scarlet cloak?" she asked. "It seemed like it was tugging at it."
"I thought so too," answered Paul. "I think there is a clear message there - a push for a new departure - just like the winds of the Spirit on Pentecost Day."

Subsequent to his consultative meetings with the priests, Cardinal Bouvier embarked on a series of diocesan meetings with groups of about seventy young people. In his letter to the bishops he stated:
'My main concern is not so much with the young people who are living their faith and attending Mass and the Sacraments. My most urgent worry is for those that are not practising, who are disillusioned, who may be angry or who feel unwanted. Please ensure that these are invited to meet me in groups of about seventy when I visit your diocese.'

"What about individuals who are involved with drugs or who are addicted? Do you want to invite them also?" he was asked.
"Yes! I would especially like to meet them and listen to them."

The cardinal got his wish. Some refused to attend, others genuinely couldn't but most were pleasantly surprised that the cardinal wanted to meet them and listen to them. Each diocese had done as he had requested and typically the groups that he met included those with varieties of jewellery, hair colours, styles and tattoos, as well as those who were clean shaven and smartly dressed. In the beginning they were reticent, sceptical and surprisingly shy in some instances but after some initial inhibitions, they did begin to speak freely and discussed issues openly and sometimes humorously.

By the time he had completed the cycle of meetings, he had a clear understanding of their outlooks and of the issues pertinent to them. In keeping with a great many people they simplistically perceived God as an all powerful fairy godmother type person in whom they ceased believing because he allowed terrible things to happen such as bombings, starvation, floods, droughts and earthquakes.
"Why doesn't God stop all that?" they asked
They did not seem to be aware that the power of evil is out there, actively promoting unhappiness and suffering nor did they understand the important responsibility that rests on all humans to work to promote good and to defeat evil. They incorrectly perceived the Church as an organisation

of priests, bishops and nuns that did some wrong things but they had little or no knowledge of the enormous good it did and is doing.

"We never knew that the Catholic Church set up hospitals and schools for the poor of Ireland," some declared after the discussion section of the meeting.

"You are not getting your message out there," declared one or two towards the end of the meetings. "You need to improve your communication."

Epilogue

Paul Bernhart Bouvier, a cardinal of the Catholic Church had learned well from the lessons of his life - lessons bought, taught or absorbed from the example of others. He remembered them well:
Eddie Whiston's accurate accusation that he, Fr. Bouvier didn't listen to himself and to his daughter Tessie....... Canon Towman's strong admonition: 'don't call that girl a harlot' as his powerful hand came crashing down on the table ....and the canon later kneeling humbly on the floor and asking for the forgiveness of the sacrament........ His own mother Gretel's measured criticism: "my reverend son refused to let me meet Jesus........ Jack Donoughue's gently taught lesson, quoting from scripture to remind him that what he restricts on earth would be similarly restricted in heaven ... The amazing improvements wrought by Fr. Thomas and the Cooley Park Community Committee by means of the call to individual, familial and communal Christian responsibility. The cardinal kept these things in his heart with gratitude and humility and they strongly influenced him throughout the subsequent years.

Following on his diocesan, consultative meetings with the priests, he initiated an annual all night prayer vigil in every parish, every Holy Thursday night through to Good Friday morning - as a 'taking on of suffering' arising from the wrongs done by priests and religious. In the interests of justice and fairness, he asked that a similar night-long vigil of prayer would be held each Pentecost in thanksgiving for the wonderful worldwide work being done by Catholics, priests, nuns, other religious and lay people.

Arising from his meeting with the young people, Cardinal Bouvier asked that the religious education curriculum would be revised to ensure accurate understanding and conceptualisation of God:
"It is important to ensure that God is not portrayed and perceived as an all-powerful fairy godmother type of person whose sole attribute is love. It is similarly important to understand the persistent, pervasive forces of evil that are continuously attempting to mislead, fool and trick them with many wiles and snares. There are but two sides and we have to chose between them."

The call to Christian responsibility - individual, family and community, became a key pillar of his work and of his vision for the Church for the remainder of his life - a vision of a Church manifestly devoid of the trappings of wealth and pomp, equipped with an ever-evolving, worldwide communication ability, a Church that is open and welcoming, merciful and informed by deep prayer and holiness and a hierarchy that is manifestly humble.
Cardinal Bouvier embodied all these things in his own life and in his person and in his spirit.

Surprisingly enough, it was during this period of his life that he was subjected to what he himself termed, the 'assault of the spirits' or 'the attack of the demons.' In the aftermath of the deaths of his mother and Jack Donoughue, the death of his old friend and colleague Bishop Thomas Kendley and more latterly, the death of his father Pierre Bouvier, the cardinal's spirit suffered bouts of tiredness, of weariness and of periodic weakness and he occasionally skipped recitation of the priestly divine office - particularly during his trip to Canada for his father's funeral and in the weeks that followed. That was a foolish mistake.

It was during this time of depleted spirit and emotional distress that the assaults of the demons began - began to implant fear thoughts in his mind. Unnoticed by him at first, the thoughts became more and more powerful through evil snares and wiles and developed into wrong spirits so powerful that he was rendered vulnerable and sometimes unable to control the fears and tension that they wrought within him.

"I did not realise in the early stages that I had become subject to attack from the spirits of darkness," he explained to me on one occasion, "and when I did realise it, the wrong spirits had established a foothold in the territory of my mind."

"There are a number of prayers that are designed to counter those forces," I said.

"Yes! There are," he agreed "and they helped to turn the tide of battle in my favour and for awhile I began to think that the demons had been defeated."

"You were mistaken," I suggested.

"Yes I was mistaken," he replied "for that enemy never gives up and of course the attacks returned - sometimes taking me by complete surprise, even in the most unlikely of occasions and places."

"Should I be surprised that a cardinal became subject to so

strong an assault of the demons?" I asked.
"You should not," he replied. "Jesus himself was attacked too, when he was in a weakened state after forty days of fasting in the desert."
"Didn't the angels come to the assistance of Jesus?" I asked.
"Yes! They are there to help but maybe I didn't ask or accept their help when I should have."
"But you eventually gained victory over those evil forces?"
"I did not gain victory but I regained control. I was reminded that Jesus gave the apostles the power to cast out demons in his name and that I also had been given that power. I went repeatedly to the foot of the cross and begged to be purified and washed clean and asked devoutly for peace in my mind."
"And that peace has been given to you," I prompted.
"Yes!" he replied. "I am stronger and wiser now."
Thanks be to God," I said.

Towards the end of his long battle with the snares and wiles of the evil enemy, his good spirits got a great boost one morning when he received in the post a report titled:
Blueprint for the Dispersal of Specific Works of Art from the Vatican to Other Continents.
The young man and the girl whom he met on the train earlier that year, and whom he now knew to be third level students, had kept their promise and sent him their report.
It was a detailed, well thought out document that trenchantly argued for a pilot scheme that would involve:
(i) The replication by four, of the seven major Vatican artworks that best reflect Christianity.

(ii) Placing these replicas in a permanent exhibition in a major city in each continent - in whichever area of that city, was most densely populated by the poor.
(iii) That the scheme would be extensively applied in poorer areas elsewhere - if following a review, the pilot scheme was deemed to be a success.

The recommendations were in line with his own thinking on the issue. It was a bold new idea and he quietly and persistently promoted that blueprint among his colleagues and peers - as he had promised to the young man and the girl.

He continued to wear the robe and slippers of a humble monk. Whenever he was in Rome, and whenever the opportunity presented itself, he would impress upon his fellow cardinals and bishops:

- ❖ The need for mercy and compassion especially for 'excluded' people who are genuinely seeking to meet with Jesus in the Eucharist.
- ❖ The incorporation of the call to responsibility and to Christian activism into a revised religious education programmes.
- ❖ The urgent need to discard stylish ceremonial garb that smacks of pomp and wealth.
- ❖ The need to disperse Vatican objects of art to other continents for the purpose of evangelisation and for the betterment of the poor.

Cardinal Bouvier was known as the 'Little Monk' among

his peers and was well liked and respected by them - even by those who did not share his views. He was featured in a number of influential publications and this helped to publicise his ideas. Referring to him as the Little Monk, they were generally supportive of his belief that the time had come to move away from ostentatious ceremonial fashion and to don the cloak of poverty and humility and especially, that the time had come for the Church - the Body of Christ on earth, to be an inexhaustible fount of mercy - just as Jesus was when he walked on earth.

There must have been a lot of support for his views among his fellow cardinals also, because when the pope died, there was scarcely a tall mitre or a silk scarlet cape to be seen at the funeral ceremony.

It was November, that time of year when Christians remember their dead. The trees, still clad in autumn's multi-varied russet leaves, stood like silent sentinels, colourful and protective all around the rural, hillside graveyard. Some branches reached in over the moss topped wall beside the grave of our brother Bishop Thomas Kendley - at rest with his beloved Mary, the twins Veronica and John and Indie his beloved son and best ever buddy.

It was the fifth anniversary of his death. Nora and Rose and I, his ageing siblings stood close together, heads bowed, praying in silence deep, beside the grave, each

absorbed with our own thoughts and with countless memories, that flit across the mind at times like this and in such places.
Peace was all pervasive - compounded but not broken, by the wood-muffled sound of running streams or by the faint, distant, intermittent barking of two farmyard dogs - barking as if in conversation with each other. A lone raven flew with purpose from east to west across the broad, blue, cloud encircled dome of the sky and I looked across at Nora and Rose wiping tears away with white tissues.
"Five years," I remarked, "the time has gone by so quickly."
"I am often saddened to think that he had to die without any of his own there to comfort him," said Rose.
"Don't let that distress you," admonished Nora. "He belonged to God and not to us and God sent Cardinal Bouvier to be with him."
There was nothing I could add to that and so I kept my peace and remained silent.

There were fresh flowers on the grave.
"I wonder who put the flowers there?" asked Nora.
Rose bent down and looked at the label.
"What does it say?" asked Nora impatiently.
Rose read the words aloud:
"Always remembered - Alessandra."

A man and a woman were coming against us as we were walking the long footpath to the graveyard gate and we would have passed them by had not the woman stopped to talk.
"I know you," she said. "Aren't you a brother of Bishop

Kendley?"
"I am indeed," I answered "and these are my sisters Nora and Rose."
"It was you that brought the mobile chapel to Cooley Park when Fr. Kendley was a priest there," she continued. "I still have a photograph on my mantelpiece of you handing over the keys to him."
"Yes, it was me - I remember it well," I replied.
"My name is Tessie Hayley," she said "and I also remember it very clearly. It made a great difference to our lives. Dan and myself are on our way down to visit the bishop's grave right now. My father, Eddie Whiston, was great friends with him when he was junior curate in Lonerton."
"Eddie Whiston - I remember the name well," I answered. "Thomas often spoke of him. May I ask how he is?"
She was struggling to respond and her husband Dan came to the rescue:
"Tessie's father Eddie died a few days after the Bishop was buried - died of a heart attack - no warning, no nothing - just dropped off suddenly."
"Sometimes I think that maybe Bishop Kendley sent for him," said Tessie.
"And he probably did too," agreed Dan, putting his strong, comforting arm around his wife's shoulders. He probably had some shrubs and flowers that needed tending up above or a wall to be plastered maybe or maybe the golden gates needed fixing."
"Any news yet about the new pope?" asked Rose
"There is no white smoke yet," answered Tessie "and St. Peter's Square is packed full with people."
"I had forgotten all about it," said Nora.

"Your brother Bishop Kendley would have made a great pope," stated Tessie.
"It wasn't meant to be," I said.

That's often the way with graveyards - you meet so many people and talk about many things but mostly you think about those who are buried therein.

Later that day we visited our old homestead and were delighted to find that so much of the old place had remained unchanged - the same winding roadway into the yard, the same old sycamores still there growing on the same old ditch across from the front of the house. The haggard was different because new buildings had been constructed there but the stall and stable and barn loft were still standing, just as it was in the long ago and we were glad.

We walked again the stony wet porsheen of our childhood - leading west out of the yard and passed the gap of the field on the right where the blue cow died. We kept on going - carefully watching our step, as far as the inch field beside the river at the bottom of our neighbour's meadow where Thomas first saw the bunch of yellow cowslips that so excited him all those years ago.
"Imagine we were only children the last time we were here together," Nora remarked.
"The time has flown so quickly," said Rose.
"I would love to find out if the cowslips still grow there among the briars," I remarked.
"You wouldn't see them now because it is November,"

said Rose "and besides the grass is wet and wet shoes would not be good for us now in our old age."
"Maybe we will come again in the summer time," said Nora, "when the fields and the grass will be dry".
"Maybe we will," said Rose and I in unison and we turned and faced for home.

When we reached the yard in front of the house, Nora suggested that we walk over to the road - the road where the colt trotted out of our lives after the man who bought him all those years ago and so we headed off - three spritely elders armed with three walking sticks. We stopped for awhile at the gap of the meadow and were relating some old meadow-stories when I got a phone call from my wife Hannah:
"Did you hear the news?" she asked.
"What news?" I queried.
"We have a new pope."
"A new pope," I repeated loud enough for Nora and Rose to hear.
"Yes! It was announced from the Vatican window just a few minutes ago. You'll never guess who it is," she stated and paused - but then continued without waiting for an answer: "Dominum Paulum Cardinalem Bouvier..."
"Who is it?" asked Rose.
I was unable to reply because a lump of joyous emotion had arisen in my throat - shutting off my ability to speak. I was surprised at the extent to which the news affected me and I was unable to say his name directly.
"It is Thomas' old friend," I said, "the man who was with him when he died."
Nora and Rose wept openly and I wept deep inside. We

were speechless for a little while - stunned into silence - we three elders standing there beside the gap of the meadow where as children we helped save the hay and picked blackberries with Thomas - that same meadow where the tractor got stuck in a soft patch, spinning its rear wheels until we all came down to push it out. There now, we three senior citizens wept for joy, for our parents, for Thomas, and for Fr. Bouvier - but mostly I think we wept in hope that a more humble, more merciful, more welcoming, activist, spirit-filled Church would guide all of humanity safely along the right path.

Printed in Poland
by Amazon Fulfillment
Poland Sp. z o.o., Wrocław